THE TOWER of LONDON
CAULDRON OF BRITAIN'S PAST

THE TOWER of LONDON

CAULDRON OF BRITAIN'S PAST

Plantagenet Somerset Fry

Quiller Press
London

ISBN 1 870948 19 X

First published 1990
by Quiller Press Ltd
46 Lillie Road
London SW6 1TN

This edition first published in U.S.A. 1990

Hippocrene Books Inc.
171 Maddison Avenue New York NY 10016

ISBN in U.S.A. 0 87052 943 9

Produced by Hugh Tempest-Radford Book Producers.
Printed in Great Britain by St Edmundsbury Press

Contents

Foreword

We at James Burroughs Distillers, producers of Beefeater, probably the world's most sought-after premium gin, are delighted to support, along with the English Tourist Board, this authoritative and pleasurable history of the Tower of London, written by Plantagenet Somerset Fry.

The Tower is one of London's most famous landmarks, visited every year by some 2½ million people from all corners of the world. Since its foundation by William the Conqueror, it has provided the setting for many of the great events of British history, and the author has told the story, not only of the building itself, but also the kings, queens, noblemen and ordinary folk whose lives were bound up with it and, in too many instances, ended within its walls. Nowadays, the tragic aspects of its history over, people may simply enjoy the sight of its magnificent buildings, the ravens and the Yeomen Warders, the famous Beefeaters after whom Burroughs London Dry Gin was named.

English people first developed a taste for gin early in the 17th century, when soldiers returning from Holland (where they had probably fought with foreign armies) brought home the Dutch distilled spirit, *genever*. The popularity of this early gin increased after the Dutch prince, William of Orange, came to the English throne in 1689, and during the 18th century distillers began improving their gins with the addition of well chosen spices and herbs. One such distiller was James Burrough, a pharmacist who had been producing excellent liquors and cordials at his Chelsea home. He soon caught the public's fancy with a highly distinctive London Dry Gin, which he called Beefeater.

By the end of the 19th century the premises in Chelsea were outgrown. So, in 1908 the firm moved to the south side of the river Thames to the present site overlooking the Houses of Parliament.

We at James Burroughs are confident that you will enjoy this book of Britain's history as seen through the eyes of the Tower of London.

A. B. Oscroft
Managing Director, James Burroughs Ltd.

May 1990

Introduction

One may well ask, why yet another book on the Tower of London? What is there to say that has not already been said dozens of times? The answer lies in the expansion of people's interest in famous buildings beyond the political and social history, and the legends associated with them, into the architectural and building history. For this we have to thank a variety of agencies, the Department of the Environment's Ancient Monuments Branch, now known as English Heritage, the National Trust, the many local history societies in Britain, the regional and county archaeological societies, television documentaries, radio programmes, HRH Prince Charles, and many others, all of whom have awakened a burgeoning interest in construction history. A fresh work on the Tower of London, it seems to me, should place its architectural history in the forefront of the overall story, and if this means that something else, not absolutely germane to the strict history, has to go, or have a much reduced presence, then so be it.

Here, then, is a political, social and architectural history of the Tower, stripped largely of the surrounding legends which of course can be read elsewhere. While the book contains no hitherto unpublished illustrations, many of those that have been used here were much more familiar to readers at the beginning of this century than to us in the closing decade.

I have had much specialized assistance and advice, notably from the late Professor Allen Brown, Professor of Medieval History at King's College, London, who was the leading authority on English castles and who inspired me enormously as always, and from Peter Hammond, Deputy Master of the Armouries at the Tower, who kindly read the text and saved me from a number of embarrassments. I am most grateful to the University Library, Cambridge (the best library in Britain), which supplied me with masses of research material with matchless speed, courtesy and efficiency, and to the Vice-Chancellor of the University of Cambridge, Professor D G T Williams, President of Wolfson College, and the College Fellows who as always provided me with an unique environment in which to write much of this book.

As always, I am very grateful to my wife for her valuable critical assistance, and for preparing the index.

Plantagenet Somerset Fry

Wolfson College, Cambridge
March 1990.

Further reading

a selective list

Bayley, John. The History and Antiquities of the Tower of London, 2 vols. 1821

Barter, Sarah. Inscriptions (Treasures of the Tower series; 1976)

Borg, Alan. Torture & Punishment (Treasures of the Tower series: 1975)

Britton, John, and Brayley, E. W. Memoirs of the Tower of London (1830)

Brown, R. Allen, Colvin, H. M., Taylor, A. J. The History of the King's Works: vols 1 & 2, (1963)

Brown, R. Allen, and P. E. Curnow. Tower of London (1984)

Colvin, H. M., Ransome, D. R., Summerson, J. The History of the King's Works, Vol. III. Part 1. (1975)

Charlton, J. (ed.). The Tower of London: Its Buildings and Institutions (1978).

Gerard, John. Autobiography of a Hunted Priest. trans. P. Caraman (1951)

Hammond, Peter. Royal Armouries (1986)

Hammond, Peter. Royal Fortress (1978)

Hentzner, Paul. A Journey into England (trans & ed. Horace Walpole 1757)

Hewitt, J. The Tower, its History, Armories & Antiquities (1845)

Hibbert, Christopher. The Tower of London (1971)

Holmes, Martin. The Crown Jewels (1974)

Maitland, W. A. History of London (1739)

Minney, R. J. The Tower of London (1970)

Royal Commission on Historical Monuments. London. Vol. V. (1930)

Sutherland-Gower, Lord Ronald. The Tower of London, 2 vols. (1901–02)

Somerset Fry, Plantagenet. David & Charles Book of Castles (1980)

The Conqueror Starts his Castle in London

The Tower of London is the best known castle in Britain and it is one of the most famous buildings in the world. What is not so widely appreciated is that even as long ago as the last years of its founder, William the Conqueror (William I of England, 1066–87), its huge, dominating rectangular stone donjon, or great tower – the White Tower as it later came to be called – was fast becoming the most talked-about building in England. The White Tower was also the most awe inspiring, perhaps even frightening, structure in the eyes of the demoralized Anglo-Saxon people trying to get used to the rule of their new Norman king who had destroyed their own ruler, Harold II, at the Battle of Hastings on 14 October 1066, and had decimated the national army of England.

Within three months of his victory the Conqueror had begun to build a timber and earth castle on the north bank of the river Thames in London – not then the capital

Building the motte-and-bailey castle in Hastings before the great battle of 1066, as portrayed on the Bayeux Tapestry. At left a Norman overseer superintends Anglo-Saxons as they are forced to erect the castle. In the early days after the Conquest, Anglo-Saxons were pressed into castle building work and received no pay!

1

city, but certainly the largest in England. It straddled the south-east corner of what remained of the old eastern and southern stone walls of the Romano-British town of Londinium. William had already ordered several other timber and earth castles to be built in the south, notably at Dover, Canterbury, Winchester, Wallingford, Berkhamsted, and two more in London. He had even put up timber and earth castles on the south coast, at Pevensey and Hastings, *before* the great battle.

This was only a start. By the end of his reign twenty years later some eighty or so castles, mostly of earth and timber and the rest built of stone, had been erected or part erected up and down the landscape of England and across the border into parts of South Wales. By the death of his successor, William II Rufus (1087–1100), the number had increased to well over a hundred. And over the next century or so the building and rebuilding went on almost unabated right to the end of the reign of John (1199–1216). Of all these buildings, whose purpose and role we look at on pages 12–15, the castle on the site of the Tower of London heads the long list. There would be bigger, perhaps more sophisticated, and even more interesting castles built in the centuries to follow, but from its earliest days the Tower of London was to occupy an unique position in the story of the development of the monarchy and the government of England, and of the new feudal order being introduced into the country by the Conqueror.

An illuminated capital 'A' from the manuscript of the 12th century Chronicle of Battle Abbey. The 'A' begins an extract mentioning ".. the most noble William, duke of the Normans ..."

What was feudalism?

What were the main features of feudalism? It was a system in which a king or lord and his vassals had a contract whereby the former (king or lord) provided protection and leased land to the latter (vassals) in return for services of one kind or another, particularly military service. In the disorders that accompanied the breakdown of central government in the various parts of Europe in the ninth century, a breakdown that was greatly accelerated by the Viking invasions, there emerged a new unit of society. This was the estate, or domain, which was controlled by a king or a lord, or in some cases the Church which of course owned huge tracts of land, and this estate became a self-reliant and self-sufficient community. It was based on land, valued not merely as a possession but as a food producing unit. The controllers of the land kept some of it for themselves and employed people to work on it, sometimes though not always under conditions of servitude. The remainder of the land was leased to tenants to work for themselves in return for payment of some kind, that is, a proportion of the produce from the land.

Some controllers, particularly the kings, owned several estates, some of them bordering on each other and others scattered, and they employed people to manage them and collect the produce from the fields. Because it was so difficult to move goods about the countryside, controllers found it less onerous to visit their estates regularly and live off the produce for short periods rather than have everything moved to a central point. Where controllers were kings (rulers of large areas) or powerful nobles (such as the counts of Anjou in France or the dukes of Normandy) they were generally accompanied on their visits by a retinue of officials who assisted with the varied business that had to be dealt with, such as administering justice, collecting taxes and dealing with rents, disputes and other estate matters. In other words, government became peripatetic (as Maurice Keen put it) but in doing so it yielded much of its authority to the more local lords who were down the scale in the social structure, for they had the advantage of being permanently resident in their domains. They had in fact their own domain law and were responsible for keeping order in their territories. Although they promised allegiance to the king or the higher nobles above them, they often ignored their authority. William himself, for example, was so powerful in his duchy of Normandy that his overlord, the king of France, was afraid of him. So, the lords became petty kings in their domains and had private armies to defend them against attack from neighbours and rivals. But private armies had to be paid for, fed, clothed, equipped, and lords expected their tenants who were protected by the armies to contribute to these expenses. Gradually, tenants surrendered many of their rights and freedoms as the price of sustained security. In effect they – and their children after them – came to be bound to the land for their lives. For the lords, this system maintained continuity in the working of the estates, that is, ensured the regular production of food and guaranteed some kind of income and wealth.

Underneath the kings and the lords, there was another level of men who were not the bound tenants. These were the professional fighting men, sometimes known as knights. They were bound to the king or the lords by oaths of loyalty to fight for them, usually on horseback, to help them in enterprises the lords might wish to undertake. In return they were protected by the king or lords in the latters' courts, they were given help to maintain their horses, equipment, weapons and armour, and they might even be granted land to run as income-producing estates or allotted the earnings from existing estates. These men, known as vassals, were important members of their communities. Sometimes they were appointed as local governors, and later on as governors of larger regions (counties as they were known), who collected taxes, presided over local courts and led local levies of troops in time of war. They were expected to help protect their neighbourhoods when these were threatened by invasion, particularly during the long period of Viking raids in Western Europe from the ninth to the eleventh centuries. Gradually, a new kind of upper class developed which was essentially a military one, and it was rendered more powerful when it became hereditary. When a vassal died his son and heir took over. He became the king's or lord's man, as the saying went, promising to serve his lord faithfully for life. In return he was given a fee (from the Latin word, *feudum*, which meant the rights and revenues that his father had enjoyed). It is from this concept that the term feudal derives.

The feudal system was not, however, foolproof and vassals could by no means always be depended upon to keep to their promises of loyalty. They could be – and many were – won over by other, more powerful lords prepared to give them a better deal. Or they could rebel and set themselves up as great lords. They were the men with the horses, the weaponry, and the training and skill in warfare, and they often had the initiative. Only a powerful king, duke or count could control his vassals, and even some of these failed to do so effectively. Indeed, the warring between lords and vassals, and also between lords and their superiors, was to be a more or less permanent feature of the European scene for hundreds of years.

The Anglo-Saxons of eleventh-century England has some knowledge of this feudal system as it operated in Western Europe. It is clear that there had been some experimenting with it in England before 1066, but England cannot in any sense be said to have had a feudal system until the William the Conqueror arrived and through the agency of an alien and aristocratic society of lords and knights imposed it upon the English. What right had he to do this to the English?

William of Normandy, ruler of England

We would be wrong in thinking that William of Normandy came over to England with his band of less than 5,000 infantrymen and between 2,000 and 3,000 knights and mounted squires with any ideas of 'civilizing' the English, of introducing them to any supposed 'benefits' of Norman culture and learning. The English required no civilizing from Europe or anywhere else, and had been contributing to the mainstream of European civilization for years. The Conquest of 1066 had to be seen for what it was, the successful attempt by the then Duke of Normandy to establish a claim to the throne of England because the throne had been promised to him by its holder from 1042 to January 1066 – that is, King Edward the Confessor. When Edward died, however, he was not succeeded by William but by his principal adviser and virtual manager of the kingdom, Harold, Earl of Wessex, who was no relation to the king. This was apparently the dying man's choice, despite his earlier promise to Duke William, and it was also the general wish of the English Council, or Witanagemot. Yet, as soon as Harold accepted the crown, he must have known he would be challenged by William, and nine months later the great confrontation took place and Harold was defeated and slain. Along with him fell most of his lords and best fighting men, and the victor was presented with a rich kingdom whose government had all but disappeared. To win the battle he had needed his lords and volunteer fighting men – that is, his vassals – and he had had to offer them lands and wealth in England. Now they were ashore and victorious, and looked for their rewards. William was a generous man but he was also a firm and, if necessary, ruthless ruler, and he doubtless felt he would have to extend the feudal system he had in Normandy to England, not only to provide the vanquished with good government now that they had lost their king and many other leaders, but also to keep his supporters under control. To that end he distributed lands as he had promised, taking care not to allot too much in one area to one vassal but rather splitting the gift into parcels distanced from each other, and granting his vassals leave to build castles which, it was always to be remembered, were his gift to them, and what he gave he could also take away. This was the beginning of the system of licensing the building of castles which later became formalized in documents, quite a few of which have survived.

The origin of castles in Britain

What was a castle exactly, and why was it usually so imposing a structure?

A castle was one of the two principal arms of feudal military power. The other was the mounted armoured knight with his shield and couched lance. The castle was a dual-purpose building, a fortified residence (or residential fortress) for a king, prince or feudal lord, and it was the symbol and the substance of feudal lordship. Its rôle was both defensive and offensive, that is, it housed and protected the lord and his family, his servants and dependants, and some if not all of his knights who were sworn in fealty to serve him in war for a number of days each year. It also acted as a base from which the lord and his knights could sally forth to control the countryside belonging to him and if necessary or desirable to attack his neighbours or enemies from further afield. It was the centre of his particular sphere of government and in it or within its boundaries all kinds of business were conducted: legal and financial, complaints could be heard, grants discussed, petitions heard, disputes brought for arbitration, and commercial transactions negotiated. It was therefore a very important building and had if possible to appear so.

The Tower of London

The castle was built to dominate the landscape, and it did so sometimes by its sheer size and the prominent position on which it was erected, sometimes just because it was the only fortified residential building anywhere in or near a town or in the countryside. The castle was thus the visual expression of the lord's authority over his lands, and his dominion was roughly measurable by the distance he and his knights could ride out on a planned raid or in response to an emergency situation and back again in one operation; and this might be anything up to about 15 miles each way. In other words, he who held the castle controlled the land immediately around it, but he had to build, or capture, the castle first. Clearly, castles were structures to give credence to conquest and occupation of territory. And in England their rapid erection (in some cases, as at Dover and York, within eight days or so) was something very few Anglo-Saxons had witnessed, since no castles had been built in Britain before Hastings and Pevensey (save for three in Herefordshire and one in Essex, all by Norman friends of Edward the Confessor invited to reside in England). Castles were thus very alarming new features on the landscape and they caused both fear and resentment among the English. As the Norman monk-chronicler Ordericus Vitalis (*c.* 1075–1143) commented in his *Ecclesiastical History*, 'castles had been very few in the English provinces, and for this reason the English, although warlike and courageous, had nevertheless shown themselves too weak to withstand their enemies.' The construction of the first castles in London – there were to be three of

Aerial view of Clifford's Tower castle in York. The tower was built in the mid-13th century upon the mound of one of the motte-and-bailey castles that William the Conqueror raised in York, 1068/9.

6

The mound of the motte-and-bailey castle built in Cambridge by the Conqueror in 1068. Later on, the site became the nucleus of an extensive castle of stone, nearly all traces of which have vanished.

them – took only a few weeks, in the period just before and just after Christmas 1066, and this caused the same sort of consternation among the Londoners. Indeed, they were meant to, as another Norman chronicler, William of Poitiers, wrote: 'while certain fortifications were completed in the city against the fickleness of the vast and fierce populace.'

The Tower of London was not a typical feudal castle like the other castles built all over England in those early days. It was not, for example, William's home, as he appears to have preferred Edward the Confessor's palace at Westminster. Nor was the relationship between the king and the City of London a strictly feudal one, then or later. True, the Tower, its establishment and the organs of government it accommodated, were feared for a long time by the city on whose eastern borders it stood. But in the 14th century, the Crown formed an alliance with the dominant merchant class in London, which prevailed thereafter. At the same time, Westminster became the real capital city of England, in government and law. The role of the Tower as a royal administrative centre developed in this context. Its military strategic role came to the fore only in times of internal[1] or external[2] threat. As important as its practical functions was its symbolic role, the principal representation of royal power – hence it became the natural place for royalist and patriotic

1 Such as the Peasants' Revolt (1381) and at times during the Wars of the Roses (1455–85).
2 It was in danger twice during the attempt by Bonnie Prince Charlie (the Young Pretender) to unseat the Hanoverians from the British throne, 1745–6.

exhibitions and displays which developed from the Restoration period onwards. Yet because it was started by a feudal prince who was introducing into England a style of feudalism centred on the person – and the personality – of the king, the Tower has to be regarded as the principal feudal structure and symbol of Norman England.

Although there are remains of over 2,000 mediaeval castles in Britain (excluding Ireland), and each castle is or was an individual building, different from the next one, they were nonetheless all of one or other of two basic types. One was an enclosure with towers and sometimes other structures in the wall perimeter, inside of which was the dominant feature of a large tower set either on a mound of earth or rising from ground level. This was the owner's fortified residence. The other type was an enclosure with towers and other structures in the wall perimeter, and with a variety of buildings free-standing inside, erected for a variety of uses – such as chapel, dining hall, residential quarters, stables, armoury and so forth, but not including a great tower. The fortifications were concentrated along the wall length, in the gate tower or gate house, and in the towers in the wall length. Of course, many castles ended up being a mixture of the two types. Most, though not all, castles began by being constructed from timber and earth, but a few had stone buildings and/or walling from scratch. If they were of timber and earth, they were either a motte-and-bailey type or an enclosure type. The motte-and-bailey consisted of a flat-topped mound of earth (motte) surmounted with a tall wooden residential and fortified tower, with an irregularly shaped enclosure, or bailey, at one side of it (or in some cases surrounding it), the whole encircled by a deep ditch, and the motte top and the bailey perimeter both being enclosed by timber palisades. The enclosure type has been described, and the timber and earth variety could provide the same kind of accommodation and services and be strongly fortified as the stone variety, though not as durably.

The beginning of the Tower of London

The Tower of London began as a simple timber and earth enclosure tucked in the south-east angle formed by the joining of the original east and south stone walls of the old Roman town of *Londinium Augusta*, which was completed by the addition of a ditch and palisade along the north and west sides. This simple enclosure then received a huge stone *donjon*, or great tower, which in time came to be called the White Tower and which was a real residential palace and fortress fit for a king. The castle was later improved further by the addition of other smaller towers, extra buildings and so forth, so that it evolved into a splendid example of a mixture of the two basic types of castle. It was also to have an inner ring of walling with towers and gates and then an outer ring of walling with towers and gates, which made it a concentric castle and, so far as England was concerned, one of the few of this very expensive type of castle to be erected.[3]

3 Some of these castles, like Dover and London, evolved into concentric castles over a long period, others like Caerphilly, Harlech, Rhuddlan, Beaumaris, were built more or less in one operation – at great cost in each case.

This is a section of 4th century AD walling of Roman London, discovered during excavations in the mid-1970s by the river front.

The chronicles tell us that after winning the battle at Hastings, Duke William gathered up his forces with the intention of marching to London, the principal city (though not yet the capital) of England. He decided, however, to go there by a circuitous route to impress on the inhabitants of the south-east corner of the country that they now had a new king whose writ was about to run throughout the land and that he would brook no opposition. If there was, it would be met with force. So he went via Dover, Canterbury, Winchester, Wallingford (on the Thames) and arrived at Berkhamsted, and as each place he ordered a timber and earth castle to be built in a commanding position. At Berkhamsted he received the submission of a number of Anglo-Saxon lords and chief men, mainly from London and the home counties, and then he began to make preparations for his coronation which was to take place, symbolically, in King Edward the Confessor's abbey at Westminster on Christmas Day. To that end he sent ahead into the city an advance party of adherents to organize the construction of fortifications (*munitiones*) in order to cower the citizenry and to protect himself and his followers. What these *munitiones* were exactly is not specified but they must have included the enclosure castle in the south-east angle of the old Roman city boundaries and also the other two castles put up at the same time, namely Baynard's to the south-west of the present Tower of London, and

Montfitchet to the north, near the present Ludgate Circus. Remains of these two are no longer visible but they have been traced and identified before being covered up again.

After celebrating his coronation, which was marred by some violence when his Norman soldiery attempted to control the London mob, William pulled out of the city and stayed for a while at what is now the eastern suburb of Barking, 'while certain fortifications were completed in the city' (see page 9). It is safe to say that these included finishing the enclosure that became the Tower of London. The south stone wall, incidentally, had had a *re-entrant* since Roman times where it met the eastern wall close to the river bank. This was discovered in recent excavations by the Department of the Environment Ancient Monuments Branch (as it was in the 1970s). Earlier excavations of the mid 1960s and 1970s had, meanwhile, uncovered two stretches of ditching, a short length that runs from immediately north of the present Bloody Tower for about 20 metres on the western side and forms part of the western defensive ditch of the original enclosure, and a longer and curving stretch that runs from the eastern Roman wall at a point just north of the White Tower westwards until it reaches a point opposite the west corner of the White Tower where is swings south-westwards curving to due southwards to a point opposite the north side of the Bloody Tower though not quite in line with the shorter length. The shorter length can still be seen today, but the longer curving stretch cannot, though we know it was about 26 feet (8 metres) wide and about 11 feet (3.5 metres) deep.

No traces have yet been found of any original timber buildings, residential or otherwise, from that first period. Possibly within twelve years, more certainly within fifteen, the foundations were laid for a substantial great tower, which was to be a major fortress-palace for the king, inside the enclosure and curiously squashed close to both the eastern Roman wall and the northern-western ditch and rampart – curiously because if you look at the plan (page 23) the builders appear to have allowed themselves very little room in which to erect scaffolding and assemble all the tools, materials, wagons, etc. on the site, except on the south flank. But build it they did, and we can still see the result today, modified in some of its exterior decoration it is true, but substantially as it will have been unfolded to the people of London when the scaffolding was finally taken down during the reign of William II.

The building of castles

We have seen that simple timber and earth castles could be erected in a matter of weeks, even days. Constructing castles in stone, such as the White Tower, took years, and each one posed a catalogue of problems for the building management organization, some of which had to be identified and solved well in advance of cutting out a single cubic foot of earth to provide a trench for wall foundation material. Construction work was supervized by the king's officials in conjunction with master masons (though the term was not known then), some of whom may have been sent for by the king from Normandy where they had had experience building

The first castle built on the site of the Tower of London by the Conqueror just before or just after Christmas 1066 was surrounded on two sides by a ditch. This is a section of the ditch near the Wakefield Tower (itself not built until the 13th century).

castles and churches for him and others in the duchy, other may have been English masons who had experience of stone building at one or other of a range of stone churches and also great hall buildings. The semi-skilled and non-skilled work was done by Anglo-Saxons pressed into service as diggers and other labourers (see the workers erecting the mound at Hastings castle, on the Bayeux Tapestry panel, page 1). The skilled men, such as carpenters, stone cutters, carvers, blacksmiths, will probably have come from both England and Normandy.

The labouring gangs had to be rounded up from the locality or if needed from nearby counties (to build the castle at Ely, in William's reign, he had to impress men from Cambridgeshire, and also from Huntingdonshire and Bedfordshire). These hired men were probably not paid, and if they were, the rates would have been low, being even lower in winter months. For this they had to work all day for six days a week, from daybreak to dusk. In Anglo-Saxon times the kings had a right to deploy labourers from their jobs, whatever these might be, to help build fortifications for the *burhs*, or fortified towns, which had to be erected against Viking assault. They received pay, and presumably their jobs were held open for them to return to. This right was known as *burh-bot*, and was almost as important as compulsory military service in the old *fyrd*. Under the Conqueror, the right of *burh-bot* was claimed in support of the practice of forced labour to build castles, in other words, as *The History of the King's Works* puts it,[4] *burh-bot* became *castelwerke*.

4 *The History of the King's Works*, Brown, R. A., Colvin, H. M. & Taylor, A. J., Vol. 1., H.M.S.O., London, 1963, p.24.

We should look at some of the other problems confronting the management organization in charge of building a castle in mid- to late-eleventh century England, for it is a matter of much wonder how well the mediaeval builder coped. In the case of the Tower of London, as indeed with many castles, the nearness of water was a major consideration. And there were other questions. Could stone be quarried on the site, or nearby, and was it suitable or was it too soft? If not, where was the nearest quarry? Did it belong to the king or to the Church? (Most quarries were royal or ecclesiastical property.) How much would it cost to use on a contract hire basis? Where was the nearest waterway both ends for transporting stone and also for other materials? Water transport was quicker than cartage by land, and it was therefore cheaper. Many of the best quarries were close to navigable rivers. What sort of stone rubble was available nearby? Were there any Roman remains, like tiles and brick fragments (at London, there were, but for the White Tower these were not much needed). Where would you be able to get the top-quality stone specifically for making the stone dressings such as the quoins (corner stones), keystones for arches, window mullions and lintels, loopholes and battlement tops? All these and other material problems were worked out by the masons, and in the case of the White Tower they settled on a coarse limestone, Kentish ragstone, for the main walls outside and inside, extracted from quarries near Maidstone on the Medway and brought in barges to the site via the Medway and the Thames. The plinth on which the White Tower stood was built from septaria (a soft, clayey limestone) found along the Thames. The ashlar dressings were made from the yellowy-white stone from the district round Caen in the Conqueror's own duchy of Normandy, since it resembled marble and it was not available in England. Quantities of Caen stone were brought from France to the Tower via ships up the Thames and cut and dressed to requirements on the site. (The dressings on the White Tower today are seventeenth- and eighteenth-century replacements and in Portland stone.)

While the masons were attending to the stone supply problems, mortar experts made arrangements for wholesale manufacture of mortar on site for cementing the stones together. Huge vats were fashioned on the river bank, in which sand and lime were to be mixed and then taken to the tower in wheelbarrows. Meanwhile, carpenters and joiners were concerned with the availability of timber. Was there a source, or were there sources, close by and were the trees tall enough to produce the required lengths of beam and plank? In some cases, castle builders contracted to purchase timber from selected suppliers, in others they leased a stretch of forest which contained appropriate trees. Oak was preferred, and in eleventh-century England this tree was plentiful and widely distributed. Of the several species available, green oak was particularly suitable for construction work, as it was easy to work, and if trees of it were cut down after about thirty years' growth, they were ready to be hewn into planks and posts and to be cut and shaped without a lot of trimming and wastage.

Other building materials were also needed, some of them in great quantity. First there was lead, used for the roofing of the tower (in the case of the White Tower there were at least two gables), and for the pipes and guttering. Iron was needed for a variety of fittings as well as for making, repairing and replacing tools for the craftsmen and labourers, and for this extra timber had to be fetched to produce charcoal for the on-site blacksmiths' forges. Today, details of requirements for all these things would be accurately estimated in advance, down to the last nail, by quantity surveyors and the whole process would be supervised by a cohesive team of architects, engineers, surveyors and others, but in the eleventh-century there was no such process and no such team. Estimating had to be guesswork, and supervision would be shared on a piecemeal basis between someone appointed by the owner (in the White Tower's case, the king) who was an administrative and financial specialist – probably a cleric, too, and the most experienced building mason actually appointed to the project.

We do not know who was the actual designer of the White Tower, though from its similarity to that of Colchester Castle's great tower (built at much the same time) it was clearly the work of the same person or group of people. Its design, moreover, together with that of Colchester which resembles it, albeit on a bigger scale, is quite

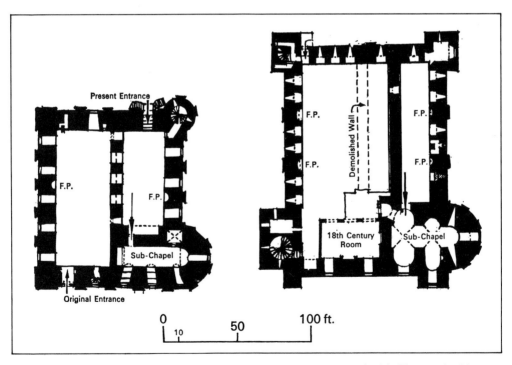

Comparative first floor plans of the White Tower (left) and Colchester great tower (right). These are the oldest great towers in England, and they are also the only ones in the UK to have a rounded apsidal extension along the east wall. Although the towers differ in some particulars, they were almost certainly designed by the same man, Gundulf, later Bishop of Rochester.

The Great Tower of Colchester Castle. This was built in roughly the same period as the White Tower, i.e. about 1076–1100, and it was the work of the same Gundulf, Bishop of Rochester. There was at least one further storey on the original building, and possibly two. Its plan is much the same as that of the White Tower, but on a larger scale. Note especially the rounded extension at the south-east corner. The great tower was sold to a local builder in the 1680s, who attempted to demolish it, but gave up the struggle when he got down to the height it is to-day.

unlike any other great tower built in England – or indeed in Europe – in the eleventh century, which has survived for us to make comparison. Since fortified residences and fortified palaces of stone were not built in England before the Conquest, then the design of the White Tower and of Colchester must be derivative of an European model which has since vanished. One suggestion is that they were modelled on the fortress palace built by the Normans at Rouen in the tenth century (but which was demolished in 1204). This in turn may have been modelled on examples built by the later Frankish kings.

With this in mind, we may connect the fact recorded in the Textus Roffensis (the register of Rochester Cathedral for the period) that work on the great tower of London was supervised by Gundulf whom the same register later describes as 'very competent and skilful at building in stone', and in so doing we arrive at the name of the man at least responsible for getting the White Tower built and presumably overseeing the arrangements, if not checking all the architectural detail (much of which would normally be decided by the mason on the spot). Who was this Gundulf?

Gundulf was born of Norman parents near Rouen in 1024. As a youngster he will have often seen the ducal palace of the Normans in the city. Gundulf entered the service of the cathedral at Rouen on the administrative side and became the cathedral clerk. Some time in the 1050s he went on a pilgrimage to Jerusalem, and on his way back, during a terrible storm in which the ship was in danger of capsizing, he vowed to enter the church as a monk. He was accepted at the great Norman abbey at Bec where he was to meet and become friends with Lanfranc (1005–89), the Italian-born scholar who had become prior at Bec in 1046. Lanfranc was appointed prior of Caen Abbey in 1063 and he invited Gundulf to join him there, and when in 1070 Lanfranc was made Archbishop of Canterbury in succession to the Anglo-Saxon Stigand, again Lanfranc asked Gundulf to accompany him. At Canterbury, Gundulf is believed to have surveyed and carried out rebuilding works at the cathedral. While he was becoming an increasingly pious and devoted man of the Church, he was also acquiring a reputation as a specialist in construction matters, notably ecclesiastical and military structures in stone.

In 1077, Gundulf was made Bishop of Rochester, obviously through the influence of Lanfranc, and he was to remain there until his death in 1108. Quite early on, Gundulf set about rebuilding the cathedral at Rochester and expanding the monastic buildings. He also built St Leonard's Tower as well as a nunnery at nearby West Malling. Evidently he had already been consulted about other buildings in stone, and these must have included the White Tower and Colchester great tower.

The year 1077 was important for Rochester. It was also a significant date for establishing approximately when the White Tower was begun. Part of the first reference to Gundulf in the Textus Roffensis (see above, page 14) mentions property in London that was given to the priory at Rochester by a London burgess who was keen to join their community. This gift was offered at some time to Gundulf, Bishop of Rochester, when the latter was staying in the house of the donor, who was one Eadmer Anhaende, 'while the same Gundulf, by command of king William the Great, was in charge of the work of the great tower of London.' The White Tower must have been started not before 1077 but surely not long afterwards, and 1078 or 1079 would seem reasonable. If Gundulf also had a hand in the work at Colchester, a starting date for which was recently put at between 1074 and 1076 (*Archaeological Journal*, 139 [1982], pp. 302–419), this fits into place well. The plans on page 13 show the striking similarities between the two buildings. Additional weight is given to Gundulf's reputation as a castle specialist by the later reference to his competence, which relates to his being commissioned to erect a castle at Rochester, under the shadow of his cathedral there, sometime between 1087 and 1089. While not responsible for the splendid twelfth-century great tower at Rochester (that came two or three decades after his death), he did raise the stone wall enclosure castle on the site inside which the great tower was subsequently built.

We now have our supervisor of the building of the White Tower with his good track record, and we may be sure he saw to it that the masons in site charge were the best that Normandy and England could furnish, for they were after all building a fortress palace for a great and powerful king. But how was the actual work done?

The ground was carefully surveyed to see if there was a buried rock base below, which might support a stone building. If not, trenches were cut by the digger gangs to ram down hardcore for foundations. For a great tower like the White Tower, the trenches would be a yard or so wider than the proposed wall thickness and the sloping or splayed plinth on which it would stand. The trenches were filled with an assortment of rubble, stone, tile and brick, and these might go down as much as 15–20 feet (4.6–6 metres). Then the tower's plinth was constructed on top of the foundations. In the White Tower's case, the material for the plinth was the septaria from Thameside (see page 12), and the plinth was splayed outwards on the south, east and west sides of the Tower (but not the north) because the Tower was erected upon sloping ground. Next, the first levels of the four walls were put together above and sitting on top of the plinth. In the White Tower the walls at these low levels were 11½–14½ feet (3.5–4.5 metres) thick.

As the first courses of walling were raised, it became necessary to erect scaffolding to continue the work. Long poles lashed together with tarred rope were anchored with horizontal poles which are called put-logs and which were let into the masonry already built. These put-logs slotted into put-logs holes, and on the surface of many great towers you can still see patterns of rows of these holes, as at Colchester and Hedingham in Essex, Guildford in Surrey, Kenilworth in Warwickshire, Portchester in Hampshire, Castle Rising in Norfolk – and here and there on the White Tower, too! This scaffolding would incorporate pulley wheel and basket lift arrangements at regular intervals, so that several sections of wall could be built at the same time.

As the walls rose vertically, consideration was given to constructing passages, chambers, staircases (usually in angles where two walls met) within the thickness of the walls, to adding pilaster or other kinds of exterior buttresses, either for wall support or to house drains from the tower's garderobes (latrines). The actual appointments within the walls and inside of the walls of the White Tower are described in the next chapter, but we can say that they are on the whole more elaborate and in many instances more spacious, as befitted the principal fortress palace of the king of England.

The White Tower is about 90 feet (27.5 metres) tall to the tops of the present battlements (which were refurbished in the seventeenth century) not including the four corner turret tops. How long did it take to build? We do not know for certain, for no-one kept a record of each year's or each season's works. Assuming it to have been started in about 1078, and that it was completed by 1096 or 1097 when William Rufus embarked upon building a surrounding stone wall for the whole castle, it looks like twenty years. Yet a careful assessment of the average time taken to build castles in the eleventh and twelfth centuries was made some years ago by D. F. Renn, who examined the building cost records of a number of castles, year by year, and arrived at an average of about 10 feet (3 metres) of tower wall height per year, allowing for long periods when little or no work was done because of climate, short periods of daylight and damage through storm or wind, careless mortaring, and so forth.[5]

On this basis the White Tower ought to have been completed inside ten years, but

5 *Norman Castles in Britain*, D. F. Renn, London, 1973.

it is clear that it was not, and we may partly account for this by emphasizing that dimensionally it was far larger than any other great tower in eleventh- and twelfth-century England, except Colchester which was about a third larger on the horizontal dimensions though about the same height vertically, that the tower includes the marvellous Chapel of St John, a small but very fine example of Romanesque architecture that on its own will have taken years to build, and that possibly some damage was done in the year 1089 when, according to the Anglo-Saxon Chronicle, England was rent by a great earthquake.

The Chapel of St John in the second floor of the White Tower. It rises two floors in height. It was built from limestone brought to London in barges and ships from Normandy. It is a fine example of Norman Romanesque architecture.

17

In the autumn of 1087 William I was in France, laying siege to Mantes, a city in the domain of his own sovereign, Philip I of France, when he stumbled and fell off his horse, sustaining severe injuries. He was taken back to Normandy and on or about 9 September he died at or near Rouen. It is tempting to think that he had details of the progress of the building of his great fortress palace in London, and that perhaps he was satisfied with the way it was coming along. Certainly his heir, his second surviving son William Rufus, who became William II, continued with the building work, which he saw to a triumphant conclusion before he also died a violent death, shot through the heart by an arrow fired at him by mistake by a friend during a day's hunting in the New Forest, on 1 August 1100.

Adding to the building

The Conqueror died leaving his duchy of Normandy to his eldest son, Robert, and his kingdom of England to his next surviving son, William Rufus. Among the properties in the inheritance of England were at least eighty castles, some of them directly owned by the Crown but managed by castellans, some in the hands of great lords but in every case ultimately belonging to the Crown. Chief of the first category was the Tower of London whose principal feature, the White Tower, was probably about half completed. There is no actual record that the Conqueror enjoined his son to continue building castles but the increase from over eighty in 1087 to well over one hundred by 1100 (though exactly how many of these were the result of direct order of the king is not known) is ample testimony to the fundamental importance with which Rufus regarded castle-building as integral with that feudalization process which he was determined to continue, as part of his father's legacy. The Conqueror had purposely left England to the tougher, sterner and more practical William rather than to his brave, easy-going but unreliable eldest son, Robert.

We have seen that the kingdom endured some unspecified climatic disaster or series of disasters in 1089, described by the Anglo-Saxon Chronicle as a great earthquake over all England, and another record tells how in 1091 the Tower itself was 'by tempest and wind sore shaken' (but also unspecified), and these natural disasters cannot but have halted progress on the completing of the White Tower. Then, an entry in the Anglo-Saxon Chronicle for the year 1097 gives us what may be a date by which the great palace-fortress was finished. After lamenting the tribulations of a very bad year, the chronicler adds, 'moreover, men from many shires, in fulfilling their labour service to the city of London, were sorely oppressed in building the wall around the Tower, and in repairing the bridge nearly all of which had been carried away.' Many historians take this to mean that, since the White Tower was now finished, the king decided to surround it with a stone wall.

As two sides of the Conqueror's 1066–7 enclosure (inside which the White Tower was later erected) were stone walls originally built in Roman times, we would not be far wrong if we assumed that the other two walls of 1066–7, of earth and timber, were now levelled and new stone walling was put up in their place. The stone wall enclosure, moreover, must have included a gate-tower or, more probably, two gate-towers, one of which would surely have been on the river side of the castle. Possibly, also, there were one or two mural towers from which guards could watch over the walls for possible intruders. Inside this enclosure stood the new White Tower, pretty much as it looks today, 900 years later.

The White Tower

The White Tower is almost rectangular, though not quite, because three of the corners are not absolutely true right angles. It is about 107 feet (33 metres) from east to west and 118 feet (36.3 metres) north-south, with a rounded turret on the north-east corner which contains a spiral staircase all the way up from the basement (ground) floor to the top. On the south-east corner is a rounded apsidal projection eastwards. This is a plan similar to that of the great tower at Colchester (whose east-west dimension is 110 feet [33.8 metres] and the north-south is 151 feet [46.5 metres] (see p. 13). Around the outside of the White Tower are pilaster buttresses at regular intervals, wider on the north-west and the south-west angle turrets than elsewhere. The tower is 90 feet (27.7 metres) high to the top of the present battlements, and the turret tops rise another 16–21 feet (6.5–7.5 metres) where they are capped with lead-covered cupolas.

Entrance to the tower was on the south wall at first-floor level, between the south-west turret and the first pilaster buttress eastwards along the wall – where it is to-day. Most great towers had their principal entrance at this level, for obvious security reasons. It is approached by an exposed staircase of wood, in three flights and three landings. This is a modern construction which stands along and close to the south wall, but the first staircase of the eleventh century will have been similar, though perhaps with fewer landings. Sometime, in the twelfth century perhaps, this original access was enhanced by the addition of a stonework forebuilding to protect the staircase and the door into the tower. There were to be other buildings grafted on to the original tower later on, which are mentioned as they become chronologically relevant, in addition to the changes made to features on the outside of the tower itself such as doorways, windows and decorative facings. The tower stands on a broad, sloping plinth which has also seen alterations during the tower's long existence.

Inside, the tower today is four storeys high, divided unequally by a crosswall rising from the basement to the top, which results in a larger western section and a smaller eastern one. A crosswall served several purposes. It strengthened the building, it allowed the floor joists and beams to be cut to far shorter lengths than the width or length of the tower itself and so reduced the need to find huge trees for excessively long timbers. And it supplied an extra obstacle for besiegers who had broken in and were fighting their way gradually up the Tower (as happened at Rochester in 1216). The eastern section is further divided by a thick wall running east-to-west which forms the north side for the sub-crypt (basement level), crypt (first floor level) and the two-storeyed Chapel of St John which has its east end and high altar in the apsidal extension. The tower walls are about 15 feet (4.6 metres) thick as basement (ground) level and about 11 feet (3.4 metres) thick in the top storey. At second floor level, in both south-west corner turret and north-west corner turret, further spiral staircases were inserted later, taking one up to the top storey and thence to the roof. The White Tower's walls were thick enough to accommodate passages, chambers, garderobes (e.g. two in the north wall at first floor level) and fireplaces.

When the tower was first built it had three floors, basement (ground), first and second. The second was two storeys high with a mural gallery all round the upper storey level. It was the same height as the two-storey Chapel of St John that filled the south-east corner of the second floor. The mural gallery continued southwards from the eastern part of the second floor and higher level into the chapel where it served as the triforium.

The second floor contained the main residential suite for the king, his family and now and again guests, and it was provided with garderobes and fireplaces. The crosswall dividing it was punctuated with connecting openings. In this floor were the great dining hall (in the western portion), the great chamber, which was more a bed-sitting room, and of course the chapel. The chapel was entered through a small opening in the southern wall of the great chamber, closest to the crosswall. The whole floor had lofty ceilings and both lower and upper stages were well lit (for their time!) by window openings with standard Romanesque round arches, the windows being of various sizes and shapes. Sometime, many centuries later, a timber floor was inserted to make a fourth floor at the mural gallery level, which meant inserting some timber pillar supports in the lower storey. This explains its 4 storey arrangement today. The timber supports on both first and second floors are 18th century, but the inserted top floor dates from the beginning of the 17th century.

Below the second floor was the first floor. Its layout was originally quite similar to the lower storey of the second floor, namely, a slightly less elaborate great dining hall in the western portion, a great chamber in the north-east, and having on the south side of that chamber the crypt of the Chapel of St John, and this was a lesser chapel. This floor was probably occupied by the constable of the Tower or his deputy, the man actually in command of the castle. The floor also contained the main entrance to the tower. It was not so well lit by windows, partly of course because there was only one level of them. The crosswall also had connecting openings between the great hall and the great chamber, but there was no direct access from the great hall into the crypt – you had to go via the great chamber. The spiral staircase in the north-east turret that served all levels was at first-floor level reached via a short passage out of the great chamber. Some time in the fourteenth century, a new spiral staircase connecting the first floor with the second floor was inserted in the south wall, to the east of the main entrance. The first floor was provided with garderobes and fireplaces. In the north wall of the crypt, exactly in line with where the eastern wall of the tower itself joins the crypt, is a small rectangular chamber which seems to have been used as a prison cell in Tudor times, but which before that had less unpleasant uses.

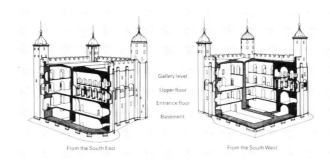

Two cut-away elevations of the White Tower; (left) from the south-east, and (right) from the south-west.

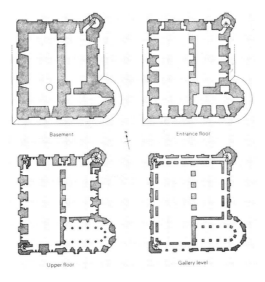

Floor plans of the White Tower in about 1100.

The basement storey, which is partly at ground floor level and partly beneath it because the whole tower is on sloping ground down towards the river's edge, is divided by the common crosswall, and the eastern section has a compartment, the sub-crypt, exactly underneath the crypt of the Chapel of St John. The whole basement storey was probably used for storage and other services, but it has to be stressed that it is likely that it was rarely if ever used for prisoners in the Middle Ages. In the larger western section is the tower's well. Access to the basement was originally only from the spiral staircase in the north-east turret (unless there was any kind of trapdoor in the flooring of the first floor), but at various times after the original building work, openings were forced from outside by altering original arrow loops, one on the north-east corner turret, two in the north wall and one in the south wall, and traces of such alterations can be seen to-day.

This then was the great tower that by the end of William Rufus' reign was dominating the skyline of London, the symbol of the Conqueror's resolution that England should be his kingdom and after him that of his successors. The tower was not of course called the White Tower then, and indeed we do not know exactly when the name first came to be used. But we do know why, and this is because in 1240 King Henry III ordered the tower to be whitewashed all over inside and outside. By the end of William's reign, other works had also been carried out, in particular the building of the wall that 'sorely oppressed' so many men from the shires who were pressed into service of *castelwerke*. In connection with the imposition of *castelwerke*, it is interesting to add that it was disliked not only by those actually pressed but also in many cases by their employers or landlords. There are records of religious establishments applying to the Crown to be granted exemption from supplying labour for *castelwerke* (and for other building work, too) at a number of sites. In William II's reign the canons of St Paul's in London successfully applied for exemption on the grounds that the king's father had not meant them to provide labour for the work on the Tower of London.

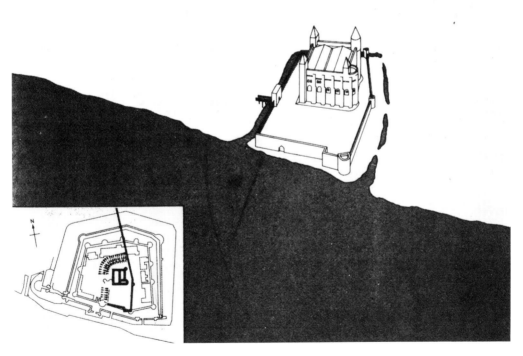

A rough elevation of the Tower as it was in about 1100, when the White Tower was complete. Plan of the Tower at the same time as above. Earlier structures (such as the old Roman wall) are in grey tint, new buildings are in black.

The First Escape from the Tower

Rufus died on 1 August 1100 and was succeeded by his next brother Henry I, the only one of the Conqueror's children who could read and write – hence his nickname Beauclerc. Cast in the same tough and uncompromising character as his father and Rufus, and more politically astute than either of them, Henry began well in English – that is, Anglo-Saxon – eyes. Mindful that his brother had made all sorts of promises of less oppressive rule and less extortionate taxation and had then broken them, the new king promptly arrested the principal agent for William's misdeeds, his chief minister Ranulf Flambard, Bishop of Durham, and put him in the White Tower. Thus Flambard became the first of a long line of distinguished (and often notorious) prisoners who spent time as a prisoner in the Tower. But within six months Flambard achieved a second record when he became the first prisoner to escape from the Tower.

Ranulf Flambard, a scholar of humble origins, became a cleric. He had a ruthless capacity for getting work done for him by other people, he was unscrupulous and dishonest and was quite unfitted to be a high dignitary of the church, which in time he became. He attracted the notice of William Rufus during the last years of the Conqueror's reign, and when Rufus succeeded, Flambard was quickly given preferment because he seemed so willing to be the agent of the new king's more outrageous and exacting policies, particularly in matters in finance, to such an extent that chroniclers talked about all justice being asleep, when 'money was the Lord'. They also tell of Flambard's habit of selling church appointments to the highest bidder. But he had his good side, too, as all men and woman do, and it is thought that he had a direct hand in supervising the completion of the White Tower, after Bishop Gundulf had settled down in Rochester attending to his diocesan work and his building schemes there. Flambard was appointed Bishop of Durham by his master, and certainly he played a major role in the work on the wonderful cathedral that was going up in that faraway northern city. When Rufus was killed in August 1100 it probably came as an alarming shock to Flambard as he will have realised at once that his enemies would be looking to the new king to redress many grievances, as indeed it happened, for almost the first act of Henry after his coronation was to order Flambard's arrest and lodgement in the White Tower.

Flambard's time in the White Tower was relatively short, and it was by no means uncomfortable. If he had had a hand in completing the building, he would have known its internal layout better than his gaolers! Two shillings a day were allotted for the expenses of keeping him (no small sum in those times), and he appears to have eaten well and entertained friends generously. Probably he was accommodated on the second floor of the White Tower, for no part of the White Tower was specifically built for imprisonment purposes, nor was any part used consistently as such. Where a prisoner was lodged depended upon his rank and how long he was likely to be kept there. Flambard was allowed to have provisions brought in from outside, especially supplies of his favourite wines which came in casks. On 2 February 1101, Candlemas

Day, Flambard held a party for his guards. He had arranged for a length of rope to be secreted in one of the wine casks due for delivery the day before. He managed to get all the guards drunk, then took the rope out of the empty cask. Tying one end to one of the pillars by a window, he let himself down the outside of the tower wall, clutching (it is said) his bishop's crozier. Unfortunately, he had misjudged the length of rope needed and it was too short by several feet. He had to jump a few yards to reach the ground where he rolled over in some discomfort. He hobbled down towards the river and there boarded a boat for the south bank where a horse was ready for him to ride as quickly as possible to the coast. From the coast he took ship to Normandy to join Robert, Duke of Normandy, Henry's eldest brother, who was plotting with disaffected nobles to invade England and seize the throne which he felt his father should have left to him. The revolt was not successful, at it turned out, but we do not know what part Flambard played or whether any retribution was visited upon him. But he had shown it was possible to escape from the Tower of London.

Henry I was an enthusiastic castle-builder – the great towers at Corfe and Norwich were among his major works – and he will undoubtedly have spent periods at the Tower. There are some financial details of money spent on works there in 1129–30, but they say nothing about what the works were and give us no clues. In 1113 the castle was damaged by fire, but whether this was the White Tower or the surrounding works is not known. The current belief is that he began, if he did not complete, the forebuilding covering the first-floor entrance to the White Tower. It was built of stone, but we have only a slight idea of what it might have looked like, as can be seen from the map of 1597 (see colour plate), which has at least got the forebuilding in the right place if not in its actual shape.

Henry died in 1135, 'a good man . . . held in great awe . . . he made peace for man and beast . . .', the Peterborough version of the Anglo-Saxon Chronicle tells us. The man who followed, his nephew Stephen, Count of Blois (whose mother was the Conqueror's daughter), was not of the same stamp. Brave, kindly, courteous, good-natured, he was also weak and vacillating, and not as we would put it today 'leadership material'.

Stephen had sworn to support Henry's daughter Matilda, whom Henry had willed should succeed him, but once the king was dead, Stephen, backed by a number of powerful English lords who probably pushed him against his will, challenged her right of succession and thus began a period of nearly twenty years of civil war between himself and his cousin and their respective supporters, many of whom thought nothing of changing sides at the drop of a lance. History has rightly condemned the period as anarchic, calling it the reign of nineteen long winters, and an extract from the Anglo-Saxon Chronicle, though extended, deserves to be quoted because of its preoccupation with castles as well as its portrait of a nation's misery.

'For every great man built him castles and held them against the king; and they filled the whole land with these castles. They sorely burdened the unhappy people

25

of the country with forced labour on the castles; and when the castles were built, they filled then with devils and wicked men. By night and day they seized those whom they believed to have any wealth, whether they were men or women; and in order to get their gold and silver, they put them into prison and tortured them with unspeakable tortures . . . they hung them up by the feet and smoked them with foul smoke. They strung them up by the thumbs, or by the head, and hung coats of mail on their feet. They tied knotted cords round their heads and twisted it till it entered the brain. They put them in dungeons wherein were adders and snakes and toads, and so destroyed them. Some they put in a 'crucethus', that is to say, into a short, narrow shallow chest into which they put sharp stones; and they crushed the man in it until they had broken every bone in his body. In many of the castles were certain instruments of torture so heavy that two or three men had enough to do to carry one . . . Many thousands they starved to death.

. . . It lasted throughout the nineteen years that Stephen was king, and always grew worse and worse. At regular intervals they levied a tax, known as 'tenserie' (protection money) upon the villages. When the wretched people had no more to give, they plundered and burned all the villages . . . Then was corn dear and flesh and cheese and butter, for there was none in the land. The wretched people perished with hunger; some who had been great men were driven to beggary . . . Never did a country endure greater misery . . . and men said openly that Christ and His saints slept . . .'[1]

For the Tower of London the reign was eventful. One of the great lords (and one who did change sides more than once) was Geoffrey de Mandeville, Earl of Essex, and he succeeded in getting control of the Tower for a period, which was confirmed in a charter of 1141 granted by Matilda. The same lord was then granted the Tower in the same year, but this time by Stephen. Such was the fluctuation of this man's loyalties. His father, also Geoffrey, had been made Constable of the Tower by the Conqueror. Nothing is recorded of works at the Tower in this turbulent reign, which came to a close in 1154.

Henry II and his Castles

Henry Plantagenet, Duke of Normandy, Duke of Aquitaine, Count of Anjou and Lord of Brittany, son of Empress Matilda and great-grandson of the Conqueror, came to the English throne as Henry II when he was only twenty-one. By then he was famous for his strong intellect, strong will and strong passions, and he had already proved himself a courageous and brilliant commander in war. Broadly built, with freckled face, fierce grey eyes and red hair cut close in Norman style, he had a harsh, cracked voice and was given to ungovernable fits of temper. His energy was boundless and it was said that he never sat down except to meals which he ate hurriedly or on horseback on which he travelled ceaselessly about his dominions in France and Britain. Finding his kingdom war-torn and miserable, he set out to

1 *The Anglo-Saxon Chronicle*; trans. G. N. Garmonsway, Everyman, London, 1953, at pp.264–5.

Henry Plantagenet, Henry II of England (1154–89), who was also Duke of Normandy, Duke of Aquitaine, Count of Anjou, Count of Touraine, Lord of Brittany. Henry was a great castle builder; among his works were Orford, Newcastle, the great tower at Dover, Nottingham, Scarborough, and Bridgnorth. Among many achievements, Henry initiated a range of legal reforms for which he is justly remembered.

restore order and to humble the unruly feudal lords who had made life so awful for Stephen and for the people for so long.

Among the many areas which commanded Henry's attention during his reign were military fortification and building. Like the Conqueror and his sons, he was a keen castle-builder, and many of those already started in earlier reigns were greatly enhanced, among them Dover and Windsor, Newcastle and Scarborough, Nottingham and Winchester. He also built a brand-new castle at Orford in Suffolk, which had – and still has – a unique great tower with twenty-one sides. Henry spent more on castles than on any other royal works (see below, page 29). But despite this activity (and there were some ninety castles where works of some kind were done during his thirty-five year reign), very little indeed seems to have been done at the Tower of London. The Exchequer accounts show only a few small sums, about £200 in all the reign, in the money of the time. (Orford Castle alone had cost him over £1,400 to build). A sum of £60 was spent on the White Tower in 1172–3, though the nature of the work is not known. In 1175–6 the roof over the Chapel of St John was covered with lead, and in 1177–8 timber was obtained from Yorkshire and used to repair the Tower, possibly to replace beams in the roof and under the floorboards. There was also money spent on repairing 'the king's houses in the bailey' in 1171–2, though what buildings these were we do not know. The twelfth-century writer (and biographer of Thomas Becket), William FitzStephen, described the White Tower as *arx palatina*, which strictly speaking means fortress palace, a phrase very sparingly

A drawing of about 1600 by the celebrated map-maker John Norden, of Orford Castle on the east coast of Suffolk. Only the tall multangular great tower remains to-day. The castle was built by Henry II between 1165 and 1173 and cost over £1400 in the money of the time.

used in that century and then only to describe buildings constructed 'for regal majesty'.

On architectural grounds there is some belief that the Wardrobe Tower (now in ruins but quite visible) may have been erected in his time. It was D-shaped, sited on the old Roman wall on the east side when that repaired walling served as the easternmost curtain of the original castle of the Conqueror's early years. It is called the Wardrobe Tower because it was part of the western end of the Royal Wardrobe building, a structure that ran west to east from the tower to the Broad Arrow Tower. The Wardrobe building can be seen on the 1597 map, but it is not there now.

Despite the dearth of evidence in the original records, William FitzStephen writes that Becket, Henry's first chancellor from 1155 to 1162 and later Archbishop of Canterbury (from 1162 to his murder in Canterbury Cathedral in December 1170), who also held the post of Constable of the Tower of London, 1161–2, carried out important works at the Tower for Henry with some speed. As the account says, 'with so many smiths, carpenters and other workmen, working so vehemently with bustle and noise that a man could hardly hear the one next to him speak'. We are unable to identify any work that might be of this short period.

At this point a look at the royal expenditure on castles in the time of Henry II may be instructive, and then at the first appearance of the skilled men who put up the buildings. The Pipe Rolls of the Exchequer, that is, the records of the king's expenditure, have survived for every year of Henry II's reign except for 1154–5, every year of Richard I's short reign, and all of King John's save for 1212–13. These rolls cover most of the sums spent on the king's works, enough certainly to present a pretty fair picture of what the kings spent on their castles. From other records we know what were the basic revenues of the kings in the same years, and this enables us to see the ratio of outgoings on castles to income generally. Henry II's basic income from Crown revenues was between £9,000 and £10,000 a year, in the money of the time. This means that he grossed about £350,000 in his reign. The total spent on his castles (some ninety of them) recorded in the Pipe Rolls for the same period (but without the year 1154–5) was about £21,000, or just over 6 per cent. Of that £21,000, incidentally, about £6,500 was spent on Dover Castle alone, and of that £6,500 about £120 only was paid to the engineer of the works (who may also have designed them). He was Mauricius ingeniator (Maurice the engineer), and his pay works out to have been about 2 per cent only of the whole costs. Today, a man in this engineer's position would be architect in charge and would expect to receive at least 10 per cent of project costs. How times have changed!

It is in Henry's reign that we begin to see the structure of a building team emerging

The ruined Wardrobe Tower, one of the earliest stone buildings in the whole complex. It was probably begun in the reign of Richard I (Lionheart). It is just to the east of the White Tower.

on major royal works. Before this time there are occasional records of men in charge of building projects, but it is in the more settled years of Henry, who restored order and stability to the kingdom in a very short time, that engineers and craftsmen appear regularly by name with the sums paid to them for this or that project. One of the features that appears is that all the building people involved, salaried or waged, were itinerant workers who travelled about the country on contract to do jobs on royal sites (and on other sites as well, if the king allowed it). Maurice the engineer, for example, whom we saw worked at Dover Castle, also superintended the building of the great tower at Newcastle-upon-Tyne, a decade or so earlier, when he was also employed for the king. At Newcastle he was Maurice the stonemason, a lower grade of employment!

The great tower at Newcastle Castle. This was built by Maurice the Stonemason, between about 1168 and 1178.

The top people in the building team were the *ingeniatores* (engineers), and probably the earliest name to be recorded on a year-to-year basis is Ailnoth. He appears first in the Pipe Roll for 1157–8 and was paid 7 pence a day. He was listed as keeper of the king's houses at Westminster (a job he held up to 1189) and he worked on a variety of royal building projects, most of them in London. From 1173 to 1174 he was employed at the Tower, though we do not know what specific operations he supervised. A year later, he was arranging for timber to be fetched from a wood at Beckenham in Kent for repairs at the Tower. Ailnoth retired, probably because of old age, in 1189, and died soon after. He was succeeded by Osbert Longchamp, a Norman craftsman, whose brother William was in 1189 to be made chancellor and justiciar of England by Richard (see page 32). We shall come across other engineers who worked at the Tower later on.

Beneath the engineers were a range of individual craftsmen, masters and ordinary skilled men. Masters could earn about 6 pence a day fully engaged and half pay on retainer waiting between jobs. Ordinary craftsmen earned 3 or 4 pence, but these sums began to increase with inflation in the thirteenth century. Among the different skills mentioned in the Pipe Rolls and other documents were stonemasons (*cementarii*), stonecutters (*petrarii*), quarrymen (*quaereatores*), carpenters (*carpentarii*), miners and diggers (*minatores, fossatores*), pickmen (*picatores*), carters (*plautrarii*), smiths (*fabri*), lime-workers (*calcarii*), glaziers (*vitrarii*), plumbers (*plumbarii*). Sometimes a stonemason was considered skilled enough to build a castle. Maurice the engineer, when he was Maurice the stonemason, supervised the building of Newcastle-upon-Tyne great tower in the 1170s.

The senior skilled men were salaried and had perks like clothes allowances, rent allowances and so forth. Lesser men did piecework, time work, even casual work, and received cash at the end of a period or the end of a job. It was tough for outside workers if the weather was bad, for many would be laid off without pay. Craftsmen, doing indoor or undercover jobs, like freemasons who fashioned the stone blocks, smiths who wrought iron in forges, and glaziers who made glass and put it in windows in covered parts of buildings, all continued to be able to work in all weathers and so collected more regular money.

Improvements in Richard I's reign

Henry II's eldest surviving son Richard (the Lionheart) succeeded.to the throne in 1189. This bold, colourful, swashbuckling warrior prince, obsessed with adventure, fighting and romance, was a born leader of men, particularly suited to command an army of crusader lords and knights bound for the Near East to win back the Holy Places in Palestine from the Moslems of Sultan Saladin, Vizier of Egypt, himself a brave, chivalrous and consummate commander of men. The two were indeed well matched. Richard spent all but half a year of his reign out of his kingdom, engaged in fighting somewhere or other, yet he lavished funds on the Tower of London. Because he expected to be out of the kingdom for some time on the Third Crusade, he put the

An 18th century likeness of Richard I (1189–99), known as Coeur de Lion (Lionheart). He spent only seven months of his ten-year reign in England, and drained the nation's resources almost to bankruptcy to get funds with which to sponsor the Third Crusade.

works under the charge of the man he had made chancellor and justiciar, William Longchamp. These works were to be the first major project on the Tower for about a century.

The man Richard appointed as chancellor and justiciar turned out to be one of the most arrogant and unpopular men ever to occupy high office in the England of the later twelfth century. That Richard also left him a free run of the Tower alarmed many Londoners who feared the worst of a man whose roots were deeply buried in Normandy. Longchamp was of humble beginnings, short in stature even for men of those days whose average height was less than that of men in Britain today. He is also said to have been lame. None of this would have mattered much but for the fact that Longchamp was also bullying, haughty, tactless and greedy. He was already Bishop of Ely, an immensely rich diocese, and to be given the two top offices of state as well was probably too much for him. One chronicler (who may have been prejudiced) said that the Church found him more than pope, the laity more than king, and both an intolerable tyrant. Even in his position at the Tower he managed to infuriate Londoners by grabbing additional acreage for extending its precincts, and by putting his brother Osbert in charge of the building operations that were to follow. These works are described below (see pages 33–35) since they represent the second major stage in the development of the castle.

Longchamp's government of England in the absence of the king soon generated opposition in the highest circles, not least among the friends of the king's brother,

Prince John, whom Richard has perhaps unwisely not left in charge. Tales of extortion, roughriding over local privileges and rights, instances of arrogance and oppression began to accumulate and were filtered through to the prince. When Longchamp, in pursuit of building works at the Tower, seized neighbouring land, the Londoners complained to the Council, and the Council listened. The chancellor was out of the city at the time, but as soon as he heard that the Council had taken side against him, he gathered up a force and headed for London, aiming to get within the Tower's walls. He managed to do this, but the Council marshalled its own army, invited supporters of Prince John to join them, advanced against the Tower, and prepared to lay siege to it (1191).

Longchamp quickly saw that the game was up and that he could expect little support and, disguised as a servant woman, he slipped out of the Tower one night, heading fast for Normandy where he sent a report of the situation to his master Richard, now in the Holy Land. The Council's forces and those of Prince John, meanwhile, joined hands and entered into the Tower, probably to celebrate the easy take-over at a great feast in the White Tower's huge second-floor Great Hall. Prince John announced that he had assumed control of his brother's kingdom in his absence and would administer it until Richard returned.

What were Longchamp's major works, especially the projects undertaken in the period autumn 1189 to autumn 1190, when the huge sum of £2,881 is recorded as having been expended? Among the first works were the digging of a very large ditch round the existing castle buildings and walling and on the north and west side pushing out the boundaries of the castle into land belonging to the city, probably to provide more space for building. Longchamp's ditch is mentioned by the chronicler Roger de Hoveden (*c.* 1150–*c.* 1201) who relates that Longchamp hoped that 'the water from the Thames would flow through it'. The ditch, however, must have failed to do that, as the slightly later chronicler Matthew Paris (*c.* 1200–1259) pointed out. Probably Longchamp overlooked that the Thames was a tidal river at that point, or his engineers got the sluice arrangements wrong.

This new ditch included enlargement of some of the original ditch of the Conqueror's time (page 10), excitingly confirmed in excavations by the Department of the Environment in the mid-1960s. The Longchamp ditch stretched from the old Roman wall on the east side of the castle (still the eastern curtain of the castle) at a point north of the White Tower, in a west-south-west direction to what is now the Beauchamp Tower and there turned south-west-south and down towards the river. The new ditch almost certainly had a stone wall built along the top of its inner bank, down to the river edge where we know a new tower, the Bell Tower, was built at this time. At the new tower the wall continued out of its south-east face towards the westerly end of the eleventh-century wall (imposed on the southern Roman wall): the meeting point was roughly where later the Bloody Tower and, adjacent to it, the Wakefield Tower were built, in the thirteenth century. The Bell Tower's plinth and the wall leading eastwards (up to the same level as the plinth) were constructed of

Purbeck marble, and the entry in the Pipe Roll for 1190–91 which refers to expenditure on stone and lime may possibly relate to this.

The Bell Tower is the second oldest mural tower in the Tower of London. It gets its name from the fact that in the days when the Tower of London was used as a state prison the bell near its top was rung at dusk to summon all state prisoners allowed to wander about the Tower precincts back to their rooms or suites. This bell was also used as an alarm to summon the garrison in case of emergency or for other necessary duties. The present bell is a seventeenth-century product installed in a seventeenth-century bell-cote, but as the Bell Tower has been so-called for longer than that, these are obvious replacements. When it was first built the tower stood at the west corner of the then castle enclosure wall, with 'the river washing its base'. It is believed that at the same time as, or soon after, its construction, a building was raised in the angle formed by the west and south walls and the Bell Tower, which provided lodgings for the Constable of the Tower.

The Bell Tower is 19½ feet (18 metres) tall on a part-splayed plinth of solid Purbeck masonry. It is octagonal in plan from its base up to the first floor, and then it is round. One interesting internal feature is the vaulted ceiling of the ground-floor

The cell occupied by Sir Thomas More, one time Henry VIII's Lord Chancellor, on the ground floor of the Bell Tower. The cell is five-sided and has a vaulted ceiling. The Bell Tower was built in the 1190s. More languished here for fifteen months before his execution in 1535.

John Plantagenet, King of England, 1199–1216. No English king has had a worse "press" than John. If half the calumny were true, his reign could not have lasted 17 years in an age when powerful feudal lords by combining resources could so easily have driven him off the throne. He was a great castle builder, and left his mark on many well-known English fortresses, such as Corfe, Kenilworth, Lancaster, Knaresborough and Odiham. He also had a sharp interest in town planning, and was the first to recognize the potential of Liverpool as a major port.

chamber, which is five-sided in plan. This is the principal room of the tower, and it was used from time to time as a prison cell. Perhaps the most famous occupant was Sir Thomas More, Henry VIII's Lord Chancellor, who was executed in 1535. He spent over a year in this room, to begin with in some comfort, but his treatment gradually deteriorated. The room above this room was occupied by prisoners, and two who spent a short time there were Princess Elizabeth (later Queen Elizabeth I) and James, Duke of Monmouth, illegitimate son of Charles II, who in 1685 raised a revolt in the West Country in an attempt to take the throne from his uncle James II.

These works of Longchamp, though considerable, are less than satisfying to the curious, for they do not seem to be worth anything like £2,881, particularly when one uses as a calculating yardstick the building cost of Orford Castle, complete with great tower, walls, mural towers and gatehouse, about thirty years before (just over £1,400), and that of Odiham Castle, also with great tower, walls, probably mural towers and gatehouse, in the first decade of the thirteenth century (well over £1,000).

Several hundred pounds were spent on the Tower by King John, though again we have no helpful information as to what was done. But while the building history is scant, there is some record of the involvement of the Tower in the reign's events.

King John is one of the most maligned of English monarchs, and we do not need to go along with the traditional notion that he had no redeeming virtues or qualities. Clearly, no man could have remained at the helm for the best part of two decades of a violent age without having some capacities, and in recent years he has been seen in a better light. He was politically wiser than most of the nobles who forced him to agree to Magna Carta. He had greater support among the English than has been allowed. Short and plump (he was hardly more than 5ft 5ins tall), John was tough, brave when it suited him, energetic when driven (for example, he once took a relieving force to a siege in France over a distance of some eighty miles in two days), and he was attractive to women. He inspired considerable loyalty and devotion from a number of powerful lords throughout his reign. Like his predecessors he had to spend what we rightly feel was an inordinate amount of time, energy and resource on curbing over-mighty lords.

John's reign is of course remembered most for the farce of Magna Carta, a document containing some sixty-three clauses, only one of which really established any kind of landmark of freedom for the individual. Once he had agreed the terms, it is interesting to record that the current pope, Innocent III, soon absolved him from keeping to his promises, while nearly 400 years later Shakespeare could write a whole play about John without even mentioning Magna Carta at all. But for the

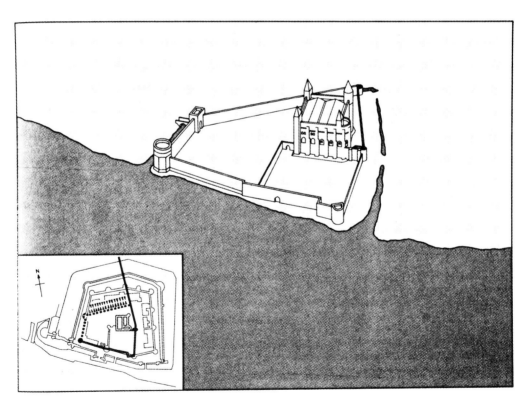

Elevation of the Tower in about 1200. Plan of the Tower in 1200. Note the alteration to the north-east/south-west ditching.

An early 14th century picture of King John on a hunt. John spent considerable sums on the Tower during his reign (1199–1216).

purposes of our story of the Tower, it is conceded that the barons certainly believed they were in the right and that they did achieve something in getting their grievances together in a document and listing their demands for their redress and forcing the king to agree to it.

The Tower figured in this conflict when, early in 1215, the barons, led by Stephen Langton, Archbishop of Canterbury, having gathered at the end of the previous year in Bury St Edmunds to draft the document and decide how to get the king's agreement, made their ways to London, seized the Tower (the king was at Windsor) and held it, deciding to use it as some kind of bargaining point. It was from the Tower that most of the nobles who were to meet the king for the presentation of the demands set out. They met eventually by arrangement on the island of Runnymede in the Thames not far from Windsor, on 15 June, and John affixed the royal seal to a number of copies of Magna Carta which were promptly gathered up and distributed to key places in the realm.

The king may have affixed his seal, but he did not intend to abide by the promises, and he had already set in motion the procedure to obtain absolution of the oath from the Pope before the Runnymede meeting. The absolution arrived a few weeks later and John began to recruit forces for the inevitable confrontation with his barons. They on their part, meanwhile, suspecting the king's intentions, held on to the Tower of London, and sent for help from the king of France, Philip Augustus, even

An aerial view of Corfe Castle in Dorset. It shows the castle plan very clearly. At the top centre is the now ruined great tower, and to its right the 'Gloriette' built by King John who regarded the castle as one of his favourite residences. The 'Gloriette' was a hall block of luxurious quality and accommodation, and was in advance of its time.

offering the English throne to the French king's son, Louis. These things were the signal for the outbreak of civil war that was only ended when John died the next year. During the war Prince Louis came up the Thames accompanied by several rebel barons of England, and actually set up court of a kind in the Tower – the only time the Tower has been held by a foreign power, provided one overlooks the fact that the Conqueror himself was a foreigner!

Henry III (1216–72) was only nine when his father King John died, and at the time he was at Corfe Castle in Dorset, one of John's favourite royal residences (John had built the Gloriette there[2]). Henry was taken to Gloucester, a town firmly in the hands of the royal faction, and in the presence of a number of loyal barons and prelates, including the two top men in England – Hubert de Burgh, the justiciar, and William the Marshal, Earl of Pembroke, the Regent – he was crowned. Both these men had been faithful to John and were superbly fitted to manage the realm during the new king's minority. Without delay, they crushed the baronial rebellion – which in many respects had been a personal squabble between John and a number of lords – and sent Prince Louis back to France.

2 The Gloriette was a luxury suite of rooms on two floors near the great tower. It was built in Gothic Style.

Louis had used the Tower as his base for over a year. Soon after his departure, the regents put in hand some repairs and possibly improvements to the 'king's houses in the bailey', which must mean free-standing buildings in the enclosure south of the White Tower and probably included kitchens, dining hall, stables, accommodation block, and the king's chamber – whatever form that took in those years. A little later, in the decade 1220–30, two new towers were built, and these were the Wakefield Tower and the original Lanthorn Tower (which was demolished in 1777 after a disastrous fire, and later replaced by the more modern structure almost on the same site). Both these towers were positioned along the southern stretch of stone wall round the castle (that is, the old Roman walling with the William II addition). The Lanthorn Tower formed an improved defence of the south-east corner of the castle, where previously there had only been a re-entrant of fortified walling. Both towers at the time rose straight up from the edge of the river.

This is the first floor of the Wakefield Tower. Originally it had been Henry III's private chamber, then it was used by later kings for private purposes, and eventually it was converted to house the Crown Jewels by Anthony Salvin, after the fire in the Tower in 1841. When the jewels were moved out of the Wakefield Tower to the present Jewel House in the Waterloo Block, the chamber was restored to much what it had been like in the Middle Ages. The oratory at right is where Henry VI was found dead in 1471.

The Wakefield Tower (left) and the Bloody Gateway. The foundations in the foreground belong to what is left of the Coldharbour Gate.

The Wakefield Tower was not the original name for this impressive cylindrical building which was started in the early 1220s and raised in two phases (you can see the different masonry on the exterior today). The second phase of building was in the 1230s. The tower was first called the Blundeville Tower, after the Constable in office during its second phase of building, John de Blundeville. This second phase involved raising its height to accommodate a second storey consisting of a private chamber for the king. Later, sometime in the fourteenth century, the records of the kingdom which had been kept in the White Tower, were moved out to the Blundeville Tower which soon came to be called the Record Tower. One of the clerks to the king, of the mid-fourteenth century, was William of Wakefield, and eventually the Record Tower got its present name.

The ground floor of the Wakefield Tower was restored during some important excavation and repair work in the 1950s and 1960s. When it had been built in the thirteenth century, the ground floor had consisted of a tall room, octagonal in plan, with round arches to the recesses in each of the eight sides. The easternmost recess contained a flight of steps up to a postern in the stretch of wall between the Wakefield and Lanthorn Towers, at the point where the wall joined the Wakefield Tower. This was a private river access gate for the king. The top floor of the tower was reached by a spiral staircase in this postern area.

The ground floor chamber had a timber frame ceiling consisting of slightly irregularly radiating spokes. It lasted until the 1860s when some major work was done to reinforce the ceiling to support the installation of a huge cage in the storey above. This case was to house and display the Crown Jewels (see page 175). By the 1860s the timber ceiling had rotted in parts, but enough was there for the well known military architect G. T. Clark to draw it as it would have looked originally. Then the ceiling was dismantled to permit replacement with a vaulted ceiling. This arrangement was altered in the 1960s when the Jewel Cage was removed to the Jewel House in the Waterloo Barracks building. A replica of the original ceiling was built in timber and inserted into place.

The storey above the ground floor chamber was the king's private chamber. It is also octagonal in plan, and it has a number of interesting features, some revealed as a result of recent restoration work after the removal of the Jewel Cage. The chamber is approached via the east recess (like the floor below) and along a short, narrow, tall passage. The recess next door (SE) has an oratory which was provided in the 1230s with a timber screen. Henry VI (1422–61), who was deposed during the Wars of the Roses, restored briefly in 1470 and deposed again in 1471, was imprisoned for the second time in the Tower of London, and occupied the Wakefield Tower. On 21 May, he was found dead in the oratory.

In 1227 Henry III declared himself of age. For another four years Hubert de Burgh continued as justiciar (he had also succeeded William the Marshal as Regent, in 1219), but in 1232 Henry, goaded by some of his less likeable nobles, arrested de Burgh on trumped up charges and stripped him of his offices. De Burgh was imprisoned, managed to escape and fled to a country church for sanctuary. The king sent a posse after him, and it broke into the church.

There were several other new works and rebuildings in the period *c*. 1220–*c*. 1240, but it is difficult to be precise about datings. Immediately west of the Wakefield Tower, a new water gate was installed in the renovated and strengthened south wall from the Bell Tower to the Wakefield Tower and to the Lanthorn. This is sometimes called the Bloody Gate, and it was an integral part of the Wakefield Tower in its lower stages. It was equipped with a portcullis. Later, it was enlarged to become a gate-tower (the Bloody Tower, see pp. 60–61) and later still was heightened to provide a comfortable prison suite for Sir Walter Ralegh (see pp. 119–24). The King also improved the domestic buildings inside the enclosure (or inner bailey, as it later became known), including building a new kitchen in about 1230 and in the 1230s a new, or at least rebuilt, Great Hall which used the enclosure wall at its southern edge. This latter building was whitewashed in 1234. There was also a new chamber for the king himself, next to the Wakefield Tower, and near that, one for the queen, both of them inside the inner bailey. There is a 1238 record that the queen's chamber was to be painted with false pointing and with flowers, and another record two years later that it was to be wainscotted and painted with roses. That was in 1240, the same year in which the order was given to whitewash the White Tower.

On the north end of the Wakefield Tower, and built into the masonry, began a northwards leading wall, the Main Guard Wall, which terminated in the Cold-harbour Gate, now only visible as foundations. It had been a conventional late-twelfth – mid-thirteenth century-style gateway flanked by a pair of round towers, the eastern tower abutting on to the west wall of the White Tower. This was the main entrance to the inner ward.

Henry III and the Royal Menagerie in the Tower

It was in the decade 1230–40 that a new rôle was accorded the Tower of London, that of the Royal Menagerie or zoo, a rôle it occupied until 1834-5. There had been a royal menagerie for several reigns, but in 1235 Henry III formally put three leopards into an enclosure in the Tower of London, and these are believed to have been the first animals introduced to the castle by an English king. In this instance, the leopards had been a gift from the Emperor Frederick II (Stupor Mundi). One may wonder how well they survived in a place so close to the river, subject to fogs, tidal breezes and polluted water. The three leopards were a tribute to the Plantagenet royal arms, namely, three lions passant guardant, which are heraldic leopards. Fifteen years later, Henry added to the 'zoo' a polar bear given him from Norway (for which the King allowed 4 pence a day to be sent on its feeding and care – and on its keeper as well!) The bear was given an iron collar and a long cord, so that it could fish in the Thames.

There is no evidence of where the early Menagerie was located, though it must have been near the water. In the reign of Edward I, an outwork on the west side, the barbican (see page 49) was erected and had near to it a wharf on the river edge. This barbican later came to be called the Lion Tower, and there is evidence that it was used for the Menagerie in the seventeenth century.

The King of France gave Henry III an elephant in 1255, and this was probably the second time that an elephant had been seen in England (the first elephant to walk on

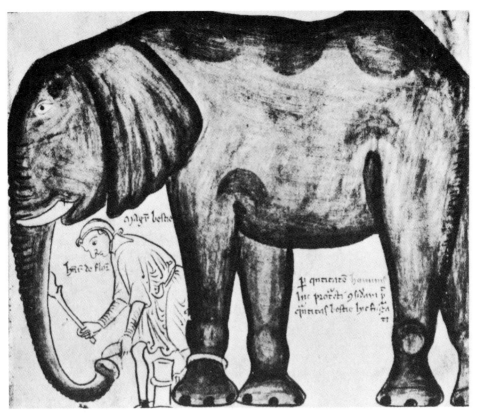

Matthew Paris (1200–59), an English historian, chronicled the history of England to the late 1250s. This picture of an elephant comes from his work, and represents the elephant given to Henry III in 1255 by Louis IX of France. The arrival of the elephant and its subsequent display signalled the opening of the Royal Menagerie to public visits.

British soil was the one brought to Camulodunum (Colchester) in 43 AD by the Emperor Claudius when he made his triumphal progress along the roads from London to Colchester during the conquest of southern Britain by his general, Aulus Plautius). Henry's elephant was given a house measuring some 40 × 20 feet (12.3 × 6 metres), according to Matthew Paris. From the 1230s, therefore, the Royal Menagerie was to be a permanent feature in the Tower up to the 1830s. Special allowances were set aside for a full-time keeper and also for animal feed.

Towards the end of the decade 1230–40, a further series of works were put in hand at the Tower, and these continued, with a short interval or two, throughout the rest of the reign. They involved a major enlargement of the whole castle on almost three sides, and were intended to strengthen the fortress. To some extent this could be said to have been because Henry's relations with the people of London were growing more strained through a general incompetence in government, and he felt less and less secure in the Tower as it was at his accession – namely, a small enclosure with only the White Tower having any real defensiveness.

Although there are many records of expenditure for this sustained period of works, they are not such as to provide us with a convenient chronological story, and a summary of what was done in the years up to 1272 may be as much as we shall ever manage to learn. One of the earlier projects was to extend the castle's area on the north-west, north and east sides and to enclose the enlarged outer ward with a curtain wall with several flanking mural towers to guard the salient points. This entailed, among other things, taking the building works beyond the east wall of Roman origin and pulling that wall down as superfluous. A continuous curtain wall with mural towers at regular intervals short enough for the wall length between two towers to be properly covered by bowshot from the towers was a much more effective defence system than a simple curtain wall.

The new curtain wall started in the north-west at the present Devereux Tower, led slightly north-eastwards, veered slightly south-eastwards and at the present Martin Tower turned sharp right and southwards in a straight line to the river to another new tower, the Salt Tower. There it turned a right angle and continued to the Lanthorn Tower to complete the southern side. A stretch of wall with a gate-tower half way along, from the Devereux Tower to the Bell Tower on the south-west completed the new enclosures. New ditching was cut just outside the three sides.

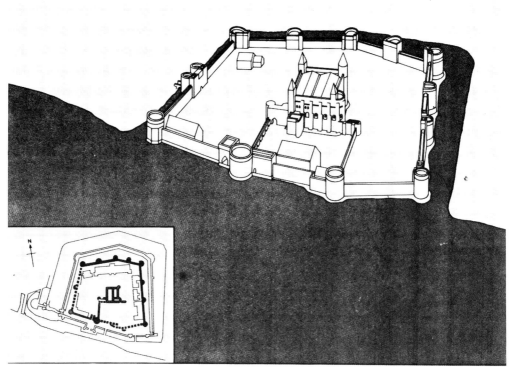

Elevation of the Tower in c. 1270. Plan of the Tower in about 1270.

Along the walling from Devereux to Salt there were six new mural towers, as follows: Flint, Bowyer, Brick, along the north wall, Martin on the angle between north and east wall, and Constable and Broad Arrow between Martin and Salt.

The new outer ward absorbed a small church, the Chapel of St Peter Vincula, in the north-west corner, just south of Devereux. St Peter was a small parish church whose beginnings are not known but which was certainly in existence in the early twelfth century. Henry had to pay some compensation to the prior of Holy Trinity, Aldgate, and other landowners in the city for the encroachment in the north-west quarter, and this was included in an overall sum of over £166 paid. He spent some money on tidying up the church but it was his son Edward I who in 1286–7 rebuilt it completely for £317.[3]

On 23 April 1240, the western gateway inserted in the new wall between Devereux and Bell Tower, 'which the king had built at great expense', as Matthew Paris wrote, collapsed 'as if it had been struck by an earthquake'. Paris also says that exactly a year later some of the walling around the gate tower fell down. Orders were given to repair the damage but there has been some doubt about what the repairs were and when they were done. The break in the wall, for example, was said to have been filled with timber palisading, which would have sufficed for a year or two but hardly much longer.

Although Henry was much concerned about the fortifying of his London castle, he found time to initiate improvements to its more domestic aspects. An earnest Christian, Henry was anxious to leave testimonials to his religious devotion – the greatest was to be his rebuilding of Westminster Abbey – and he directed some attention to the Chapel of St John in the White Tower, which had been neglected. In 1240 he ordered it to be repaired and decorated. This entailed whitewashing the walls, putting stained glass in some of the windows, and having a marble font with columns specially made ('well carved').

3 St Peter ad Vincula was almost totally rebuilt in the Tudor period and was restored in the 1870s.

III

Grandeur and decline of its feudal rôle

The Tower had been begun in 1066–7 as a simple enclosure castle erected during William the Conqueror's first months as King of England, to overawe his (to him) foreign subjects in London. He may have stayed there now and again, but monarchs of his day never remained long at one address. The only way to keep order was personally to spend time in all sorts of places, and to be seen at them. By the death of Henry III just over two centuries later, the Norman conquest was way beyond the reaches of the memory of anyone. Normans, Angevins, other Frenchmen, Anglo-Saxons, even some Celts, had begun to become fused into a single people (though not a single class). Government of England was really no longer peripatetic. If not actually declared formally as such, London had become for practical purposes the capital of England, and most organs of government had become based there. To cap it all, the Great Council of England, summoned to meet by Simon de Montfort in 1265 after he had defeated and captured the king, Henry III, and his son Prince Edward at Lewes, had been joined by two representatives summoned from every English shire and most of the larger English towns, and all had gathered at Westminster in London. This is rightly regarded as the beginning of the English Parliament.

As for the Tower, it had already been greatly extended in physical area, with numerous buildings and wall lengths added. It was the home of the royal menagerie and it housed the royal regalia and jewels, part of the royal treasury and armoury and some national records. It was the place where distinguished state prisoners were held, usually in some style, and it provided the accommodation for the king's justices to hear pleas of the Crown for the City of London. And it had been used as a war store – that is, arsenal – since about 1200. It had a set of apartments for the king and his family, including the king's chamber, which were quarters of some magnificence. These had been located between the White Tower and the south stretch of the great inner wall, but they are no longer there today.

It was during the reign of Henry III's son, Edward I (1272–1307), that the last major phase of improvement and extension was carried out at the Tower, when the Tower became a major treasury and record repository, and national arsenal. This majestic, iron-willed warrior king, 'Longshanks' as he was called because at 6 feet 2 inches he was one of the tallest men in England, devoted his thirty-five years on the throne to two principal but contrasting activities, warfare and legal reform. The latter does not concern us here as it has little to do with the development of the Tower, but Edward's obsession with campaigning and conquest spilled out into military engineering and architecture, in particular castle-building. More famous for the great new Edwardian castles put up or started during or soon after his campaign in and conquest of Wales (1277–83), notably Aberystwyth, Beaumaris, Builth, Caernarfon, Conwy, Fflint, Harlech, Hope, Rhuddlan and Ruthin, he also attended to castles in England, where his works including making improvements at Cambridge, Chester, Corfe, Dover, Nottingham and Winchester. Top of the list, however, was the Tower. There, Edward completed his father's reconstruction work, by making it concentric and substituting, 'for the original entrance an indirect approach interrupted by no fewer than four gateways and exposed throughout its length to effective flanking fire'. His works which are outlined below and which were completed within the ten years 1275 to 1285, cost him £21,000, twice the amount spent by his father over fifty years!

Edward I makes the Tower concentric

One of the interesting facts about Edward's works at the Tower is the date when they were first put in hand – 1275. The king had succeeded to the throne in 1272 but was abroad on the Seventh Crusade at the time, and he did not return to his country until mid–1274. We may be right in assuming that when he came to London for the first time as king, to await his coronation, he spent his first days in the royal apartments in the Tower. Almost at once he recognized the need to finish his father's works and to develop new ideas of his own. His years on crusade took him to the Near East and enabled him to see at first hand crusader castle architecture. Many of the crusader castles were concentric – that is, having a concentric arrangement of perimeter walls with flanking towers and gates. One example widely quoted and illustrated is the Krak des Chevaliers in Syria. This type of fortification was not new in the Near East. It had been employed by the ancient Romans, and possibly even before that. It had been introduced into France, notably at Carcassonne, and the idea was not new even in England. Henry II and his son John had begun, if not finished, the job of making Dover castle concentric and Henry III certainly started to convert the Tower of London into a concentric fortress.

Edward I's works involved the enlargement still further of the area occupied by the Tower in London, this time on all four sides. The most dramatic improvement was the extension on the south (river edge) side, and it involved very complex earthwork and reshaping of existing geography of the river frontage, including pushing back the river line so as to make the Bloody Gate (hitherto a water-gate) into a landward gate, and to convert the space immediately outside the original south wall into a dry outer bailey from Bell Tower to Salt Tower, and to build a new outer wall with a new water-gate and other flanking structures against which the Thames was to lap.

Aerial view of Dover Castle. It began as a motte-and-bailey erected in eight days by the Conqueror while on his circuitous route from Hastings to London after his great victory in October 1066. The Dover site had already been used for key fortifications by both the Romans in their occupation of Britain (1st–5th centuries AD) and later by Anglo-Saxons. Dover Castle began to acquire its stonework in the time of Henry II who had the splendid great tower built. Dover was to be one of the few castles of England to develop into a concentric castle.

The new water-gate was called St Thomas's Tower, and later became better known as the Traitor's Gate. This tower superseded the old Bloody Gate as the river entrance to the Tower, and the Bloody Gate itself was enlarged by adding an extra storey (see page 60). At the west end of the new south front a twin-cylindrical gate tower was built, and this was called the Byward Tower. Into its eastern rectangular block ran both southern walls. At the other (eastern) end of the south front, two small rectangular towers were erected, about 49 feet (15 metres) apart, and these became known as the Well Tower and the Develin Tower.

On the three landward sides of the Tower of London, major changes were also made. The ditch in front of Henry III's perimeter wall with flanking towers (page 44) was filled in to create a narrow outer bailey, and more or less along the outer edge of the infilling an outer wall, lower in height than Henry's, was built. It was given no new towers on the landward sides (except the Byward at the extreme south–west and Develin at the extreme south east). It was built lower so that defenders along the wall-walk behind the parapet on Henry's wall could provide covering fire with bow and arrow (and, later, with firearms) over the heads of other defenders manning the wall-walk along the outer wall. This allowed the lower-level soldiers to adopt a more offensive role by opening up on hostile forces outside the castle, and even to come down from the wall and engage the enemy at ground level. This was one of the aims of the concentric principle, to turn defensiveness wherever possible into attack.

Outside the new perimeter Edward had a new and much wider ditch dug all round the landward sides. The new perimeter wall, meanwhile, provided the water front on the Thames and at the same height, though this arrangement was altered later on.

In connection with this major improvement, we should look at the interesting new barbican, or outwork, and its associated buildings on the west side. Where the new ditch passed in front of the Byward Tower, the land on the far side was cut away in a semi-circle and the river let in to fill it. Before the water was let in, a complex arrangement was erected to provide a fearsomely deterrent entrance to the Tower. Out of the Byward Tower's west front projected a stone-walled passage bridge that led to a second twin-cylindered tower gatehouse, the Middle Tower, and from the west side of that the passage bridge continued into a half-moon-shaped outwork, the barbican, which was situated in the middle of the cut-away semi-circle. This barbican was a semi-circular open building (that is, without roof) with a wall-walk round the top protected by a battlemented parapet. The barbican was later known as the Lion Tower, and it was at some time in its existence used to house the Royal Menagerie (see page 172). The barbican had at its north side a fortified gateway leading to a stone-walled passage bridge across the north side of the semi-circle over the land side, where it let into a second fortified gateway. Both gateways had drawbridges and portcullises and there were also more drawbridges and portcullises along the passage bridge from the Lion Tower's east side to the Byward Tower, whose portcullis and its operating wheels and mechanism are still those *in situ* today. The Lion Tower itself has now disappeared, but enough of it was seen in excavations

An engraving of the late 18th century of Edward I.

to show that it was very similar in design to the barbican at Goodrich castle in Herefordshire added at much the same time. A similar barbican was also erected at Sandal Castle in Yorkshire, a generation earlier.

When these structures at the Tower had been completed, the Thames was let in to surround them. The digging of the great ditch or moat began very early in the ten-year scheme, and it cost over £4,100, about £2,500 of that spent in the first eighteen months, and both sums relate only to payment of wages to the diggers. The king also hired a Flemish water engineer, Master Walter of Flanders, to ensure that the level control and sluice arrangements worked, as Longchamp's system of 1190 had not. The ditch excavation was a tremendous exercise resulting in one of the biggest earth-moving undertakings of even this king's castle-building programme, and Londoners must have been startled at the huge heaps created on both sides of the channel. The king was astute enough, moreover, to sell off as much of the earth as he could to help defray the diggers' wages bill, and much of this excavated earth was rich in London Clay, which he sold to local tile-makers and brick-makers. We don't know whether they were equally astute in making the tiles and then selling them to the king to roof some of his new buildings!

Also started in this period was the St Thomas's Tower, at the time more simply known as the 'new chamber above the water'. St Thomas's began as a two-storeyed rectangular tower of noble proportions, wider than it was tall, which jutted out into the Thames, and which had projecting rounded turrets on both south corners flanking the wide entrance arch. This arch fronted a tunnel over a water basin that admitted boats through to a landing stage with a flight of steps leading back and up

A model of the Krak des Chevaliers, one of the most famous of the castles built by the Crusaders in the Near East. The Krak was begun in the late 11th century, and had been made concentric by the end of the 12th. It resisted siege by the forces of Islam for a long time, but eventually succumbed in 1271.

The mechanism that operates the portcullis in the Byward Tower. Much of it is original, though the ropes have been renewed.

into the outer bailey. The tower was intended to be an impressive entrance suitable for a king and his royal visitors. For a time it contained a sumptuous first floor consisting of hall and chamber with glazed windows, most of which opened and some of which had coloured glass. The storey also had tiled floors. The eastern chamber had a small vaulted room leading off its east corner in the south-east turret, and this was an oratory. A bridge connected the rear of this storey to the vaulted chamber storey in the Wakefield Tower behind. As that was for a time the king's private chamber, it suggests that the first floor in St Thomas's Tower was also intended for his personal use. Indeed, St. Thomas's Tower was to supplant the Wakefield Tower as the king's privy chamber.

Edward I used the Tower of London as a prison as much as any of his predecessors. Even before the great building programme of the beginning of his reign had been completed, the Tower had been employed to confine numbers of unfortunate Jews, men, women and children, from all over England. It was an age when Jews were not widely welcomed in the country. That they had been tolerated at all was chiefly because the kings found them good sources for funds, from taxation and from payments for rights which were accorded to others free. Both Henry III and Edward imprisoned many families for failing to pay all their dues. One of the buildings they occupied was the Elephant House built specially to accommodate

51

Henry III's present from Louis IX of France in 1255 (see pp. 42–43). The elephant died three years afterwards and was not replaced, and the 40 × 20 feet (12.3 × 6 metres) shed became a convenient prison hut. In 1279 Edward had several hundred Jews herded into the Tower for allegedly having clipped coins of the realm. It is thought that more than 200 were eventually put to death. The survivors, and with them all the remaining Jews in England (except a handful of indispensable doctors) were formally expelled from the country in 1290. Jews were not re-admitted into England until the time of the great Cromwell, nearly four centuries later.

The only major political figure to spend time in the Tower in this reign, however, was the King of Scotland, John Baliol. Edward, known as 'The Hammer of the Scots', had intervened – quite illegally – in 1286 when King Alexander III of Scotland was killed from a fall from his horse over a cliff near Burntisland in Fife. He was succeeded by his granddaughter, a little girl of only four. She was Margaret, daughter of King Eric of Norway who had married Alexander's daughter, also called Margaret. Guardians were appointed to govern Scotland. Four years later, Margaret was brought to her homeland by ship, but when the ship stopped at Orkney she died, aged only eight.

When Alexander had been killed – one of Scotland's greatest tragedies – the English king heard the news with some pleasure. He had had his eyes on Scotland ever since he had conquered Wales in 1282, and dreamed of an united Britain – under the Plantagenets, of course. The tragedy, and more particularly the succession of a minor, presented Edward with a chance to see his dream come true. Little Margaret's father had asked Edward (did Edward put the idea into Eric's head?) to keep an eye on the guardians in charge of Scotland. Edward obliged and also got Eric to agree that Margaret should be betrothed to Edward's son, Edward, the new Prince of Wales. This would ensure that one day young Edward would be king of both countries. Margaret's death in 1290 threatened to upset the arrangement, but Edward came up with an ingenious alternative.

There were at least three good successors to Margaret, all of them direct descendants of King David I of Scotland (1123–54). All owed something to the English but none was acceptable to the other two. So Edward offered to arbitrate and choose a successor whom they would all have to accept. He made a condition: no matter whom he chose, that king would have to acknowledge him (Edward) as overlord of Scotland. Foolishly, the heirs agreed. Edward chose John Baliol, a great-great-great-grandson of David I, a weak and unreliable lord of mixed Norman and Scottish blood, whom he thought would be bound before long to provoke rebellion among the Scottish nobles. Just to make this more probable, Edward actively underminded Baliol's authority in a number of ways.

When in 1294 Edward went to war with France, and summoned his lords and knights for their feudal duties, he included Baliol in the list. But Baliol had had enough and he refused. Instead, he made a treaty with France – the first of a long succession of such arrangements between the two kingdoms to be known as the Auld

Alliance. Edward was furious and immediately marshalled forces to invade Scotland. He reached Berwick, then a Scottish town, besieged the castle and took it, treating the garrison and the citizens of the town around with appalling savagery. Other outrages followed at Dunbar, Roxburgh, Stirling and Edinburgh and at the capture of Edinburgh, in 1295–6, Baliol himself was taken along with his son and a number of loyal lords and knights. They were all sent on the long journey to the Tower of London. Edward, in the meanwhile, went on to Scone and seized the sacred Stone of Destiny, an ancient Scottish symbolic relic, and sent it to London where it was placed in Westminster Abbey.

Baliol was forced to abdicate and the English king took over the throne himself, holding it until his death in 1307, but governing Scotland through a viceroy. In the Tower, Baliol was lodged in rooms off the Great Hall in the White Tower, and he stayed there for six months. It was a relatively easy time for him. Indeed, he had so many privileges to begin with (being given a chaplain, assistant chaplain, tailor, pantler, butler, two chamberlains, a barber, and allowed to have a stable of horses with grooms to tend them, and a pack of hounds with a huntsman – and an allowance of 17 shillings a day for the maintenance of this establishment) that Edward felt obliged to reduce it soon afterwards, but to a new level that was still tolerable. Baliol managed to get the Pope to intercede for his release and was freed.

Two other buildings round off the main part of Edward I's works at the Tower, the new Beauchamp Tower and the rebuilding of the Chapel of St Peter ad Vincula (so

The Beauchamp Tower was built by Edward I on the site of an earlier gateway into the Tower.

named because the date of its original consecration was 1 August sometime in the earlier twelfth century, the day of the year when St Peter was first imprisoned in Jerusalem, *ad vincula* (in chains). The Beauchamp Tower, named later for Thomas Beauchamp, Earl of Warwick (d.1401), who resisted Richard II and spent time in the tower for his pains, was raised in 1281 on the site of the gate-tower which had fallen down in 1240 (see page 45). It was built to a height of about 60 feet (18.5 meters) and is exceptionally wide. It is three-storeyed, with a semi-circular front to the outer bailey. Its north-east and south-east corners on the inward side (in line with the inner wall of Henry III) have rectangular plan turrets. The whole tower appears to have been begun and completed inside the year. The internal appointments were luxurious for those times. The tower was extensively restored in the 1850s by the well-known historical architect Salvin who also restored, among other buildings, the massive great tower at Norwich Castle.

In its time the Beauchamp Tower accommodated many famous prisoners, and nearly a hundred inscriptions carved into stonework in the walling inside by some of the famous and also many less distinguished prisoners can be seen today. Some of the inscriptions are not now in the places where they had originally been carved, since they have been moved in more modern rebuildings and redecorations. For example, the Middle Chamber on the first floor, the star feature of the tower, which accommodated possibly more celebrated people than any other part of the Tower, has more inscriptions than perhaps it actually witnessed being executed. Among the

The first floor chamber of the Beauchamp Tower, as seen by an engraver in 1821. It has its own private garderobe (latrine) reached via a passage at right. This chamber contains a number of the famous Tower inscriptions, not all of which were originally carved in this particular chamber.

An early 19th century picture of the first floor chamber in the Beauchamp Tower. Note the inscriptions on many of the walls.

famous ones is the John Dudley inscription, consisting of a device with a central bear and ragged staff and lion with two tails in a cartouche border of roses, oakleaves and honeysuckle, under which is a verse, four lines long. John Dudley was the eldest son of the Duke of Northumberland who in 1553 tried to put Lady Jane Grey on the throne of England when young Edward VI died. Jane was married to Northumberland's second son, Lord Guilford Dudley. Northumberland, Jane and Lord Guilford were arrested when the Duke's coup failed, and very soon afterwards Northumberland's four sons were also taken and put into the Tower, including John Dudley. Northumberland, Jane and Lord Guilford were all put to death, but the others were let out, and John Dudley died a few days after his release. This Dudley inscription is in the Middle Chamber of the first floor of the Beauchamp Tower. So is another, the simple four-lettered name IANE (Jane). This was long said to have been carved in the stonework by the hapless 'Nine-Days Queen' herself, but it is not at all probable since women prisoners were not usually lodged in the Beauchamp Tower, but more often than not were kept in the lodgings of the Gentleman Gaoler on Tower Green, inside the western inner wall. Her name is much more likely to have been carved by Lord Guilford who may have shared the Middle Chamber with at least one of his other brothers, as well as John.

The Beauchamp Tower was also the place where Sir Walter Ralegh spent his second, much shorter, term in 1618 before his execution.

The Chapel of St Peter ad Vincula today bears little resemblance to the rebuilt chapel of Edward I, since the latter was almost completely destroyed in a fire in 1512 and was rebuilt (again) in 1519, in a style quite different from the Edwardian. Moreover, the Tudor rebuilding was restored, with alterations, in the 1870s.

The Royal Mint is established at the Tower

It was in Edward I's time that the royal mint found its first home in the Tower, sometime during the great first building decade. There is a reference to *domus eschambrii* in the building accounts for 1278–9, and in the Pipe Rolls for 1279–80 a sum of £729.17s.8½d. is shown for works on building and equipping the Mint, which included a 'little tower where the treasure. . . is kept' and timber used 'for the workshops. . . for the needs of the moneyers'. We do not know where the Mint was first set up, but it may have been in what is still called Mint Street, in the west part of the outer bailey, perhaps not far from the barbican. About fifteen years later, a special structure was put up, possibly near the north-west corner of the outer bailey wall, next to what is called Legge's Mount. The Mint remained inside the Tower for centuries. Its activities required a growing amount of accommodation, which spilled out along the outer bailey, for workshops, mills, melting houses and presses. The Mint was finally moved out in 1812.

The royal records were kept from the earliest period of the castle in the White Tower (once that was completed). But as time went on the number of records increased – Pipe Rolls, Close Rolls, Liberate Rolls, Issue Rolls and so on – and these took up more space in a building that already had to cater for royal occupation and guest accommodation, space for military garrison, legal and administrative functions, and so on.

In considering the works of Edward I, particularly the programme of the decade 1275–85, we are fortunate in knowing the names of some of the officials and craftsmen in charge, and even some biographical details. One of the officials, Giles de Oudenard, described as a king's clerk, was the keeper of the works at the Tower throughout the decade. In effect Giles was administrative controller of the works at the Tower, which meant he had to be responsible for the accounting – and presumably paying the bills and collecting the dues and other cash sums raised. Giles had once been controller of Henry III's Wardrobe, and was also purveyor (chief buyer) to the Great Wardrobe from 1274–82. Although he had overall responsibility for the works at the Tower, there was also Robert of Beverley in charge of building operations. Robert was master mason (perhaps chief architect in today's terms) at the Tower (and also at Westminster Abbey) during the period 1275–85, and was paid 1 shilling a day, later raised to 2 shillings a day. He died in 1285.

Edward I died in 1307 while on his way up to Scotland to lead yet another punitive expedition against a people determined not to put up with foreign domination. The

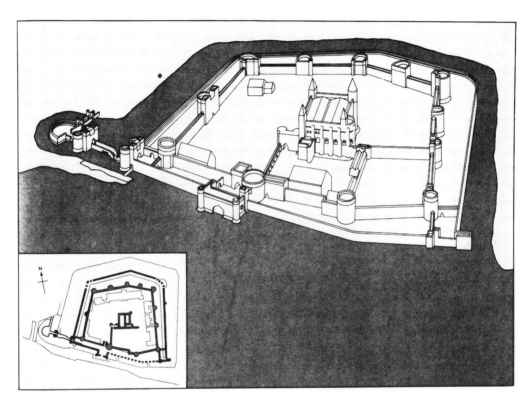

Elevation of the Tower in about 1300, after Edward I's major works. Note the enlarged ditch. Plan of the Tower, 1300. The Tower has become fully concentric. Note the half-moon shaped barbican (Lion Tower).

Tower of London, whose buildings, walls and ditches covered some 18 acres of the capital – approximately what the Tower covers today – was not to receive any further significant additions. Changes there would be, in every succeeding century, even in our own, but withal, Edward died leaving the castle more or less as he wanted it. His son, Edward II, different from his brilliant and imperious father, was a likeable young man, artistic, loyal to his friends, but lazy, unreliable, extravagant and weak-willed, and yet perhaps is to be pitied rather than despised, certainly for the manner of his death.

Although the new king had little taste for war and found the business of government so irksome that he left it mostly to ill-chosen favourites, he did show some interest in castle-building. He built the great tower at Knaresborough Castle and spent large sums on Pickering Castle, both in Yorkshire, and he spent money at Beeston Castle in Cheshire. At the Tower of London he strengthened, by widening and heightening, that part of the outer wall between his father's St Thomas's Tower and the Well Tower on the east. He also added battlements to the four towers on the east side of the inner wall, Martin, Constable, Broad Arrow and Salt. He also stayed

Edward II

at the Tower fairly regularly, often with his wife Isabel, daughter of the king of France. They had two children, Edward (later, Edward III) and Joan, and the latter was actually born in the royal apartments. Edward also displayed an interest in the royal menagerie, and in 1314 made formal arrangements for the royal lion to have a quarter of mutton every day and for the lion's keeper to receive 3½ pence a day. It was Edward who instructed that the growing corpus of exchequer records piling up in the chests in the treasury office should be sorted out and filed properly.

Probably the first time a woman was sent to the Tower for imprisonment was when in 1321 Lady Bedlesmere, wife of Bartholomew of Bedlesmere, lord of Leeds Castle near Maidstone in Kent, grossly insulted the queen, Isabel. The queen had just been on a pilgrimage to St Thomas à Becket's tomb in Canterbury Cathedral and was returning to London, when bad weather forced her party to look for somewhere to stay for the night. She descended upon Leeds Castle, but Lady Bedlesmere, whose husband was away at the time, refused to admit the imperious queen, and even allowed her retainers to attack the royal party, and some of them were killed. The queen was thoroughly frightened and fled, reaching the Tower where she complained to the king. He sent a posse to deal with Lady Bedlesmere. The castle was stormed and taken, and the castellan was hanged. Lady Bedlesmere was brought back to the Tower to cool her heels.

In 1327 Edward II was deposed as the result of a coup led by his faithless wife and her lover, Roger Mortimer, first Earl of March. The king was taken to Berkeley Castle where in September he was brutally murdered. He was succeeded by his

Edward III

fourteen-year-old son Edward, and the country was left in the hands of his mother and her paramour. Three years later young Edward asserted himself, contrived to entrap Mortimer and his mother in Nottingham Castle and they were arrested. Mortimer was hanged at Tyburn, and Isabel was sent to honourable confinement in Castle Rising in Norfolk.

Edward III was to reign for fifty years. The convulsions of the period are not the subject of this work, but among the major features of the reign were the start of the Hundred Years War with France (in 1337) and the first glorious victories of the English at sea (Sluys, 1340) and on land (Crécy, 1346, and Poitiers, 1356), and the Black Death, the dreaded bubonic and pneumonic plague, which affected all Europe and first struck England in 1348–9. Edward was also involved in war with Scotland. The Tower of London held a variety of prisoners in the reign, many of them princes, lords, and knights captured in war. Two of the prisoners were kings, David II of Scotland and John II of France. Works at the Tower were also a major item in the royal building accounts for the period, though none were on the dramatic scale of earlier reigns.

The works of Edward III

One of Edward III's first projects involving the Tower was a detailed survey of the state of the buildings, defences and facilities, which was begun towards the end of 1335. This had become essential because of a series of deteriorations in many parts of the fabric, due partly to neglect in the time of his father. It has been alleged that much of the neglect was the fault of a lazy and unhelpful Constable, John of Cromwell (1308–21), who appears to have allowed more than £500 worth of damage to remain undealt with, particularly in the royal apartments. A further £1,200 was the responsibility of other equally culpable constables. All these renovations were carried out between 1336–1342.

One of the principal undertakings of new work (including reconstruction work) was further strengthening the outer wall and raising its height on the south side, this time between the west side of St Thomas's Tower and the Byward Tower. The south side of the inner wall was also heightened along the full stretch between the Bell Tower and the Salt Tower, and this involved inserting a new gate tower between Lanthorn and Salt. We have no name for this tower and there are now no remains to be seen. It was a new entrance to the royal apartments in the inmost ward and was built between 1339 and 1341. Eight years later the king had a new water-gate put in the stretch of outer wall along the south side, about 100 feet (31 metres) west of the Well Tower. This was the Cradle Tower and it took seven years to finish, clearly to some extent because of the Black Death which caused major interruptions to every kind of activity, civil and military. The Cradle Tower has since been extensively restored (the top part rebuilt altogether). It was used from time to time as a prison, and is perhaps most famously associated with the daring escape of Father John Gerard in 1599 (See pp. 114–117) which he described in detail in his subsequent autobiography.

Further improvement were made in Edward's reign to the Bloody Tower (then the Bloody Gate). The development of the Bloody Tower is a complicated one to trace but the building is one of the most famous (or notorious) of the whole castle, and its history should be summarised.

The Bloody Tower

We have seen (see page 42) that the origins of the Bloody Tower were a water-gate inserted in the wall between the Bell and the Wakefield Towers sometime in the 1220s, and that its lower stages were an integral part of the adjoining Wakefield Tower on the east. The gate had a portcullis on the south (river) side from the start and so must have had some kind of chamber above to house the apparatus to raise and lower the grid. The portcullis indicates an important role for the gate as an access to and exit from the Tower. This water–gate is usually referred to as the Bloody Gate in architectural descriptions, though there is no evidence at all of such a name in the Middle Ages. It was not a tower, and its only accommodation, apart from the housing for the portcullis mechanism, was a porter's lodge.

Half a century later, during Edward I's great Tower-building decade of 1275–85, the Bloody gate was converted into a gate tower when the river foreshore in front of the wall from the Bell Tower to the Wakefield Tower was embanked and the outer (south) wall built between the new Byward Tower and new St Thomas's Tower. The conversion involved extending the archway into a gatehouse and raising its height.

We do not know how high, or what sort of structure was put on top of the arch of the gatehouse passage (the vaulted ceiling of the gatehouse is a later addition). Today, the archways at the south and north ends have a squat look, due to the fact that the level of the ground along the passage is 2 feet (.5 metres) higher than it was in Edward's time. The enlarged gate tower rose up with its eastern side abutting directly on the Wakefield Tower which was then taller and which thus acted as an extra protection. At this time, the tower was still not known as the Bloody Tower, and almost certainly was not equipped to house prisoners.

An engraving of 1821 of the gateway in the Bloody Tower. It shows the vaulting inserted in 1360–62 by Robert Yevele.

Tower Wharf

The third building phase at the Bloody Tower was during the reign of Edward III. This new work was designed by Robert Yevele, warden of the Tower masons and brother of the more celebrated master mason and designer of cathedrals and castles, Henry Yevele. Robert Yevele later worked at Wallingford Castle in Berkshire. These Tower works were undertaken in the early 1360s. We cannot be certain of the full extent of them, but they definitely included the very fine vaulted ceiling over the passage, decorated with ribs with recessed lion's head bosses – a typical design style of the mid-fourteenth century – and above the ceiling a chamber, of which some of the components (of similar date) are still *in situ*, such as the floor made up from a variety of patterned tiles (enclosed in a framework of brick) revealed very recently and which are thought to have been made at Penn, near Beaconsfield in Buckinghamshire, and the square-headed fireplace (with bread oven) on the west wall. This chamber (later modified) was clearly constructed for use by a key official of the tower, perhaps even the Constable himself, as the tower was the main gate from the outer ward into the inner ward.

The Bloody Tower was for a time known as the Garden Tower – long before it got its present name – because it led into the gardens of the Queen's House to the west. The more dramatic name was applied to it at the end of the sixteenth century (the first known reference is 1571) probably from its association with so many prisoners of Tudor monarchs who spent time there before ending up on the execution block. It was to be modified again at the very beginning of the seventeenth century to accommodate one of the Tower's most famous of all prisoners, Sir Walter Ralegh (pp. 119–124).

During the king's reign the royal apartments were moved from the area of the Wakefield Tower corner further east to the area by the Lanthorn Tower. Little is known of its precise details but it must presumably be linked with the insertion of the waterside Cradle Tower and also the unnamed landward gate-tower slightly north-east.

The last of Edward III's works was the construction of a great part of the Tower Wharf, which has survived very largely as it was to the present day. It was built in stages. The earliest section, built of timber, had been begun by Edward I as part of the Lion Tower barbican complex, and stretched from west of the Lion Tower down to the Byward Tower. The second stage, also in timber, was from the Byward eastwards to the west corner of St Thomas's, and was erected in 1338. These two stretches were rebuilt in stonework in the years 1365 to 1370, and sometime in the reign of Edward III's successor, Richard II (1377–99), the wharf was completed in stone from St Thomas's down to beyond the Develin Tower. The last stretch was begun in 1389 under the direction of Henry Yevele who was at the time master mason at the Tower. It is interesting to note that at this time most if not all royal building works were subject to the overall administrative supervision of a single official, the Clerk of the King's Works. It was a new office, created in 1378, and the first holder was John Blake. The Clerk of the King's Works at the time of the last Wharf project was none other than Geoffrey Chaucer, the greatest poet of mediaeval England. He held the office for two years.

Among the many prisoners in the Tower in Edward's long reign were the two kings, David II of Scotland and John II of France, both captured in battle. David was the son of the illustrious Robert Bruce, king of Scotland from 1306 to 1329, who won the glorious victory of Bannockburn against Edward II in 1314, which established Scotland's independence. In 1346, the same year in which Edward III had won the crushing victory over the French at Crécy, David was persuaded by the French king to mount a diversionary invasion of England, to take some of the heat off the French forces. David agreed, and led a badly planned and clumsily organized raid into Northumberland and Durham, and was defeated at the battle of Neville's Cross, near the great northern city. Worse, he was captured along with many lords and knights, while many more knights were slain. By all accounts the young king – still only twenty-two – struggled fiercely, sustained two arrow wounds, and yet wrestled with several English captors before being finally overpowered. He was sent to London where he was imprisoned in the Tower, to await the decision of Edward III about his future. David was lodged in the White Tower, in some comfort, in the royal apartments. The English king demanded a ransom of £100,000 for his release, but this took many years to raise. David remained in the Tower for much of the time, in what has been described as gentle captivity. Some Scottish authorities suggest that he was treated more as a royal guest than prisoner, and had considerable freedom of movement, so long as there was no attempt at escape or movement in Scotland to plot his abduction from the Tower.

Ten years after the victory at Crécy, the English won another decisive victory over France, this time at the battle of Poitiers where the English army was commanded by the King's eldest son, Edward, the Black Prince. At the end of the day, the English had taken a huge number of prisoners, foremost among them King John II of France himself, together with one of his sons, and over thirty top lords and hundreds of knights. The whole bag was shipped to England up the Thames to the Tower. King John and his son were lodged in the royal apartments in the White Tower (the Scottish king David had been transferred to Odiham castle in Hampshire to make room). For the French king, Edward III demanded 3,000,000 crowns ransom, and this took four years to raise. A sad postscript to this tale is that when King John was allowed to return to France in 1360, leaving his son behind as a hostage for the remainder of the ransom, the son, who was the Duke of Anjou, absconded three years later. The noble king thereupon volunteered to return to London as a prisoner again and to stay until the whole ransom had been paid. He returned to London but was not held in the Tower but transferred to the country where after a few months he died.

Edward III's alterations in the location of the royal apartments included some renovation work on the Great Hall which bordered the inside of the inner bailey wall.

It was reroofed and the windows facing northwards (towards the White Tower) were enlarged and raised. New accommodation was also built for the Constable during the years 1361–66, and this included quarters that required over 100 feet of glass 'worked with fleurs-de-lys and borders of the king's arms'. These quarters were erected on the site of the present Queen's House, adjacent to the Bell Tower (see page 89).

Edward III died in 1377. His eldest son, the Black Prince, had died the year before, and the new king, Richard II, was the Black Prince's ten-year-old son. Some say that the boy was 'angelic'. When news was brought to his lodgings at Sheen palace that his grandfather had died, he was at once taken to the royal apartments in the Tower, accompanied by his mother. Less than a month later, clothed in white, he made a splendid processional journey to Westminster Abbey for his coronation. He was the first king known for certain to have made the coronation journey straight from the Tower.

Richard's reign was to be filled with difficulties and tragedies, many of which, sadly, have to be recognized as being his own fault. He grew up into a man of violent temper (there is an account of his having hurled a pair of slippers at a foreign ambassador during an important diplomatic meeting), capricious, weak in judgement, given to extravagances of all kinds, who nursed grievances over years and then exacted peculiarly cunning and unpleasant revenge. In his last years, he was dangerously unbalanced, with a craving for absolute power. The slightest opposition to his wishes sent him over the top: he detected conspiracies at every turn. Yet he was also extremely brave, highly artistic, and he was faithful, courteous and attentive both to his first and his second wife. The death of his first wife, Ann of Bohemia, hit him so hard that it is widely regarded as the main cause of his character degeneration over the last years. As for his courage, it was first put to the test when he was still only a boy of fourteen living at the time in the Tower. This was when he intervened personally in the serious uprisings, collectively known as the Peasants' Revolt, of 1381, the causes of which are complex and were based on longstanding grievances. The culminating event was the imposition of yet one more poll tax in 1380, which impinged upon every adult, rich and poor, and the percentages assessed per head were hopelessly unfair.[1]

The Tower during the Peasants' Revolt of 1381

The Peasants' Revolt began in Essex, where several minor priests had begun preaching revolutionary sermons advocating very socialist ideas. Some of these were delivered by a remarkable demagogue, John Ball, who used as his text the couplet

When Adam delv'd and Eve span,
Who was then the gentleman?

John Ball was eventually arrested and so were many others. This was the signal for revolt in several parts of the country, notably in Kent where thousands of peasants

1 The assessments for the poll tax of 1990 do not appear to be much less unfair.

marched on Rochester castle and seized it. This encouraged them to march on to London to present demands to the government, to the king himself if need be. They chose as their leader Wat the Tyler, a builder's artisan from Maidstone who had served in France, and behind him they set out for the capital, gathering more support along the road. Meanwhile, the men of Essex, led by Jack Straw, headed into north London and encamped on Hampstead Heath, having sacked and burned many nobles' houses on the way.

Wat Tyler's force, meanwhile, reached the Strand, and attacked the Savoy Palace, the London home of the king's uncle, John of Gaunt, and ransacked it. Peasants were ordered by Tyler not to loot, but they could hurl clothing, artefacts, furnishings and so on into the street for burning or smashing: the demonstration was against inequalities, not for personal enrichment. Then the mob came up to the Tower itself where Richard and his Council had already been holding emergency meetings to decide how to contain the revolt. The capital was surrounded by angry peasants, many of them armed. Soon, the Tower would be encircled. The king had the gates closed, so the rebels encamped where they could find spaces outside the walls. It was mid-June and warm. They would wait until the men of Essex reached them from Hampstead.

In the morning, the king and his councillors looked out over the battlements of the Tower walls and saw all round them groups of peasants, thousands and thousands of them. Inside, the Tower's garrison was incomplete, probably not more than a few hundred men with arms, obviously no match for the throngs outside. To this day we do not know who decided the next move, but the young king left the Tower with a procession of officials, heading for Mile End. He may have done this to pull away some of the crowds round the Tower. At Mile End he came upon further gatherings, and with great courage rode up to the foremost, raising his hand to still the noise of angry talk and shouting.

He reminded them that he was their king, and asked what they wanted. The leaders came forward, much impressed by his boldness, but yet anxious about the large gathering of officials behind him. Briefly, they summarized their grievances, which in effect were hardly less than a demand for the end of serfdom, the cancellation of the Statute of Labourers and much else. The king replied that he would grant their demands. He also agreed to pardon all the leaders if the multitudes would disperse and go home quietly. It seems that many were ready to make the agreement, but the leaders, including Wat Tyler, were not so trusting, and some of them went back to the Tower. There the leaders were admitted, probably because the king was in effect a hostage, and they allowed some of the mob to rush in. Hundreds of angry people poured into the castle, and many headed for the royal apartments, frightening the occupants. They barged into the king's own quarters, and ransacked the royal wardrobe.[2] They also burst into St John's Chapel in the White Tower where Archbishop Sudbury of Canterbury had sought sanctuary along with the Treasurer, Sir Robert Hales. They dragged him out and to Tower Hill where they put him to death. They raided the armoury (the king's privy wardrobe, as it then was) and took more than 100 coats of mail, more than 900 bows with quivers of arrows, and two cannons. They also dragged Hales to Tower Hill and killed him, too.

The young king again attempted to meet the rebels to persuade them to go home. The next day they met at Smithfield and during the discussions Wat Tyler was struck down by William Walworth, London's Lord Mayor, who thought he was about to assault the king. The crowd was very angry indeed and might have overwhelmed the king and his party, but for Richard's presence of mind. He stepped forward and cried out that as they had lost their leader, they should follow him instead: he would be their leader. And so they did, down the streets and out of the city, many of them heading for home.

But the king was not as good as his word. Perhaps he may have wanted to be, but heavy pressure was on him to teach the rebels a lesson. The promised pardons were cancelled. Many of the leaders were hunted down and put to death, among them Jack Straw and John Ball. But if the revolt had been a failure after all, it had also thoroughly frightened the ruling classes.

In 1389 Richard, now twenty-one, insisted on taking on the government of England himself. He dismissed his uncle, Thomas, Duke of Gloucester, youngest son of Edward III, and his associates who had been managing the nation and doing it very badly, and for the first half of the next eight years the chronicles generally agree that England enjoyed a semblance of good government. For a time Richard had the support of his devoted wife, Anne, but she died in 1394 and the event unhinged an already unstable personality. His immediate reaction was to burn to the ground the manor at Sheen where she died. A few days later, when the Earl of Arundel arrived late for her funeral, the grief-stricken king personally assaulted him. As the years went by, he became progressively more unbalanced. All the while he nursed a series of grievances against those members of his family, their friends and those associates who had had anything to do with the government of his uncle Gloucester and in 1397 he suddenly lashed out. Gloucester and his colleagues were arrested for conspiracy and some were immediately beheaded, including Arundel who was executed on Tower Hill. Gloucester was taken to Calais where he was soon afterwards murdered. Then it was the turn of the Earl of Derby (Richard's cousin, Henry Plantagenet, eldest son of John of Gaunt) and he, too, was banished. When old Gaunt died early in 1399, Richard, having previously promised Henry that he should be allowed to inherit his father's estates, now decided to seize them, with all the manors and castles. It was a stupid act of vindictiveness and it gained for Henry a large measure of sympathy.

In the spring of 1399 Richard sailed for Ireland to deal with unrest in the eastern part. This was the signal for Henry, now Duke of Lancaster, to come home and claim his inheritance. He landed at Ravenspur in Yorkshire and moved rapidly inland,

Grandeur and decline of its feudal rôle

A small painting from Froissart's Chronicle, written c. 1390–1400. Froissart, a French scholar from Valenciennes in northern France, spent time in England, Scotland, Flanders and Italy, and was a friend of Chaucer, the Black Prince and Richard II. His Chronicle covers the years 1325–1400 in England, Scotland, Flanders and France, with information also on Italy and Germany and Spain. The picture above depicts the scene where Walworth, Lord Mayor of London, slew Wat Tyler during a meeting between Tyler and the young king, Richard II, during the Peasants' Revolt, 1381. When Tyler fell to the ground, the furious peasants moved forward as if to lynch Mayor Walworth, and even threatened the king, but with great courage and presence of mind, Richard stepped forward and offered to be their leader.

gathering considerable support on the way. Richard left Ireland as soon as he heard of his cousin's landing, but through one accident after another he failed to muster any appreciable forces with which to resist Henry and he was compelled to surrender at Flint Castle. Henry, who probably had not had any designs upon the throne when he first landed in Yorkshire – he was not the direct heir (that was Edward Mortimer, Earl of March, great-grandson of Lionel of Clarence, Edward III's third son; Henry was grandson of Edward III through his fourth son, Gaunt) – may now have decided that he should make a bid for the throne. He may have been put up to it by magnates who hoped to gain from a change of monarch. He had much other support, and of course he had the king in his power. Richard had offended so many of the lords, whether allies or opponents, that it was not difficult to get together enough of them to clamour for his abdication. Richard was taken to the Tower where he remained for a few weeks. At the end of September he formally signed the abdication document in the White Tower. That enabled a hastily convened parliament at Westminster (made up largely of those discontented magnates and their associates who had accompanied Henry and the king back to London from Wales) formally to declare the King deposed and then to invite Henry equally formally to step forward to claim the crown, 'since it was evident that the kingdom of England was vacant.'

There was no groundswell of support for Richard at the time, and the London mob seemed happy at the elevation of Duke Henry to the throne. Yet it was recognized that Richard's presence in London did constitute a danger, perhaps a focal point for unrest among the supporters of Henry if the latter failed to come up with what they might have expected as payment for their support. At the end of October it was decided to move Richard out of the capital to confinement in the countryside. Taken first to places in Kent, he was eventually installed at Pontefract Castle in Yorkshire, one of the castles inherited by Henry from his father. It was here that Richard died, early in 1400. To this day the manner of his death has never been satisfactorily established, though the suggestion that he was murdered at Henry's orders is now generally discounted.

Henry IV was crowned in October 1399. He followed his cousin's example by spending the last nights before the ceremony in the Tower and proceeded from the barbican to Westminster on the appointed day. Before doing so, he created a number of knights. It was an old custom just before a coronation, but for this occasion the new king ordered that every candidate should have a bath the evening before the investiture. Forty-six candidates were provided with bath tubs, as the chronicler Froissart put it, 'every squire had his own bain [bath] by himself, and the next day the duke of Lancaster made them all knights at the mass time.'

Henry IV fared little better than his cousin in the governing of England. Although he died in his bed at Westminster, his reign was filled with conspiracies, rebellions, troubles with Owain Glyndŵr in Wales, and finally rows with his son and heir, Henry of Monmouth, who even let himself be persuaded by his Beaufort half-uncles to urge his father to abdicate. Yet Henry IV held firmly to his throne, listening rather more than his predecessors to the advice and pleas of his parliaments (it had after all been a parliament that had offered him the throne in the first place).

Although fifteenth-century England was inherently a turbulent, violent place in which to live, it cannot be shown that the few resorts to armed conflict that did occur made any significant contribution to the violence one way or the other. Between the Norman Conquest of 1066 and the deposition of Richard II in 1399 there had been only two periods of more than thirty years without fighting in some part of England, and the extent of civil war in the fifteenth century was small compared with the conflicts of previous centuries – or of later ages. The total period of active fighting between the first Battle of St Albans which opened the Wars of the Roses in 1455 and the battle of Stoke which ended them in 1487, amounted to only about twelve or thirteen weeks in thirty-two years, or one week in two-and-a-half years. Yet people at all levels lived in a constant state of fear – fear lest the delicate balance between

A mediaeval French manuscript picture of Richard II of England kneeling before his cousin, Henry of Bolingbroke, to resign the throne and offer his crown to Henry. After Richard had resigned he was imprisoned in the Tower while the Council decided what to do with him. Henry, meanwhile, was proclaimed Henry IV. Eventually Richard was imprisoned at Pontefract Castle where he died, probably from self-inflicted starvation.

strong, good government and disorder should suddenly give way. As Professor J. Lander has put it, thoughtful men recognized the dreadful weakness of the forces of government even in normal times. Once upon a time the Church had provided the moral support governments needed for enforcing some level of law and order by constant appeals for spiritual obedience to secular authority. All the same, the French statesman and historian, Philip de Commines, a contemporary of Henry VI, Edward IV and Richard III, wrote that 'England enjoyed this peculiar mercy above all other kingdoms, that neither the country, nor the people, nor the houses were wasted, destroyed or demolished but the calamities and misfortunes of the war fell

Henry IV

only on the soldiers and especially on the nobility.' This may help to explain why numerous castles up and down the country were in the fifteenth century repaired, extended, strengthened – and even new ones built, like Raglan, Tattershall and Baconsthorpe – but very few in fact were attacked and besieged.

As for the Tower of London, despite the turbulence of the scene, little was spent in the years from Henry IV to Richard III, the largest amount by far being spent by Edward IV (1461–83) who among other works added the brick-built Bulwark, an outwork on Tower Hill beyond the Lion Tower, as an extra defence of the main entrance to the Tower. It is probably coincidental, but of all these kings, Edward IV used the Tower more than any other.

The Tower was assaulted at least three times in this period. First was during Jack Cade's rebellion of 1450. The Duke of Suffolk, chief minister to Henry VI from 1447, already unpopular for arranging the marriage of the king to Margaret of Anjou which entailed England giving up some of its possessions in France, was finally impeached for having negotiated a treasonable arrangement with France, but to save his life Henry banished him for five years. Suffolk's enemies, however, intercepted his ship to France and executed him in an open boat outside Calais. When the news reached England, a general scare followed that the king was bent on taking revenge on the men of the Kent shipyards who had provided ships to pursue Suffolk across the Channel, and under Jack Cade, who assumed the name of Mortimer, they rose and marched on London. They got as far as the Tower but were beaten off by the garrison. A second skirmish followed on London Bridge where Cade's force was decimated. Cade was offered a free pardon, then it was withdrawn (just as Richard II had withdrawn his pardons after the Mile End and Smithfield meetings in 1381, see page 66), and Cade was pursued and caught. In 1460, the Tower was besieged and bombarded by the Yorkists and the walls were damaged. Eleven years later, the garrison had to help repel an attack by Lord Fauconberg.

Some Tower prisoners in the Late Middle Ages

Throughout the period from 1413 to 1485, a considerable number of famous prisoners spent time in the Tower, and some of them were put to death. First of the

A number of mediaeval pictures of building operations on castles and cathedrals have survived. In this one, of the 15th century, an octagonal tower is being raised inside pole and rope scaffolding. The shed at left is where the masons worked on the blocks of rough stone to make smaller and smoother ones for building work.

important prisoners of Henry V (1413–22) was Sir John Oldcastle, in the first years of the fifteenth century one of the leaders of the Lollards, that group of sincere people who criticized the Mass, questioned papal supremacy and pleaded for a return to biblical teachings and practices in the Church. Oldcastle had been a gallant commander in France and had even defeated the Duke of Orleans at Paris. But he fell foul of Henry V once the latter became king, though when Prince of Wales Henry had been tolerant of Oldcastle's beliefs. The king had him arrested and taken to the Tower where he was sentenced to be burned at the stake, the standard punishment for heresy. But Oldcastle managed to escape and fled to Wales where he hid for nearly four years. In 1417 his hiding place was betrayed and he was taken again to the Tower, and this time he was hanged, and his body, together with the gallows from which it was suspended, was burned.

In 1415, meanwhile, Henry V had covered himself with glory by winning a devastating victory against France at the battle of Agincourt, in which about 6,000 French were killed and 1,500 taken prisoner, for the loss of only 150 English and Welsh archers and troops. Among the 1,500 were Charles, Duke of Orleans, son of the Orleans defeated by Oldcastle (see above), who was nephew of Charles VI, King of France. This Orleans was only twenty-four and for his release the English king put a very high ransom, 50,000 livres. For one reason or another the sum was not collected for a quarter of a century, and the luckless prince had to spend the whole time in confinement in England. He was held for a few months in the White Tower, to begin with, and then transferred to other castles, one after the other, including Windsor and Pontefract. His stay in the White Tower was depicted in a well-known manuscript painting of about 1490 (see colour plate).

The Tower accommodated another high personage in honourable confinement in the years 1406 to 1423, and that was James I, King of Scotland. James Stewart, eldest son of Robert III, was only ten when in 1406 his father was taken seriously ill and reckoned not to survive for long. In this event, the boy would be king as a minor, and thus become the focal point for fighting among the Scottish nobility who would vie with one another to govern in his name. Principal among these nobles was Robert's brother, the brilliant but unscrupulous Duke of Albany, who was already acting as Regent in all but name. So Robert sent James to France for safety, but the ship never reached the Continent. English pirates boarded it off Flamborough Head in Yorkshire, seized the young prince and sent him to London. There, he was put in the Tower by Henry IV who yet decided to treat him in the manner befitting a royal prince. Further, he went to much trouble to bring the boy up, encouraging him in learning and in martial arts. James's father Robert III died soon after the news of the boy's capture was brought to him, and so the prince became James I while in captivity. Henry allowed him to have a household of Scottish men and women servants and friends. He was finally allowed to go home to his kingdom in 1424.

The Tower also played a rôle during the dynastic struggle between the two branches of the House of Plantagenet and their respective supporters, that is, the

Lancastrians whose titular head was Henry VI and the Yorkists who were actively commanded by Richard Plantagenet, Duke of York, and afterwards by his sons Edward IV and then Richard III.

The principal victim of the Wars of the Roses was undoubtedly Henry VI (1422–61) who was to meet his end in the Tower. This virtuous, gentle, and simple-minded man would have been far better employed as master mason or designer of one of the great buildings he commissioned than titular and intended manager of a thriving western European kingdom in the fifteenth century. His reign was a catalogue of disasters for himself, his family and his countrymen. Only nine months old at his accession, he grew up in an atmosphere of bitterness, faction and deceit. His father's conquests and settlement in France were all undone and frittered away, and in his own land law and order were persistently abused in the highest places, which set the very worst of examples to everyone else. Pushed around by self-seeking ministers, many of them members of the large, sprawling mass of the Plantagenet family, forced to sign this and that act of Parliament, treated as a half-wit, this pathetic ruler endured almost continual misery. He was devoted to religion and to study, loved the arts, absorbed himself in great building projects, sometimes beggaring the exchequer to fund them, among which are the glories of King's College Chapel, Cambridge, and Eton College. Possibly these things kept him for some years from going out of his mind entirely. In 1445 he was inveigled into a marriage with Margaret, daughter of the Duke of Anjou, a positive firebrand utterly different from him in every particular, who soon bent him to her will. The last years of his life were completely dominated by her ambitions.

In 1453, Henry was stricken with mental illness, becoming for a time little more than an imbecile. Parliament therefore chose Richard Plantagenet, Duke of York, as Protector of the Realm, but in a few months the king miraculously recovered, and at once his wife got him to sack York and replace him with a ministry made up of members of the Beaufort family, cousins through their descent from John of Gaunt by his third marriage (Henry was great-grandson of Gaunt through Gaunt's first marriage). The displacement of York who had been a popular choice, coupled with the final collapse of England's cause in France, led to the outbreak of the Wars of the Roses. The York faction had been anxious for a peaceful solution to the problems of government by an orderly transfer of executive power from Lancaster, clearly unfitted to manage, to York, who at least had some qualifications to try. But Margaret, in 1455, suddenly produced a son, Prince Edward, which altered the position completely. She was not having England managed by Yorkists when there was now an heir to Lancaster.

The course of the war is not the subject of this book. For about six years, fighting was to say the least spasmodic, with long intervals between several battles with indecisive results. The unfortunate Henry was carted about from battlefield to battlefield as some sort of Lancastrian emblem of just war, was captured, released, captured, released again, and finally driven out of England after the Yorkist victory at Towton in 1461. The Duke of York had been killed at the battle of Wakefield at the end of 1460 and his place as head of the faction taken by his bold, cunning, able but often indolent son Edward, who became Edward IV. This Edward spent several days living at the Tower before proceeding to Westminster for his coronation.

Four years later, while Margaret had been leaving no stone unturned to get her husband back to his throne, the hapless Henry was discovered in Lancashire and brought to the Tower where he was made to endure considerable indignities on his way in. He was imprisoned in the Wakefield Tower, where conditions were better, though not in keeping with his station for, as one report has it, his visitors found him 'not so worshipfully arrayed nor so cleanly kept as should be such a prince'. In 1470 he was set free when Richard Neville, Earl of Warwick, the great kingmaker and one of the more attractive heroes (or rogues) of the Wars of the Roses, changed sides from being the champion of the Yorkists and their foremost commander to supporting Queen Margaret's persistent cause. Warwick defeated Edward in battle and drove him out of England, so that Henry could become king once more. But it was for a few months only, for in April 1471 Edward returned, rallied the Yorkists and at Barnet crushed Warwick in a great battle in which the Kingmaker was slain. A month later, Edward won again, this time against the queen, at Tewkesbury. Her son, Prince Edward, was killed. Her husband had, sometime before Barnet, been recaptured and replaced in the Wakefield Tower. And now, after Tewkesbury, it was Henry's turn to make the supreme sacrifice and he was found dead in the oratory of the Wakefield Tower, on 21 May. To this day no one knows what happened, but when his remains were exhumed at Windsor, the back of his skull was found to be damaged. Tudor historians, anxious to blacken still further the name of Richard III – at this time Duke of Gloucester – accused him of killing the king, but they ignored the fact that he was miles away in Yorkshire at the time.

For the next twelve years, there was relative peace in England, though intrigue and conspiracy were not far away. In 1478, George, Duke of Clarence, Edward IV's younger brother, having quarrelled with his other brother Richard, now fell out with the king, who had him attainted for treason by Parliament and sent him to the Tower. Clarence was held in the Bowyer Tower and there he was privately put to death. One story at the time was that he had been drowned in a butt of malmsey wine, his favourite drink.

Edward died in 1483, at Westminster Palace. He was succeeded by his young son, Edward, who at the time was staying with his mother's family in Ludlow, and was brought down towards London. On the way, the party was stopped at Stony Stratford by Richard, Duke of Gloucester, who had been appointed Protector of England in his brother's will. Various members of the Ludlow party were arrested, with the connivance of the Duke of Buckingham, one of Gloucester's cousins, and young Edward was escorted on the remainder of the journey to London by Gloucester and Buckingham. His coronation date was fixed, but there was to be no coronation. Instead, Edward, now joined by his younger brother Richard, Duke of

Edward IV

York, aged only nine, was lodged in the Tower, according to tradition in the Bloody Tower, although this is now generally disputed. He had been declared illegitimate by Parliament at the instigation of Gloucester, who had produced evidence that the boys' father had been previously betrothed to another woman when he married their mother, Elizabeth Woodville, in the 1460s. Neither of them therefore could succeed, the throne should pass to Richard, and Parliament petitioned Richard to accept the crown, which he did. From that moment on, the boys were allegedly never seen alive again (nor were they seen dead, either).

The question of whether Richard III murdered his nephews in the Tower, or anywhere else, has interested historians for five hundred years. Tudor historians of course claimed that he did and produced all manner of spurious evidence to support them. There was a reversal of view when the Stuarts came to the throne in the seventeenth century, and the question is argued heatedly even today, with societies up and down England devoted to proving one thing or another, but not yet succeeding in getting much closer to the truth than Richard's contemporaries did. It would of course have been helpful if Richard had said something at the time, but he did not.

There is evidence, however, that England was in for a renewal of the York versus Lancaster rivalry even before the end of Edward IV's reign, and the political stability of the country still rested on the capriciousness of the great lords, who were as always ready to betray their king at the drop of a hat. The spectacle of Stanley with his retainers lined up along the edge of the battlefield at Bosworth in 1485 to see which way the actual conflict between Richard III and Henry Tudor was going, before deciding on which side to throw in his support, may shock us today, but was something kings of the fifteenth century had to reckon with. The Duke of Buckingham backed Richard III in the deposing of young Edward V, but within months was marshalling forces to attack his erstwhile liege lord, probably on behalf of Henry Tudor, still in France, whose opportunity had not in fact yet come. If the princes were murdered, Richard paid in the end whether he did it or no, for two years later he lost the battle of Bosworth against Henry Tudor, not through bad generalship but as a result of this capriciousness.

Henry Tudor won at Bosworth in a half-day battle in which he had some 8,000 men against Richard's 12,000. It was quite an achievement, but it is likely that the result – namely, winning an entire kingdom with a small band of men – served to make him suspicious and withdrawn for the rest of his life. What one could achieve with so small a number could equally be lost at a subsequent trial. And the treachery of Stanley was not lost on him, even if at the time he was grateful for it. From the moment of victory to the end of the century, Henry had to reckon with one conspiracy after another, and to devise schemes to thwart them and maintain his security.

Bosworth is generally regarded as the last of the battles of the Wars of the Roses, but this is not so. The actual end is in dispute to this day. It can be argued with some conviction that the Pilgrimage of Grace in 1536 represents the last embers of Yorkist revolt against Lancaster, but this is beyond the scope of this book. The last of the conflicts of the Wars of the Roses, however, was the battle of Stoke, in 1487. Certainly it was the last engagement in the field.

The mechanism for operating the portcullis at the Bloody Tower. It has been altered and restored.

IV

Tudor home and gaol

Soon after Henry Tudor had won the battle of Bosworth and thus become Henry VII, he arranged for the last Plantagenet heir in the male line, Edward, Earl of Warwick, Clarence's son, who was already in custody as a result of an order by Richard III, to be brought to London for safe-keeping in the Tower. Henry himself came to the Tower in October 1485 and stayed there to await his coronation. Like earlier kings, he appointed a number of new knights and he also took the opportunity to formalize certain honours to higher lords who had helped him to triumph at Bosworth. Lord Stanley, arch-betrayer of Richard III, was advanced to the earldom of Derby. Henry was crowned at Westminster after a procession from the Tower. A few months later he married Elizabeth Plantagenet, daughter of Edward IV and his wife, Elizabeth Woodville, thus uniting the house of Lancaster with the house of York. Soon afterwards, Elizabeth was crowned as Queen.

Henry VII: the last king to make the Tower his home

Henry, who was to spend a lot of time at the Tower in his twenty-four years as king, made a number of improvements to the castle's facilities. These include a gallery known as the King's Gallery, which was built in 1506. It was a structure between the Lanthorn Tower and the Salt Tower and appears to have contained several apartments, a private chamber for the king, a library, and a council chamber among them. In some form it incorporated the old curtain wall between the two towers. The 1597 map (see colour plate) shows the structure (described of course as the Queen's Gallery!), but what we see for that date is a mix of the Henry VII work and the subsequent improvements and additions known to have been made by Henry VIII and Elizabeth I (see pp. 83–87, 110–111).

At the beginning of 1487, word reached Henry of a plot to depose him and put in his place a ten-year-old child, Lambert Simnel, who was a baker's son with a resemblance to the young Earl of Warwick. The conspiracy was headed by John de la Pole, Earl of Lincoln, a nephew of Edward IV (and a Plantagenet heir on the female side), with Francis, Viscount Lovell, one of Richard III's dearest friends who had got away after the defeat at Bosworth. Lincoln was a member of the king's Council and of all people would have known perfectly well that Warwick was alive and well in the Tower. As soon as he discovered that Henry knew about the plot he left the country, taking Simnel with him, and went to the court of Margaret, Duchess of Burgundy, Lincoln's mother and also the sister of Edward IV. Henry's immediate reaction was to have young Warwick paraded in the streets outside the Tower for Londoners to see that the boy was alive and well-treated. It is believed that the people were even encouraged to talk to him if they wanted. Henry then stood firm to await the next move of the conspirators; presumably he will have arranged for them to be informed of his 'exhibiting' Warwick to Londoners. He will also doubtless have organized agents to try to find out Lincoln's intentions.

On 5 May 1487 the conspirators played their hand, and a desperate and foolhardy one it was. With support from Margaret of Burgundy in the form of ships, money and a force of 2,000 German mercenaries, Lincoln and Lovell sailed to Ireland and on 24 May had Simnel crowned as King Edward VI of England, in Dublin. The ceremony was watched (and approved) by Garet Mor, Earl of Kildare, the most powerful of the Irish lords. Then the new 'king', in the company of Lincoln and Lovell, set out across the Irish Sea to Lancashire, with the 2,000 Germans who were accompanied by a force of half-clothed Irish troops. Henry VII, meanwhile, prepared for a confrontation, was waiting for the invaders at Nottingham. The two armies met in battle at Stoke and in a half-day struggle Henry triumphed. Lincoln was killed; Lovell escaped and was never seen again, though for generations his ghost was said to haunt the charming little waterside church and community of Minster Lovell, on the Windrush near Burford in Oxfordshire. Simnel was captured and spared. Henry decided to make a mockery of him: he was sent to work in the royal kitchens – in the Tower, perhaps? Later, Simnel became a trainer of the king's falcons. It was a sensible way for Henry to have handled the episode.

The Elizabethan historian John Stow (1525–1605) described the Tower as a 'citadell, to defend or command the Citie: a royale place for assemblies, and treaties. A Prison of Estate, for the most dangerous offenders: the onely place of coynage for all England at this time: the armourie for warlike provision; the Treasurie of the ornaments and jewels of the crowne, and generall conserver of the most Recordes of the King's Courts of justice at Westminster.' 'The armourie for warlike provision' is another phrase for state arsenal, and certainly since about 1200 the Tower had among its rôles the job of providing the king's armies (and navies) with weapons and missiles (crossbows, bolts, quivers, longbows, arrows, among others) and also siege engines such as mangonels, trebuchets and ballistas.

The introduction of gunpowder in the late thirteenth century and the resulting evolution of artillery and firearms from the fourteenth century onwards heightened the importance of the arsenal rôle: armies and navies sent by the Crown into battle or into hostile environments were often supplied from the Tower. As early as 1275 the Tower staff list contained a Chief Smith who made armaments. The first was Master Henry of Lewes, who died in 1291. Half a century later, Master Walter the Smith, along with a carpenter, Reginald of St Albans, were on the payroll for making firearms for Edward III to use at Crécy in 1346. These firearms were 'ribalds'. A ribald was a number of guns (of iron) joined together in a wooden frame. Gunpowder was being manufactured in the Tower from the 1340s, and increasingly so as the years went by. And by the end of Edward III's reign, smiths in the Tower were making hand-guns entirely of metal.

At the beginning of the fifteenth century a new state post appeared in the Tower's payroll, as it were, and that was the Master of the Works of the King's Engines and Guns of the Ordnance. This became shortened to Master of the Ordnance. To begin with, the new official was not the sole person with this duty. In the middle of the century Henry VI granted licences to Christopher Barton and Sigmund Shyrwode to manufacture ordnance on Tower Wharf, beginning a tradition of gun-making on the Wharf that went on into the seventeenth century.

In Henry VII's reign, the Ordnance department began to assume a more important place in the Tower functions, coinciding with the new king's interest in gunpowder manufacture and his anxiety that that should be monopolized by the state. Attempts had been made to control gunpowder-making in the middle of the Wars of the Roses, when in 1461 it had been ordained that gunpowder should only be made in the Tower. But as the turbulence of the war period showed, the monopoly had not been enforceable.

Sometime in the first years of Henry VII's reign, the Ordnance department acquired quarters in the Tower, which are mentioned by reference in a record as the House of Ordnance. This was presumably a storehouse for gunpowder and weapons. The building, about which there are no details, is known to have been on Tower Green.

We have seen that Henry VII's position as first Tudor king was continually being threatened by plots of one kind or another, so much so that some observers reckon that it made him suspicious and withdrawn for the rest of his life. The Simnel episode was followed some three years later by a more dangerous conspiracy which spread over eight years. In 1491, Perkin Warbeck, the son of a Flemish citizen of Tournai in Flanders, appeared at the court of Margaret of Burgundy, pretending to be Richard Plantagenet, Duke of York, younger of the two princes in the Tower. The Duchess affected to believe him – certainly he had acquired a grace of manner more befitting a prince than one of his class. She did so, too, because she was always anxious to make as many difficulties for Henry VII as she could. Warbeck was sent to Cork in the south of Ireland where he formally made his claim. It was accepted by some, but rejected by a greater number who drove him out of the country. Warbeck returned to Europe where over the next few years he made the rounds of the enemies of Henry, including Charles VIII of France and Emperor Maximilian. The French king entertained him in Paris and even acknowleged him as the rightful heir to the English throne. But before long, Henry, whose intelligence network was fully appraised of Warbeck's movements and intentions, succeeded in persuading Charles to drop this support, making it one of the conditions of the Treaty of Étaples which ended a war between England and France.

Warbeck had to leave France, and then went to the Emperor Maximilian who also welcomed him, promising him aid in the furtherance of his claim. From Maximilian he proceeded to Margaret of Burgundy who renewed her support and offered help. By now, Warbeck had acquired the backing of a handful of disaffected English magnates, among whom was Sir William Stanley, brother of the Lord Stanley who had changed sides at Bosworth in 1485 and thus assured Henry's triumph over Richard III. Henry's agents, however, detected this part of the Warbeck conspiracy and Stanley and his colleagues were arrested, Stanley being taken to the White Tower. A quick trial was followed by equally quick justice – execution. Warbeck, meanwhile, equipped with a small force by Margaret and by Maximilian, landed in Kent but was driven off by loyal county folk (1495). He went on to Ireland, but at Waterford was met by an equally determined and loyal force who defeated him in a skirmish. He would have been taken prisoner but for the timely assistance of members of the Fitzgerald family (leaders of Irish opposition to English rule) who helped to get him away and sent him off to Scotland.

Warbeck arrived in Scotland in November 1495 and was at once offered asylum by James IV, who had been for some time at loggerheads with Henry because the latter, while not actually at war was nonetheless encouraging warlike acts against Scotland. These included attacks by privateers on Scottish ships in the Firth of Forth, and support for the Highland Chiefs, led by John MacDonald of the Isles, in their struggle with James. The Scottish king went so far as to offer Warbeck one of his kinswomen, Lady Catherine Gordon, as wife and they were married soon afterwards. James IV launched an invasion of England on Warbeck's behalf, but it was beaten off and the king decided to tone down and then finally to withdraw his backing of the Warbeck cause.

Warbeck left Scotland and considered returning to Burgundy, but in the meanwhile Henry had negotiated a trade agreement with Burgundy, the well-known Magnus Intercursus which practically guaranteed free trade between the two countries, an agreement which had a specific clause, 'that Warbeck should not be received in Burgundy'. So Warbeck decided the time had come to invade England in the south, confident that he could raise support because of some discontent in the western counties. He went to Ireland yet again, raised some troops, and then landed at St Michael's Mount just off the Cornish mainland. His march through Cornwall was uneventful and he reached Exeter which he tried to storm. But the king brought an army against him and broke up his small force. Warbeck fled and took sanctuary in Beaulieu Abbey in Hampshire where he soon surrendered on receiving a promise that he would be spared. Even this far the king was disposed to being lenient, and Warbeck was taken to the Tower while Henry considered what to do with him (1496).

Henry's inclination to spare Warbeck lay in his realizing that Warbeck, for all his troublemaking, was but a tool in the hands of the remnants of the Yorkist party who had still not accepted the verdict of Bosworth. Once in the Tower, however,

Warbeck continued to scheme, and during his confinement succeeded in making contact with Edward, Earl of Warwick. For this to have been possible it is likely that the warders responsible for the two young prisoners had succumbed to bribes. The young men appear to have had a number of meetings, in which they hatched a plot to escape. It is possible that some if not all of the warders involved may have been accomplices. The plot was a daring one, and included seizing and murdering the Constable of the Tower, Sir John Digby, but it was detected. Warbeck was taken to trial and sentenced to be hanged at Tyburn: Warwick, because he was of royal blood, was executed on Tower Hill (1499). There is an alternate view, namely, that though Warbeck certainly plotted to escape, Warwick's complicity was faked in order to provide the king with just cause for putting Warwick to death.

The king may have felt that perhaps this was the last of the challenges to his title. Certainly, no more conspiracies were uncovered during the remainder of his reign. Henry continued to use the Tower regularly for his residence, and in February 1503 his wife, Elizabeth, sister of the princes in the Tower, gave birth to another daughter who died almost at once, and less than a fortnight later the Queen herself died in the royal apartments. She was taken to lie in state in St John's Chapel in the White Tower, and then conveyed to Westminster Abbey to be buried.

Six years later, Henry VII himself died, though not in the Tower but at Richmond. He was not much mourned or missed – sadly, as later historians have often thought, because his contribution as ruler of England was among the most beneficial of all English monarchs. His financial skills and his careful management of royal funds – some have called it parsimony – enabled him to convert an almost bankrupt exchequer into one of the healthiest of any reign, and yet he was in many respects a generous benefactor. He curbed the power of the nobility by banning private armies and by monopolizing gunpowder, he advanced the middle class, put landless middle-class men into the business of government – men who owed everything to him and so were unlikely to conspire (and indeed none did) – and he encouraged commerce, trade, voyages of exploration (notably the father-son partnership of John and Sebastian Cabot who discovered Newfoundland), and made commercial treaties with European powers.

Henry was succeeded by his second son, Henry (his eldest, Prince Arthur, had died young in 1502). The new king was eighteen. The reign that was to follow was to some historians, including this one, among the most appalling periods of English history. When he acceded he was received with great enthusiasm. He had been popular as Prince of Wales when his outgoing and jovial nature was a happy contrast to the reserved and morose disposition of his father. Large, powerfully built, handsome and athletic, he was also well read, could speak several languages, could play the lute and the organ, (and was later to compose music), and could discuss a wide range of erudite subjects with the cleverest men in the land. When he died, thirty-eight years later, he was hated and feared by almost everyone, high and low, and was mourned by no one. He had impoverished the nation with his extravagances and his vainglorious posturings on the European scene, had frequently manipulated the country's laws (though never actually setting them aside) to justify frightful acts, and had behaved time and time again with the utmost severity and cruelty, both to individuals (including two of his wives) and to whole sections of the community. As far as the Tower was concerned, his reign – more than any before or since – was characterized by the expansion of its rôle as a state prison, a place of execution and a repository of instruments of torture that were frequently and relentlessly applied.

Torture in the Tower of London

It may be useful to look at this point at the problem of torture in England. While we have seen that the Tower was used as a prison since the early twelfth century at least, this was only a secondary part of the castle's function right through the Middle Ages and up to the beginning of the sixteenth century. Obviously some prisoners will have been subjected to torture though there is little evidence in records or chronicles other than vague references to inmates being burdened with chains or kept in small cells without light. It is hard to believe, for example, that no prisoners put in the Tower through the agency of John Tiptoft, Earl of Worcester (*c*.1427–1470), an effective administrator holding high office in the time of Edward IV (1461–83), who was

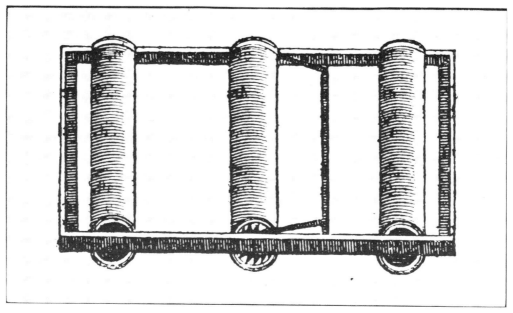

A drawing of the mechanism of a rack. 'It consists of a strong iron frame about six feet long, with three rollers of wood within it. The middle one of these, which has iron teeth at each end, is governed by two steps of iron, and was probably that part of the machine which suspended the powers of the rest when the unhappy sufferer was sufficiently strained by the cords . . . to begin confession.' This description is taken from Isaac Reed's edition of Shakespeare, of 1799.

notorious for ruthlessness and cruelty, were tortured. At the time there was in the Tower a relatively new instrument of torture, the rack, later known as the Duke of Exeter's Daughter because it had been invented, in the mid-fifteenth century's by John Holland, Duke of Exeter, who was for a time Constable of the Tower. Yet it would be quite wrong to look upon the mediaeval Tower as an infamous place of torture and execution - the almost total lack of inscriptions upon cell or chamber walls dating from any of the first four centuries is ample testimony. Nor is it easy to see Henry VII, who spent so much time living in the Tower, a man capable of the kind of clemency traditionally associated with Julius Caesar, tolerating torture on any scale.

It is the Tudor Age after Henry VII that may with some justice be regarded as an age of torture, beginning notoriously with the new king, the first king to fill the Tower with prisoners on a large scale, and often of a different type than before, and the first to allow torture almost as a matter of course. He made a start within a few weeks of accession. The two principal ministers who had done so much to fill the national coffers with funds, many of them obtained by pretty severe and often questionable methods, Edmund Dudley and Richard Empson, were arrested and sent to the Tower and a hasty trial for 'treason' followed, although whatever else they might have done, they had certainly not committed treason. Dudley tried to escape but was stopped. Both men were executed shortly after, though neither had been tortured. The growth of the use of imprisonment and/or torture in the Tower in this king's reign was not exclusively due to the odious nature of the king. We have also to allow that the break with Rome in the 1530s and the impact of the Reformation generally created a new kind of opposition to the Crown, one based on ideology – or conscience, and this opposition had to be contained.

The forms of torture applied in the sixteenth century included the rack, the Scavenger's Daughter (otherwise called Skeffington's Gyves, after Leonard Skeffington who was Lieutenant of the Tower in the time of Henry VIII), manacles, shackles, pilliwinks (a handcrusher), thumb-screws and spiked iron collars. There was also solitary confinement in an inhospitable cell in either the White Tower or in one or other of the smaller towers. The Scavenger's Daughter crushed the victim while the rack stretched him. One Scavenger's victim was the Irish rebel Thomas Miagh who was imprisoned in 1581 and tortured. He inscribed a comment on his punishment on the walls of the Beauchamp Tower, where he was held for two or more years, but he was eventually liberated and returned to Ireland where he found a job – as a gaoler!

Henry VIII, some of whose enormities we shall allude to in the appropriate places, carried out several important repairs, modifications and new works at the Tower. He was also responsible for ordering a detailed survey of the state of the fabric, in the period 1531–3. The survey (overseen by his chief minister, Thomas Cromwell) was followed straightaway by a programme of reparation to the walling and the towers, and also major improvements to the royal lodgings in the south-east.

To take his works, however, in their chronological order, we should first mention the Brick Tower on the northern side of the inner curtain wall. This had been first built by Henry III (see page 44) and now, in the period *c*.1510–20, it was rebuilt, this time using brick – hence its name ('new repayred with bryck', as Cromwell's survey described it). It was thenceforth, as it may have been beforehand, occupied by the Master of the Ordnance, at least up to 1641. The Brick Tower was to be reconstructed again, this time in the later nineteenth century.

The next work was a major rebuild of the Chapel of St Peter ad Vincula, after a disastrous fire in 1512. The rebuild was probably carried out in 1519–20, and was of course done in Tudor style, It cost some £260 in the money of the time, and the work was supervised by Walter Forster, Comptroller of the King's Works. Just outside the chapel, to the south, was (and is) Tower Green where some of the very highest victims of the execution block met their ends. In Henry VIII's time these included two of his six wives, Anne Boleyn (the second) in 1536 and Catherine Howard (the fifth) in 1542. They also included Margaret Plantagenet, Countess of Salisbury, daughter of Edward IV's brother, the Duke of Clarence, who was spitefully put to death by the gross king for no better reason than that he had a personal quarrel with her son, Reginald Pole. The latter had been planning to arrange an invasion of

Margaret Plantagenet, Countess of Salisbury, daughter of George, Duke of Clarence, younger brother of Edward IV (1461–83), who in 1541 was executed at Tower Green when she was 68, for no better reason than that her son Reginald Pole had been made a cardinal and was a leader of Catholic opposition to Henry VIII.

Figure of Elizabeth of York, daughter of Edward IV and sister of the Princes in the Tower. She married Henry VII in 1486, thus uniting the Houses of York and Lancaster, and she had several children including Henry VIII, and Margaret Tudor who was married to James IV of Scotland. She lived with Henry in the Tower and died there in 1503. The sculpture is part of her tomb in Westminster Abbey, and was executed by Pietro Torrigiano, the Florentine sculptor who after punching the nose of his fellow student Michaelangelo had to leave the city. He spent some time in England.

England. These victims, together with Jane, Lady Rochford (executed in 1542), were buried without any monument in the chancel of the chapel.

The alterations to the royal lodgings in the south-east of the castle followed soon after the Cromwell survey. By this time there were apartments for the king and another set for the Queen consort, and these had originated and evolved earlier in the mediaeval period. Since the entire range of structures was pulled down in the later seventeenth century, we have little to go on in describing what they were like. Even their depiction in the 1597 map (see colour plate) is not much help, for the roofing obscures almost everything underneath. There are records mentioning works on various individual apartments such as the King's Gallery, the Royal Wardrobe, the Great Chamber, the Privy Chamber, Council Chamber, Dining Chamber, and references to decorative features replacing earlier features, even to the re-use of panelling from one room in another, but all of them are tantalizingly incomplete and we are really no better off.

The alterations of 1532–3 were carried out quickly enough for the apartments to be ready for Henry and Anne Boleyn to stay in on the eve of Anne's coronation in May 1533. Repairs and modifications were also made to St Thomas's Tower, among them strengthening the very wide mediaeval arch in the north wall of the tower, altering the window arrangement in the storey above the arch, and inserting in the water passage underneath the tower a new pair of gates. These gates very much later came to be called Traitor's Gate. They protected the river approach to the Tower which in the Tudor Age was a suitable landing place for prisoners on their return from trial and conviction at Westminster. They would be conducted through the gates and under the north arch to their prison cells.

Another alteration was to the timber-framed apartment on the north side of the tower: this was rebuilt and then partitioned into four quarters to make rooms for the Lord Great Chamberlain (the Earl of Oxford) and the king's chamberlain (Lord Sandys).

To begin with, all these and other works were supervized by Thomas Flower, Surveyor of the King's Works (1528–32). One of the master craftsmen he employed was the Hertfordshire carpenter, James Nedeham (fl. 1514–44) who won the contract to rebuild the St Thomas's Tower lodgings, sometime in June 1532. Four months later, Nedeham was promoted to become Surveyor of the King's Works in succession to Flower who had been sacked. Nedeham remained in this official post until his death in 1544. He was one of the very few craftsmen about whom we have quite a lot of biographical information and it is interesting that he first appears in the Tower's records not as a craftsman but as a 'gunner', which may have been a sinecure acting as a pension for service in the war with France.

Nedeham got his sinecure in 1525. He had become a carpenter in the decade 1510–20, and was actually warden of the London Carpenters' Company for a spell. He was probably employed as a carpenter on war service and so when he came to the Tower he was a very skilled man, not only in woodwork, carving and joinery but also, like many carpenters, knowledgeable and proficient in stone masonry. He was hired to work for Cardinal Wolsey at York Place, part of the Whitehall Palace complex that was under construction, and by 1531 he had become 'the king's carpenter'. When he was made Surveyor, he appears to have been the first craftsman to be elevated to this relatively influential post: his predecessors had invariably been clerics and not blue collar workers. Nedeham's advancement was due partly to his association with Thomas Cromwell who had been supervisor of some of Wolsey's principal building operations. Cromwell succeeded Wolsey (when the latter was disgraced in 1529 ostensibly for failing to obtain for the king the annulment he required of his marriage to Queen Catherine of Aragon) as chief adviser to the king. Nedeham worked at Hampton Court. He also worked at Cromwell's new mansion going up in Throgmorton Street (which later came to be the Drapers' Hall). It was at this mansion that Cromwell, in order to enlarge his garden, actually had a neighbouring house moved, lock, stock and barrel, on rollers some 22 feet (6.8

The White Tower more or less as it looked when it was completed at the end of the 11th century. There are later alterations to the facings, windows, battlements, turret tops, but essentially it is what William the Conqueror and his son William Rufus wanted. The staircase in front is a new one, but probably conforms to the one put up in the original building period.

An attempt to escape ends in disaster. Gruffydd, elder son of Llywelyn Fawr (the Great), Prince of all Wales (1194–1240), is captured in a skirmish with England, and is sent to the Tower, in 1241. In 1244 he attempts to escape but is killed when his rope snaps and he falls and breaks his neck. The picture comes from Matthew Paris's Chronica Majora.

Richard II being put into the Tower after he had abdicated, in 1399. The king at right is his cousin Henry IV who had compelled him to give up the throne.

Pontefract Castle, Yorkshire, by Alexander Keirinx, c. 1625, where Richard II was imprisoned and soon afterwards died. For a long time it was one of the principal royal castles in the northern half of England.

The rooms in the Bloody Tower occupied by Sir Walter Ralegh for thirteen years (1603–16). The upper room was his bedroom, which he was allowed to share with his wife for several years. The bed is not the original. The lower room was a study/sitting room, in which among other things, he wrote his History of the World, *and gave lessons to the Prince of Wales.*

Thomas Wentworth, Earl of Strafford.

An aquatint of the Tower in the early 19th century. There is a lot of activity among the ships in the Thames in front of Tower Wharf. As usual, the White Tower dominates the scene.

In this coloured engraving the artist has dramatically captured the night of 30th October 1841 when the fire in the Bowyer Tower spread to engulf the Grand Storehouse, at the Tower. It is easy to see how the lead piping and flashings on the north side of the White Tower melted in the heat.

This is a late 19th century colour print of the famous 15th century small painting showing Charles, Duke of Orleans (who was captured at Agincourt in 1415), writing at a table when he was a prisoner at the Tower (1415–1440). Orleans was a gifted poet, and he produced a variety of verses, some in English but mostly in French. Nearly half a century after his release on payment of a huge ransom, a collection of his verses was presented to Henry VII bound in a volume which had this picture as one of the main illustrations. It is a complex picture, for it attempts to show a variety of things, telescoped historically and topographically, such as what it was like inside the White Tower (note the fireplace, for example), what Orleans did with his time, what was going on in the Tower precincts, what sort of buildings surrounded the Tower (notably, London Bridge and a spread of church spires), how Orleans greeted the courier who brought the ransom money after 25 years, and so forth.

Henry Wriothesley, third Earl of Southampton (1573–1624), the Elizabethan soldier and patron of Shakespeare, who joined the conspiracy of the Earl of Essex against the government in 1601 – and so incurred a charge of high treason. Southampton spent two years in the Tower. Shakespeare dedicated some of his works to Southampton, including his first poem, Venus and Adonis, *in 1593. Note the inset picture of the Tower at top right corner.*

The inset in the above enlarged. When Southampton was released from the Tower he sat for the portrait, and the artist commemorated the release with the inset picture.

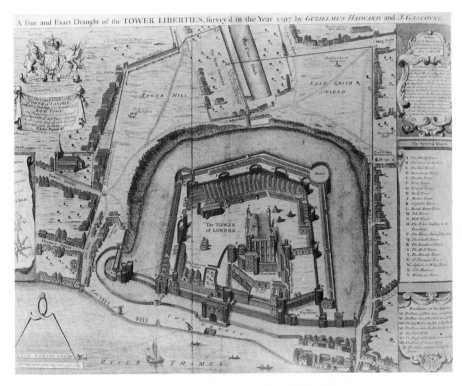

A plan of the Tower drawn in 1597 by William Hayward and John Gascoigne.

The Brick Tower after it had been damaged in the 1841 fire at the Tower.

A recent aerial photograph of the Tower, seen from the north-east.

meters) northwards to provide more space. Readers may recall a similar exercise just outside Sudbury in Suffolk in the early 1970s, when the owner of Ballingdon Manor, a sixteenth-century timber-framed mansion, moved his house several yards uphill on wheels, in order to get away from a new estate of houses being built further downhill, which spoiled his view.

After finishing the St Thomas's Tower improvements, Nedeham turned to other buildings on the list needing restoration. Among these was the White Tower which required a new roof, the Lieutenant's Lodgings which had to be rebuilt altogether, some new drawbridges across the ditch by the barbican on the south-west and across the ditch by the Develin Tower on the south-east of the castle. Most interesting of all, he built a new Jewel House for Cromwell (for the king) who, in addition to his many other offices of state, was Master of the Jewels. This new structure stood between the south side of the White Tower and the north side of the Great Hall, somewhere near the previous Jewel House which, though abandoned, had not been pulled down. The new building was constructed of brickwork with dressings of stone from Reigate quarries and also from Caen in Normandy.

Nedeham seems to have done less and less at the Tower and more elsewhere in his later years. He died while serving with the army on campaign in France in 1544 and was buried at Boulogne.

It should also be mentioned that repair work was carried out on several of the castle's towers during the years running up to the Cromwell Survey and after, and these included the Salt Tower (then known as Julius Caesar's Tower), the Broad Arrow Tower, Bowyer's Tower, Flint Tower, Develin Tower and the Cradle Tower. In 1536 Cromwell was able to report that the king had 'repaired the Tower of London'.

Despite all these works the king was losing interest in the Tower as a royal palace-residence, and probably never stayed there again after the night or two before Anne Boleyn's coronation. Gradually, its rôle as a palace subsided and eventually all but disappeared as its other functions assumed greater importance – especially as a prison and an ordnance depot. The Elizabethan historian Raphael Holinshed (d.1580) described the Tower as 'rather an armorie and house of munition, and thereunto a place for the safekeeping of offenders, then a palace roiall for a king or queen to soiourne in. . . '.

One more set of new works was undertaken in the 1540s, and that was a storehouse for the Ordnance. The first one was built 'north of the Mynt', and it was raised not by the Surveyor who followed Nedeham (Sir Richard Lee) but by the Lieutenant of the Ordnance, Sir Francis Fleming. This followed a survey of the existing Ordnance buildings undertaken in 1536 by the Master of the Ordnance, Sir Christopher Morrice, who consulted James Nedeham and took him on the survey. They found that the 'long howse of Ordenaunce upon the grene is redy to ffall'. But it was nearly a decade before the Ordnance requirements were met, during the years 1545–7, when Fleming was commissioned to 'erect and newe buylde one house wherein all

The monument to Sir Richard Cholmondeley, in the Chapel of St. Peter ad Vincula. He was Lieutenant of the Tower during the reign of Henry VIII, for whom he had fought at the battle of Flodden Field, in 1513. Beside him lies a monument to his wife.

the kinges maiestie's store and provicion of Artillerie Ordinaunce and other Municions maye be kepte garded. . . .' The new building was of brick and timber, and had a tiled roof and lead guttering and pipes. Racks were installed on which weapons could be stored. There was a special room partitioned off for the king's own weapons.

The armour of Henry VIII

Mention of the king's weapons brings one to the armours of Henry VIII. There has been armour in the Tower since the beginning. The Norman and early Plantagenet kings took their chain mail garments with them wherever they went. Armour and arms for the Tower garrison were kept in the Royal Wardrobe, the Norman ones so wonderfully illustrated in so many panels of the Bayeux Tapestry. The garments included a long shirt from neck to knees, called the hauberk, and a pair of leggings, and some knights wore shorter coats. The mail consisted of iron wire rings interlinked and riveted, the rings being in some cases interspersed with solid rings.

This provided a very flexible garment, and sometimes an undergarment would be worn below, made of stuffed wool and cloth, known as a gambeson. But these garments were also heavy on the shoulders. Gradually, in the thirteenth century, mail armour came to be reinforced with iron plates, which on the limbs were then combined with articulated plates. By the time of the battle of Agincourt in 1415, mail had been superseded altogether by 'a full harness of plate from head to foot', known as white armour.

Most mediaeval armour of quality was made in Southern Germany, Flanders or northern Italy, which meant that monarchs and top nobles had to get it from these manufacturers and pay a high price. Some armour was made in other countries, and England had its own armourers from the fourteenth century, but none of it was to be comparable with the wonders of Nuremberg or Milan or Brussels until the sixteenth century, and in England it was Henry VIII, who had marvelled at some of the armour he had seen, especially the suit presented to him by Emperor Maximilian I in 1514, who decided to encourage high quality armour-making in his own kingdom, setting the example by having some made for himself. He attracted a number of German craftsmen to come and work in Greenwich, providing them with suitable workshops near the royal palace. He also gave encouragement to Flemish and German armourers.

The King had a number of suits of armour made for him over the years of his reign, and while we are not able to say how many he commissioned, there are five surviving

The Queen's House from the north-east. These buildings, which have restoration work of several periods, are in the south-west corner of the Inner Ward, roughly occupying an 'L' between the Beauchamp, Bell and Bloody Towers. The earliest surviving buildings are of Henry VIII's time. It is now the house of the Resident Governor. For centuries it was the residence of the Lieutenant (the Lieutenant's Lodgings). Though still called the Queen's House, it has never been a royal home.

suits in England, one at Windsor and four in the Tower. Two of these are foot-combat suits of 1520, one made for him by German craftsmen at the workshop at Greenwich, the others by Flemings and Italians.

No account of the Tower of London's history can be considered complete without some mention of the sad procession of high-born and distinguished people of both sexes, who spent time in the Tower in Henry VIII's reign, sent there by the king, many of whom also went to their deaths within or just outside the Tower precincts. But in alluding to these events, it is equally important for the proper understanding of the history and rôle of the Tower that whatever the level of sadness generated by contemplation of the fate of people like Sir Thomas More, Queen Anne Boleyn, even the odious Thomas Cromwell himself (who had played some part in consigning so many others to the Tower), in no way does this Tudor period excess represent anything more than a fraction of the sum total of the Tower's contribution to the story of England.

   Sir Thomas More was the most celebrated victim of Henry VIII's monstrous and pathological career of blood-shedding among those who crossed him even in the slightest degree. Born in London in 1478 the son of a judge, he was a page for a time in the household of Cardinal John Morton, Archbishop of Canterbury and chief adviser to Henry VII. More went to Oxford and then read law at Lincoln's Inn in

Thomas Cromwell, Earl of Essex, Henry VIII's secretary, Vicar-General, Lord Great Chamberlain, Lord Privy Seal, and principal agent for the dissolution of the monasteries (1536–9). He took the responsibility for a number of the king's grosser measures, and when he made the mistake of pressing the king to marry Anne of Cleves, a union that was doomed from the start, he was arrested on a charge of treason, which it certainly was not. He was executed at Tyburn, after a short spell in the Tower.

Thos. Moor L'Chancelour.

Sir Thomas More (1478–1535), one of the greatest Englishmen of the 16th century. Lawyer, author, statesman, philosopher, friend of Erasmus, he was Henry VIII's Lord Chancellor from 1529 to 1532, the first layman to hold that office. When he refused to recognize the king's claim to be the Supreme Head of the English Church, he was tried for treason, imprisoned in the Tower and finally executed.

London. He soon became known for his skills as a pleader of cases in the courts, and belonged to a circle of scholars among whom the leading lights were Erasmus and Dean Colet, the great humanists. In 1504, More became an MP In the next reign, Henry VIII was struck by More's arguments in a particular Star Chamber case, and in 1514 the king made him Master of Requests, and a few years later a Privy Councillor. More also impressed Cardinal Wolsey, who took him along to several important diplomatic meetings abroad, and in 1523 More was elected Speaker of the House of Commons.

When Wolsey was disgraced in 1529, the king pressed More to accept the vacant Lord Chancellorship, almost the highest office in the land. More hesitated as he was reluctant to get involved with the king at that high level because he had already detected signs that Henry was heading for a break with the Church of Rome, something More was unwilling to countenance. Yet he did recognize the need for some reform of the Church. In 1532 matters came to a head when the king announced his intention of having himself declared Supreme Head of the English Church, displacing the Pope, and he expected More, along with others, to swear an oath accepting the declaration. More, however, would not be moved, and he resigned the Lord Chancellorship, but he did not make any attempt whatever to influence anyone else likewise to refuse to swear. Ordinarily, he might have been allowed to live out his days quietly in retirement, away from the Court. But the king demanded universal support for his stand among the leaders in government, the Church and the law, and much as Henry respected More and admired his intellectual gifts which transcended those of all his English contemporaries, he refused to tolerate even silent opposition and he had More arrested. More was presumed guilty of misprision of treason, but he was not charged with treason until after more than a year.

More was committed to the Tower, where he was imprisoned in the Bell Tower, in the large vaulted chamber on the ground floor. This had three arrow loops. There was another chamber above, which was to accommodate Bishop Fisher of Rochester, another martyr to the king's vengeance, at much the same time. More was harshly treated, forbidden to write, deprived of books, and kept in the dark, like a common felon – and yet he had been Lord Chancellor! After more than a year, he was tried at Westminster Hall. He was taken by boat from the Tower to Westminster, and at the trial he was found guilty, chiefly through the perjury of the chief witness for the prosecution, Sir Richard Rice, which was necessary precisely because the proper procedures were being followed. The new Lord Chancellor, Sir

The well-known drawing of the family of Sir Thomas More, by Hans Holbein (the Younger), in 1527. It is at the Kunstmuseum, Basel, in Switzerland. Judge More, Sir Thomas's father, is seated at third left; More is next to him, and More's wife Alice is at extreme right.

Queen Anne Boleyn, second wife of Henry VIII and mother of Elizabeth I. Anne Boleyn, having failed to give the king a son and he tiring of her, turned to a lover for consolation. But they were caught. She was executed on Tower Green in 1536.

Thomas Audley, pronounced sentence, that he should be hanged, drawn and quartered. He was taken back to the Tower, this time by barge, to await the barbarous sentence. Less than a week later he was told that the king had commuted the sentence to simple (!) execution on the block on Tower Hill, and on the 6th July 1535 he was despatched. His body was buried in St Peter ad Vincula and his head affixed to London Bridge.

The story of Anne Boleyn is so well known that it does not merit yet another account here. But it is of interest that, unlike almost all major state prisoners who spent time in the Tower before and after trial at Westminster Hall or elsewhere during the Tudor period, Anne was actually tried in the Tower itself. Wherever it was, the room had to be rearranged to provide seating for a number of lords selected to hear the case against her, namely, that by committing adultery while she was the wife of the king she had committed high treason as well. She was sentenced to death, first by burning at the stake, but this was later altered to execution on Tower Green, outside the Chapel of St Peter ad Vincula. She had asked if she could be executed by sword rather than by axe, and her wish was granted. But it took some days to find an executioner capable of doing it properly with a sword, and when he was found he came not from England but from France.

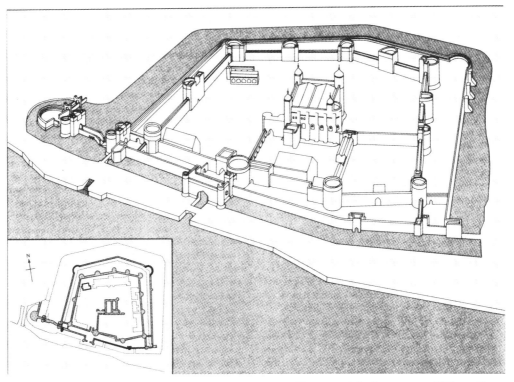

Elevation of the Tower at the end of Henry VIII's reign, in 1547. The principal development since 1300 was Tower Wharf, in the foreground. Plan of the Tower in c. 1547.

Some famous prisoners of the 16th century

To the relief of most Englishmen, Henry VIII at last died in 1547. 'He left his realm in a condition of great misery, and for all its troubles he was personally responsible . . . of his unbounded selfishness, of his ingratitude to those who had served him best, of his ruthless cruelty to all those who stood in his way . . . the story

A picture portraying some of the Tudors. It was painted in 1667 by van Leemput from an original by Holbein which had been painted for Whitehall Palace but which was burnt in a fire in 1698. Clockwise from left are: Henry VIII, Henry VII, Elizabeth of York, wife of Henry VII, and Jane Seymour, Henry VIII's third wife.

of his reign develops each of these traits in its own particular blackness.' Thus wrote Sir Charles Oman over half a century ago, and although much research has been done on his reign since then, Henry remains no more likeable, even if a little easier to understand. Despite the king's efforts to assure the succession in the male line – which included divorce, marriage to commoners, execution of wives – he was in the end succeeded by a sickly underdeveloped boy of nine, Prince Edward, child of his marriage with Jane Seymour who died in childbirth. It was obvious he was not long for this world.

The governance of England was put in the hands of the Council, headed by Jane's elder brother Edward Seymour, Earl of Hertford, who soon had himself advanced to become Duke of Somerset. The new king was to reign for only six years, but he began to show signs of sharp intelligence as well as a slightly sinister hardness of character that had he lived might have led him to emulate his repulsive father. Edward entered the Tower about a week after Henry's death to receive a great welcome from a gathering of the great men of England. A week later, he was solemnly created a knight by his uncle Hertford following the wishes of the late king, and the boy then handed out honours to many of the leading men, pre-eminent among them the dukedom of Hertford, and a barony for Hertford's younger brother, Thomas Seymour. An earldom was given to John Dudley, son of the Dudley executed at the start of Henry's reign, who will figure prominently later on (see pp. 99–102).

Young King Edward made the solemn procession from the Tower to Westminster Abbey for his coronation on 19 February 1547 (see below) but it is unlikely that thereafter he stayed very much at the Tower, as his father had practically given up the palace buildings there and preferred the new palace buildings that were going up

The procession accompanying Edward VI to Westminster for his coronation, in 1547. It is leaving the Tower. The White Tower is at extreme left.

in Whitehall. The history of the Tower as a royal fortress-residence in use as a castle may be said by this time to have come to an end. The rôle of the castle in support of the feudal order of society had virtually disappeared as the system of feudalism itself gave way to a different and perhaps more unpleasant arrangement. Yet as a structure the Tower was to survive and to undergo alteration, improvement and adjustment to meet both the older rôles it continued to play (Ordnance, Mint, Menagerie, Crown Jewel repository, state prison) and also new ones. We need therefore to look at its subsequent history, right to the present time when it has become by far the most popular historic monument in the kingdom.

Use of the Tower as the headquarters of the Royal Ordnance inevitably put the whole complex of buildings continuously at risk because of the storage of gunpowder within. There was a disaster on the evening of 22 November 1548 when some barrels of gunpowder stored in one of the towers, possibly the Lion Tower, were accidently set alight and blew up the whole building. The wrecked tower is recorded as having been 'next the drawbridge', but which drawbridge is not identified. The historian Stow says the tower was rebuilt.

Little else seems to have been done to the Tower's fabric in young Edward's reign, but the human history of the Tower was an eventful one. Among the important people of the period who spent time there were Stephen Gardiner (1483–1555), Bishop of Winchester, for his championing of the continuation of holding Mass, Thomas Seymour (1508–49), his brother Edward Seymour, Duke of Somerset, Protector of England, and three other bishops, Worcester, Chichester and Durham.

Thomas, Lord Seymour of Sudeley, was an attractive, bold, swashbuckling adventurer, who had held command of the Channel fleet during the last years of Henry VIII. But he was jealous of his elder brother, Edward, Duke of Somerset's position as Protector and set out from the beginning to undermine him, and if possible supplant him in office. Thomas's envy was not in the least assuaged when Somerset made him Lord High Admiral, with an influential seat on the royal Council. On the other side of the coin of his qualities, Thomas Seymour was both indiscreet and impetuous, and these were before long to lead to his downfall and execution.

When it became clear early on in the young king's reign that he was not going to survive for long, the Council began to think about the succession. The king had two half-sisters. One was Mary Tudor, daughter of Henry VIII and his first wife, Catherine of Aragon, who was a Catholic. Mary had had to endure many years of humiliation and countryside exile because of the break-up of her parents' marriage in the early 1530s and Henry's subsequent marriage to Anne Boleyn, and by the 1540s (her mother had died in 1536) Mary had become a hard and embittered woman, filled with suspicion. The other half-sister was Elizabeth Tudor, daughter of Henry VIII and Anne Boleyn, and she was born in 1533. She, too, had been pushed into the background when she was hardly three years old, when her mother was disgraced and executed in 1536.

Thomas Seymour, one of the Council members concerned about the succession, immediately began to champion the claim of Elizabeth, coupling this with a proposal that he should marry her. It was brazenly indiscreet, and his brother Edward swiftly scotched the idea with a threat of arrest. So Thomas turned his attention to the widow of Henry VIII, Catherine Parr, whom he apparently loved before she became Henry's last queen in 1543. Thomas and Catherine were married late in 1547 and they took Elizabeth to live with them at their conjugal home. We need not be surprised at Thomas Seymour's part in this explosive idea, but historians have always wondered what prompted the widowed queen, now newly married, to go along with it.

The presence in the house of a young and good-looking girl (Elizabeth was then about fifteen) was a diversion that any newly married couple could well do without. It was natural that Elizabeth would develop an interest in Thomas, for he was an attractive man, with a way with women, and in this case he did nothing to discourage this interest. Elizabeth on her part was old enough to understand some of the mysteries of love, though that does not make her precocious. Thomas cannot be entirely blamed for taking advantage of a situation that not only he but his wife set up. Even in the early days of the marriage, Thomas would go into Elizabeth's bedroom in the early morning. If she were dressed, 'he would bid her good morrow . . . and strike her upon . . . the buttocks familiarly . . . and sometimes go through to the maidens and play with them.' Sometimes it was too early, and she had not yet got up, whereupon 'he would . . . make as though he would come at her, and she would go further into the bed so that he could not come at her'. This was harmless, provided the familiarities did not get out of hand, and that they kept quiet about them. But Thomas was not capable of discretion; horseplay with a princess had an element of exciting danger, and it was something to boast about among his friends, which he did.

Eventually, Catherine by now pregnant, thought the business had gone far enough and she sent Elizabeth away. A few months later, Catherine died in childbirth, and after an indecently short interval Thomas turned his attentions again to Elizabeth, this time in furtherance of a wildly ambitious scheme to oust his own brother from the Protectorate and also to marry Elizabeth. He allowed himself to believe that he would get the support of the young king. Plunging headlong down the high-treason path, he began to canvass support among friends and among discontents to back a *coup d'état*, but Somerset was kept well informed. In some respects he had little need of secret service watching: Thomas made no effort to cover up his tracks. In due course, the Protector had Kate Ashley, Elizabeth's governess, and Thomas Parry, her cofferer, arrested and questioned about the scheme, in particular about Elizabeth's part in it, if any. Both were circumspect with their answer: they admitted what the Council already knew, namely, the details of the frolics with Elizabeth in the Seymour household while Catherine Parr was alive, but they said little else. Yet the Council was convinced that she was implicated, and on several occasions invited Thomas to 'discuss' the matters, and each time he treated the Council members with scorn. Then, on 17 January 1549, he was formally arrested at his house in the Strand and taken to the Tower. On 25 February a bill of attainder against him was brought before Parliament, but he was forbidden to defend himself against the charges. His conviction for high treason followed, and on 20 March he was executed on Tower Hill. According to Bishop Hugh Latimer of Worcester (himself later to die at the stake), Thomas died 'irksomely, horribly . . . God had clean forsaken him'. It was said at the time that the fall of one of the Seymour brothers would lead to the overthrow of the other, and so it did.

Edward Seymour, Duke of Somerset

Barely half a year later, Protector Somerset was unseated in a *coup* headed by John Dudley, Earl of Warwick. A false charge of treason was engineered and Somerset was taken to the Beauchamp Tower to await trial. Miraculously, proceedings were not brought, and after cooling his heels for a few months, during which the worst that happened was that part of his huge income-producing estates were taken from him, he was reconciled with Dudley, now Duke of Northumberland and Protector of England. The character of this John Dudley is worth a mention, for he came from a family several of whose members were sometime or other in trouble with the monarch and who spent time in the Tower of London.

John Dudley was of that middle class of Englishmen from whom the Tudor monarchs preferred to choose the men who worked with them and for them in the governing of the country. Though his young life had been spent in an atmosphere of disgrace through the attainder and execution of his father, Edmund Dudley, he managed to make his way into the top echelons of the royal service. By 1538 he was Deputy Governor of Calais and by 1542 Warden of the Scottish Marches, with the peerage of Viscount Lisle. He was already known as an avaricious and unscrupulous self-seeker, and possibly these qualities appealed to Henry VIII. But Dudley was also a first-rate soldier and no mean commander of men at sea. At the accession of Edward VI he was one of the top men in England and enjoyed an influence as a member of the Council almost as dominant as Somerset himself. He also had qualities that the latter did not, was ruthless and courageous, fearing no man on earth.

In February 1550, Dudley (created Earl of Warwick in 1547) allowed Somerset to leave the Tower and even restored him to membership of the Council. But Somerset, who was personally much better liked by people of all classes than the more unrelenting Dudley, clearly posed a running threat to Dudley and before long he was arrested again and taken to the Tower, again on high treason charges. This was in the autumn of 1551, by which time Dudley had persuaded the young King Edward VI to advance his own peerage to a dukedom, of Northumberland. Somerset was alleged to have headed a conspiracy to murder Northumberland and lead a revolt against the young king himself, using (it was said) a troop of some two thousand soldiers to seize the Tower and cower the city of London.

At the beginning of December, Somerset was taken from his cell, which may have been the same one in the Beauchamp Tower that he had occupied in 1549, and escorted to Westminster, preceded (according to the historian Stow who may have witnessed the procession) by a guard carrying the official execution axe and accompanied by a large squadron of weapon-carrying men ready to engage the two thousand troops said to have been assembled by the Duke. At Westminster Hall, Somerset denied the charges against him effectively enough to win an acquittal on the high treason counts, but being convicted of felony which did not normally carry the death sentence. As he then returned to the Tower, this time preceded by the guard carrying the official axe pointing away from him, the crowds, who had always held Somerset in some affection as a man who at least meant well, cheered enthusiastically, believing that he had been acquitted altogether. It is likely that this spontaneous demonstration in his favour actually ensured that he would be put to death. Northumberland, while eschewing popularity himself – to such an extent that one specialist on the period, Milton Waldman, wrote, 'as an example of the power of sheer unscrupulous genius to get on without popularity he stands alone in English history' – was not moved by jealousy but rather by the need to crush opposition from whatever quarter it threatened. Believing that an attempt would be made to rescue Somerset as he proceeded towards the block on Tower Hill for execution on 22 January 1552, Northumberland took the unprecedented step of ordering the citizens of London to stay indoors until two hours after the actual execution, 8 a.m. But the orders were ignored widely, and in a series of confrontations with the ring of armed troops round the execution block, more than a hundred would-be spectators were driven into the outer ditch of the Tower and only scrambled out with difficulty.

Shortly after 8 o'clock Somerset was executed, amid groans and tears, and afterwards many of the crowd surged forward to dip handkerchiefs into his blood. He was later buried unceremoniously in the Chapel of St Peter ad Vincula, next to the remains of his brother Thomas Seymour.

Northumberland now ruled supreme. He managed to keep himself in power for about eighteen months, largely because he never hesitated to strike down all who stood in his way. Yet it was a time of great uncertainty and terror, when no man trusted his neighbour and few his own family, the while England wondered what would happen to the king, Edward, and more concernedly, who would succeed him. As the months went by, Edward's health showed no signs of improvement at all; he developed additional and more sinister symptoms, more characteristic of poisoning than of the tuberculosis widely understood to be the complaint from which he suffered.

Lady Jane Grey – Nine Days Queen

Northumberland's thoughts, meanwhile, had for some time been occupied with the succession, and he conceived a daring plan for ensuring that he would hold on to the Protectorate if the young king died. He arranged for his fourth son, Lord Guilford Dudley, to marry Lady Jane Grey, the fifteen-year-old cousin of Edward, who was the nearest direct Protestant heir. Lady Jane Grey, intelligent and good-looking, pious and keen on her books, was the grand-daughter of Henry VIII's sister Mary, who had married Charles Brandon, Duke of Suffolk. Northumberland virtually compelled the young couple to marry in May 1553, and then prevailed upon the sickly Edward to write a new testament, leaving the throne to Lady Jane, thus excluding Mary, daughter of Henry VIII and Catherine of Aragon, because she was a Catholic.

At the beginning of July 1553, Edward took a turn for the worse and on the 6th he died, aged only fifteen. Legend immediately took up the tale that he was poisoned, but it is clear that he was sickly enough not to have lasted for long as things were. As soon as news reached Northumberland at his Thames-side home, Syon House at Isleworth (which today is still the London home of the dukes of Northumberland), where Lady Jane and her husband Lord Guilford were also staying, he called a meeting of the Council. On 9 July, Lady Jane was formally told she was Queen and then conveyed in state on a barge to the Tower. It was the first of less than eleven days that she would spend in the Tower as Queen.

The proclamation of Lady Jane Grey was received by Londoners with singular lack of enthusiasm; they had nothing against her personally but they dreaded the continuation of Northumberland's Protectorate. Even the royal cannon salutes from the Tower walls – 'a shott of gunnes . . . as had not been seen oft' – created no stir. Little wonder, for the city had already rumbled that the virtuous Jane was usurping the claim of the rightful heir, Mary Tudor, who meanwhile was waiting at her Hertfordshire home for the summons to come to London. It did not come; indeed, Mary soon discovered that she was in great danger of arrest by Northumberland, and so she left for East Anglia, heading for Framlingham Castle in Suffolk, a well-defended fortress which had only a few months before been given to her by her half-brother, the king. Once there, she was able to rally considerable support among the nobles and gentry, and within a few days could count on an army of several thousands to help her establish her claim. It is a reflection more of the odium in which Northumberland was held than of any liking for Mary that the shires of Norfolk and Suffolk, though predominantly Protestant, readily supported the Catholic daughter of Henry VIII.

Northumberland assembled a small force at the Tower and set out for East Anglia to confront Mary: whatever else one may say of him, he never lacked courage. At Bury St Edmunds, he realized that his cause was lost, as his force had deserted almost to a man, and he retreated into Cambridge. There he was apprehended and brought to London, and put into the Bloody Tower. The 'Nine Days Queen' Jane was moved out of the royal apartments and lodged in the Lieutenant's House on the Green, while her husband Lord Guilford together with his four brothers (all of whom were picked up by Mary's forces) were put into the Beauchamp Tower. Mary Tudor

Portrait of Lady Jane Grey who was held in the Gaoler's lodgings in the Tower before her execution in 1554. Her husband, Lord Guilford Dudley, was kept at the same time in the Beauchamp Tower, and it may have been he who carved her name, IANE, in the wall there, where it can be seen to-day.

was proclaimed Queen on Tower Hill. She herself reached London on 3 August and took up residence in the Tower. She stayed for about two weeks, and then left for the more comfortable Whitehall Palace.

On 18 August, Northumberland was taken to Westminster Hall and tried, convicted and sentenced. He was returned to the Tower and put in with his sons in the Beauchamp Tower, where the inscriptions carved into the walls by members of the Dudley family can still be seen. Northumberland tried to recant, forsaking his Protestant faith, but to no avail. He could expect no mercy and did not receive it, and was executed. Lady Jane was kept in confinement while Mary considered what to do with her.

The story of Lady Jane Grey's miniscule reign as queen and her subsequent fate has always been regarded as particularly tragic. Tradition, if not history, has portrayed her as an innocent, helpless and unwilling party to her ruthless father-in-law's schemes, but we may without unduly denigrating her memory question the totality of this innocence. During the few days she spent at the Tower as queen she signed a quantity of official documents, letters to lords-lieutenant in the shires and so on, appointed officials and even had a coronation medal struck in the Royal Mint within the Tower precincts (though it has been argued that this last was done without her knowledge). Sometime during those days she also received the royal regalia and State Crown. Could all this – and perhaps more – have been done without any collusion on her part? The new queen, Mary, evidently considered there were enough grounds for trial for high treason, and 13 November 1553, about six weeks after Mary's own coronation, Lady Jane Grey, her husband Lord Guilford Dudley and others were arraigned at Westminster Hall, tried and found guilty, and sentenced to death. They were returned to the Tower.

The 'tragedy' tradition also leads us to believe that Mary, consumed with anger at the schemes of Northumberland in his efforts to deprive her of her rightful succession, was bent on making the unfortunate teenage queen pay with her life, but this is not supported by facts. There is correspondence showing how Mary resisted

Henry Grey, Duke of Suffolk, father of Lady Jane Grey, the Nine Days Queen. He was executed in 1554 for his part in the rebellion led by Sir Thomas Wyatt against Mary I (1553–58).

pressure to put Jane to death, and that when in the end she had to agree to do so, she was moved not by feelings of vengeance but because of continued though futile efforts by members of Jane's family to raise revolts in her favour, thus implicating her, however unwittingly.

During her imprisonment in the Tower after the collapse of Northumberland's scheme, Jane was accorded much freedom (if one can ever use this word in the context of imprisonment). She was allowed to walk about every day in the Privy Garden of the royal apartments and in the Lieutenant's House garden, and even, under escort, to walk around Tower Hill. She was also allowed to receive visitors.

Wyatt's Rebellion

Very early in 1554 news reached the people of London and the south that the queen was planning to marry. Her intended husband was Prince Philip of Spain, son of Charles V, Emperor of the Holy Roman Empire and also King of Spain, and the foremost champion of the Catholic cause in Europe. The news produced great alarm among the English, high and low. The marriage would make England no more than another part of the fast-growing Spanish empire; the nation would soon be feeling the sharp end of the Spanish Inquisition and all that this entailed; and terrible persecution and deaths would result for heretics. Very soon, a number of spontaneous demonstrations erupted against the projected marriage. The best-known one, which probably constituted the greatest danger to the queen, was that organized by Sir Thomas Wyatt, sometime in January, down in Kent. There is evidence that Wyatt was given encouragement, perhaps even offered material support, by the French court which dreaded the Anglo-Spanish match.

By the beginning of February 1554, Wyatt and his force were occupying positions on the south bank of the Thames, directly opposite the Tower. The garrison at the Tower, meanwhile, had been put on alert and reinforced, ready to resist assault. Quantities of ammunition are said to have been brought in. On 4 February, some of the Tower artillery, positioned on the tops of the White Tower and St Thomas's Tower, opened fire on the Wyatt encampment across the river. Wyatt tried to get his force across, but found London Bridge nearby well defended by troops loyal to the Queen, so he had to take his force along the south bank as far west as Kingston to be able to get across the Thames safely. From there he marched via Brentford to the Westminster region and the first clashes with royal troops took place there and in the Strand. On the 7th Wyatt himself was captured near Ludgate, as his revolt collapsed and the troops fell away, many into hiding. He was taken by barge along the Thames to the Tower, with other leaders, and entered the Tower through Traitor's Gate. There were so many rebels with him that some of the existing Tower prisoners had to be moved from their rooms, some to other parts of the Tower, some taken outside the Tower to other city prisons. Among those moved was Bishop Latimer of Worcester, who was moved to join Archbishop Cranmer in the Bloody Tower (see pages 107).

As soon as news of Wyatt's rising reached the queen (who was at Whitehall

Palace), she sent for the Duke of Suffolk (Lady Jane Grey's father) to come and command the royal forces to be marshalled against the rebels. But Suffolk chose that moment to take up Wyatt's cause, and rode swiftly to his estates in the Midlands hoping to raise an army in support. The paltry force he did manage to recruit was however quickly dispersed by loyal troops nearby, and Suffolk himself was captured and brought to the Tower. By now, Mary – understandably – had had enough. Suffolk, Wyatt and others would have to die, and for the safety and stability of the kingdom Lady Jane Grey and her husband would also have to go. Even at this late stage Mary hesitated before signing Jane's death warrant, but on 12 February Jane was executed on Tower Green (because she was of royal blood) and her husband, Lord Guilford, on Tower Hill because he was not. Suffolk was tried at Westminster Hall on 17 February and executed on 23rd.

Princess Elizabeth

Wyatt's rebellion was a protest against the intended marriage of Mary with Philip of Spain. It was not any part of Wyatt's plan to put Lady Jane Grey on the throne again, even though the rising coincided with Suffolk's treason. Rather Wyatt aimed to support the idea of displacing Mary with her half-sister Elizabeth, and when, after his arrest at Ludgate and imprisonment in the Tower he was threatened with torture, it was to get him to implicate Elizabeth, and not Lady Jane Grey, whose fate was already sealed. Mary's advisers, chiefly Simon Renard, ambassador of Charles V to Mary's court, were convinced that Elizabeth herself knew of the aim of Wyatt and others to put her on the throne – or if they were not, they chose to affect so, because they were after all promoting Mary's marriage with Philip. But Wyatt held firm and revealed nothing. Mary, by now thoroughly frightened by the series of events since the death of Edward VI, began to think of the awful possibility that her half-sister might have to be eliminated. Certainly, Elizabeth would have to be taken out of the area of conspiracy.

Elizabeth had been living quietly in the country throughout Edward VI's reign, and during the Northumberland conspiracy she had remained aloof. Indeed, as soon as she heard that Northumberland had been taken at Cambridge, she wrote to her half-sister Mary with congratulations on her overcoming the attempt to stop her acceding to the throne, and then joined her when Mary triumphantly entered London at the beginning of August, 1553. But the 'honeymoon' was soon over, and the two half-sisters began to view one another with growing distrust. Mary wanted Elizabeth to give up her Protestant beliefs and convert to Roman Catholicism: Elizabeth did not want to but was willing to go through the motions of trying, to attend Mass and sit through lectures on the old faith. Mary may even have hinted to Elizabeth that her future might be at risk if she did not abjure Protestantism, and was not, it seems, really taken in by Elizabeth's attempts to placate her. Certainly, Mary's advisers, especially Renard who had by now become more important in Mary's entourage than any of her English councillors, except possibly Gardiner, her

105

Lord Chancellor, and the two of them worked on her suspicion of Elizabeth, eventually prevailing upon the queen to arrest her on charges of high treason and commit her to the Tower.

The future queen of England was not altogether surprised at this turn in events, though she was certainly mortified. As she actually passed through Traitor's Gate on Palm Sunday, 1554, she exclaimed, 'I never thought to have come in here as prisoner . . . bear me witness that I come in no traitor but as true a woman to the Queen's majestie as any is now living'. Once the government had Elizabeth safely inside the Tower, it continued to search for proof of Elizabeth's implication in the Wyatt conspiracy. This was when Wyatt was racked, as we have seen, and others were, too. One was Sir James Croft (who was 'marvellously tossed and examined'). Elizabeth herself was rigorously catechized several times and for long sessions, but she confessed to nothing. She was confined in the royal lodgings under guard, and

A view of Traitor's Gate, the principal entrance to the Tower from the Thames, through which state prisoners were conveyed. This is an early 19th century picture.

under stringent conditions. She was not allowed to leave her room for the first weeks. Everything brought in to her or collected from her was closely examined. No contact was permitted with friends other than those approved by the Constable, Sir John Gage, and because of her widespread popularity she was at all times hidden from the public whenever she was taken for a walk in the Privy Garden, and she was kept away from any windows in the royal lodgings that looked out over the public places. It was said that during this period of strict supervision, she scratched on a window pane the famous couplet:

Much suspected of me;
Nothing proved can be.

Mary and her councillors deliberated long as to what to do with Elizabeth. A suggestion that Parliament should be asked to bring an act of attainder against her was dropped after an enquiry among members revealed that few would support the idea. And so, reluctantly, Mary accepted that she could not have Elizabeth put to death. And on 19 May Elizabeth was released from the Tower and taken to Richmond Palace and thence to the royal manor at Woodstock, near Oxford, under the close guard of Sir Henry Bedingfield. There, strict precautions were taken to prevent any attempt to rescue her or even to let her have any communication with people outside.

Mary went on to reign for a further four years. In that time she directed her energies chiefly to reversing the Protestant Reformation of England, which had begun in her father's reign and continued with increasing vigour in the time of her half-brother Edward VI. The Archbishop of Canterbury under Henry VIII and Edward VI, Thomas Cranmer, and several bishops including Hugh Latimer (Worcester) and Nicholas Ridley (London), were dismissed and then sent to the Tower, and Stephen Gardiner, formerly Bishop of Winchester but deprived in Edward VI's reign, was restored to his see and made Lord Chancellor as well. Many other clergy were dismissed. The new Book of Common Prayer was banned and the Latin Mass was formally restored. There followed an intense persecution of Protestants in all walks of life – university teachers, lawyers, merchants, preachers, gentlemen farmers, ordinary men and women. More than 300 were burnt at the stake as heretics. For a while, Cranmer, Latimer and Ridley were confined together in the Bloody Tower in the Tower of London, until at the end of March 1554, the three of them were taken to Oxford where, eighteen months later, Latimer and Ridley were burnt at the stake, and a few months after that Cranmer too suffered the same fate. There were some more conspiracies against Mary which led to more imprisonments and more instances of torture.

The rebellion of Wyatt failed to change the queen's determination to marry Philip of Spain, and in July 1554 they were married in Winchester Cathedral. The new couple did not visit the capital for some weeks thereafter, and the Spanish prince did not see inside England's premier fortress until the following summer. The French ambassador to England, Antoine de Noailles, wrote that Philip rode on a horse

Mary I (1553–58).

beside his wife who was carried in a litter, as she had been ill for some months with dropsy. They did not stay in the Tower for long, and continued to Greenwich Palace.

Mary I died in November 1558. Her marriage to Philip of Spain, who had succeeded to the Spanish throne in 1556, had not been a happy one. She had longed for a child – even believed that she was pregnant only to find that a distended abdomen proved not to be evidence of an embryo but a symptom of dropsy that was to be the eventual cause of her death. Philip had left England in 1557, never to return. Mary worked out her salvation through the persecution of others by faggot and stake, and died leaving her kingdom Catholic only in name, for the bulk of the people were at heart anxious to follow the newer Protestant faith. She was succeeded by her half-sister Elizabeth, and this time there was no argument as to the succession, despite the fact that Elizabeth had in Catholic eyes been invalidated because of the unacceptability of the marriage between her father and her mother.

For the last months of Mary's reign, Elizabeth had been lying low at Hatfield House in Hertfordshire. When it was clear that Mary was in the terminal phase of her illness, ministers and other statesmen began to visit Elizabeth, promising help and guidance for her forthcoming reign. Among them was one whose 'guidance' was not at all welcome. He was Count Feria, ambassador of Philip of Spain, a proud, humourless man. He seems to have antagonized Elizabeth by boasting that her forthcoming accession was only going to be possible because of the good graces of his master, Philip. Perhaps he even hinted that once Mary was dead Philip would be prepared to marry Elizabeth. She regarded this stance with some disdain, forcefully enough to prompt Feria to write to Philip about her widespread popularity; 'everyone is on her side'.

In spite of the welcome the new queen was about to receive from her people in London and throughout the country, things were anything but easy for her. From the first day she had to reckon with a still-powerful Catholic faction with members in the highest places of government. England was still at war with France, and the ties with Spain were not as strong as Catholics would have liked. Not surprisingly, for Englishmen did not like Spaniards on the whole, a feeling aggravated by the growing numbers of Spaniards of varying importance appearing in London as the years went by in Mary's reign, many of them strutting about in military dress. After Mary's death, it was some time before these people were persuaded one way or another to go home. Indeed, as it turned out, the relationship between England and Spain was to dominate the entire reign of Elizabeth, only five years short of a half a century. It was

The Protestant priest and martyr, Cuthbert Simpson, who was imprisoned in the Tower during the persecution of Protestants in the reign of Mary I (1553–58), was tortured on the rack. This is an engraving of his suffering, which he himself described afterwards.

to be a relationship highlighted at frequent intervals by conspiracies against Elizabeth, in which in almost every case the hand of Spain could in some way or other be detected.

One of the principal results of this continuous Spanish irritant was a marked increase in the use of the Tower of London as a prison for political and religious offenders at all levels of society. Through its gates passed a well-nigh endless stream of victims, some eventually to perish in the Tower or outside by execution or from other causes. Many more were to languish for long periods of confinement in a variety of degrees of comfort (or discomfort). Thomas Sherwood was in 1577 consigned to the 'dongeon amongst the ratts'. This was supposed to have been a cave some 20 feet (6 metres) deep with no ventilation or light, and was near the river, though the actual site is not known. This increase in the use of the Tower in a changed rôle is also reflected in a number of building improvements and additions, to which reference will be made in the course of the rest of this chapter.

As for the queen herself, though she followed the custom of many of her predecessors in staying at the Tower during the days running up to her coronation, thereafter she hardly ever visited or stayed at the Tower during her long reign – not surprisingly in view of her earlier experiences there, when she had for a time been so close to execution within its walls. She heard the news of Mary's death on 17 November. Ten days later, dressed in purple velvet, she rode in procession to the Tower and stayed there for a week. Then she moved out to Somerset House in the Strand until just before Christmas, which she spent at Whitehall. On 12 January 1559 she returned to the Tower, this time by barge on the Thames, stayed in the royal apartments and two days later left in a splendid procession, consisting of some 1,000 people, on horseback towards Westminster Abbey for her coronation on the 15th.

The first major work at the Tower in her reign was begun in 1560 when a new building was put up for the Mint which already occupied several structures within the Tower. This new building was erected near the Salt Tower, was later referred to as 'the newe upper Mynte within the Tower', and later still as the Irish Mint. Two new refining houses were also built, but only one was actually within the Tower precincts, in this case next to the Coldharbour Tower beside the White Tower. Here, a team of metal refiners from Germany worked to refine the base coinage which had been manufactured in the time of Henry VIII who had debased the national currency to help cope with severe financial difficulties during his last years. None of these buildings is still standing.

A few months before the 1560 building work began, a report on the condition of the royal armouries in the Tower was presented to the queen's chief secretary of state, William Cecil (later Lord Burghley). It recommended the erection of a new armoury building, suggesting it should be sited in the Mint or elsewhere. The report also suggested that the 'greate myll' of Parson Brooke, a coiner and apparently a somewhat fly businessman who had helped Henry VIII in his coinage debasement activities and then (later on) got involved in setting up machinery to make coins during the reign of Mary I (when because of her marriage with Philip of Spain improvements could be carried out through the importing of quantities of silver from the Spanish mines in South America), should be broken up and the ironwork sold to pay for the new armoury building. After the 1560 building work, there were further improvements to the Mint structures, the last being in 1586.

Eventually, the new armoury building was probably the two modifications carried out in the White Tower in the years 1565–6 of which no traces have yet been determined. Some of the White Tower today holds a considerable range of exhibits of royal arms and armour, much of it from the Tudor period. In the years 1565–6 some £2,000 was expended on a variety of repair works at the Tower generally, and this involved the purchase of 240 loads of stone from the site of the decayed abbey at Reading, a Benedictine foundation dissolved in the 1530s.

Queen Elizabeth's prisoners

So many people were imprisoned in the Tower during Elizabeth's reign for such a variety of reasons that we should not entirely dismiss the record. She began quite dramatically by imprisoning no less than six bishops for remaining Catholic after her acession. They were the Archbishop of York, and the Bishops of Bath, Ely, Exeter, Lincoln and Worcester, and they were still there two years later. Some examples illustrate the sorts of difficulty that 'earned' a spell in the great fortress for displeasing the queen, whether or not they broke the law.

When Elizabeth came to the throne she had no acceptable heir. She was not married and there were no other children of Henry VIII. The next in line were cousins, some Protestant, some Catholic. Among the closest heirs were grand-children of Mary, Duchess of Suffolk, Henry VIII's younger sister. One of these grand-children had been Lady Jane Grey, who had been executed in 1554. But there were two further sisters. One was Catherine, the other Mary. In 1561 the position had not changed. Any one of them could have become the focal point for a *coup d'état* in their favour. And in that year Catherine Grey had secretly married the Earl of Hertford, elder son of the Protector Somerset, of Edward VI's time. After several months, Catherine could no longer hide the fact that she was pregnant, the secret slipped out, and the queen heard about it. She immediately became apprehensive at the prospect of yet another heir to the throne, a direct one, and her reaction was extreme. She had Catherine arrested, but for the time being Hertford was left alone although he will certainly have been watched. The marriage was declared null and void, chiefly because it had taken place without the queen's permission, though no statutory leave was required. Catherine was put in the Bell Tower where in September 1561 she gave birth to a boy. A few days later the boy was baptized in the Chapel of St Peter ad Vincula and given the name Edward (after his grandfather, the Protector Somerset). Hertford, meanwhile, had been taken to the Tower and imprisoned, not in the Bell Tower with his wife but in another tower, and the

Lieutenant of the Tower, Sir Edward Warner, had been charged with ensuring that the young couple did not meet. Evidently, however, Warner did not follow his orders closely, and seems to have let the couple meet alone and spend time together, for in February 1563 Catherine gave birth to another boy, who was also christened in the Chapel of St Peter and called Thomas. When the queen got to hear about this, she exploded with rage. Hertford was fined heavily. Warner was promptly dismissed and imprisoned in the Tower.

Catherine was released in the summer of 1563 but Hertford had to wait until 1569. Catherine died in 1568, but her two sons survived, the elder one, Edward, becoming Lord Beauchamp. He died in 1612, before his father Hertford, and his eldest son Edward (born in 1586) succeeded Hertford in 1621, and lived to become the second Duke of Somerset, as late as 1660. He was the ancestor of the present twentieth duke.

Many Roman Catholics were imprisoned in Elizabeth's reign, charged with treason or suspected of treason, under the increasingly stringent treason legislation of her time. The queen, mindful of the tribulations of Catholics when her half-brother Edward VI was king and the gross suffering of Protestants under her half-sister Mary, chose to pursue a middle course in which she required outward conformity to the Church of England but otherwise allowed a considerable measure of freedom of conscience. Roman Catholics who refused to conform to the Act were fined but otherwise generally left alone provided they did not get involved in more active opposition to the newly established religion.

Some of the more determined Catholics saw the new settlement as a threat to the survival of Catholicism itself. Catholics who conformed to the requirement to attend English Church worship would, they believed, sooner or later depart forever from their Catholicism. It would be better for Catholics to become victims of organized persecution, for that would provoke them to rebel, in which case material aid would be forthcoming from Catholic powers in Europe, particularly France and Spain, in the hope that ultimately the faith would be restored. This was the strange thinking of the Catholic revivalist preacher and missionary, William Allen, one-time Fellow of Oriel College at Oxford, who in 1568 set up an English college at Douai in the Netherlands specifically to train selected young English Catholics for a very dangerous life. They were to learn how to infiltrate English society and attempt to get people to return to the Catholic faith. Allen was looking for martyrs as well as servants, and he inculcated into their hearts that it was their supreme duty to die if need be for the faith. Among these new 'missionaries' to be sent over to England by Allen was Edmund Campion, who was to become one of the best known of the Catholic martyrs – a college was named after him at Oxford early in this century.

Campion came to England in 1580. For a year he moved about the country preaching among sympathetic groups in various districts and then more boldly addressing public audiences in country districts where the local gentry were known to be in favour of the old religion, even if they were not practising it. He wrote letters to Rome in which he described the welcome he and some of his fellow infiltrators

The Tower of London in the middle of the 16th century – perhaps just as Elizabeth I knew it. This is a drawing by Wyngaerde. Note the cannons on Tower Wharf, in the foreground.

were receiving, how unpopular the Protestant settlement was, how many longed to come back into the Roman fold. Undoubtedly he exaggerated the position, and as it turned out he achieved very little. In the summer of 1581, after having been watched carefully by agents of Francis Walsingham, Elizabeth's secretary of state from 1573–90 and founder of England's secret service system, Campion was arrested after addressing a meeting in Oxford. He was taken by various routes to the Tower, decked in a paper hat which carried the inscription 'Campion, the seditious Jesuit'. In the Tower he was brutally treated – several sessions on the rack are believed to have stretched his body by about four inches – and he was also thumb-screwed and suspended by the hands. All this took place in the vaults of the White Tower which were often (though not always) used at the time for prisoner torture. Then in December he was hanged, drawn and quartered at Tyburn.

A prisoner of a very different kind was William Davison, who in 1587 was assistant secretary of state to the queen, and effectively Walsingham's deputy. For a long time the queen had been dithering about whether to sign the warrant for the execution of Mary, Queen of Scots, but on 1 February 1587 she finally put her signature on the document, regretting almost immediately that she had done so despite the ample grounds for the Scottish queen's paying the supreme penalty. Davison took the document and despatched it to Fotheringay Castle for the sentence to be carried out, which it was one week later. When the news of Mary's execution reached London, all the church bells were rung, cannons were discharged and bonfires were lit in the streets. But Elizabeth grieved; as she said in answer to foreign heads of state and others who protested, she had never meant to send the warrant. Someone therefore had to be scapegoat, and the lot fell upon the wretched Davison. He was arrested, tried in the Star Chamber, and sent to the Tower to be imprisoned during the queen's pleasure. He was also fined almost to the point of destitution. He remained a prisoner for eighteen months, though very probably under the most lenient regime of confinement, and released after the collapse of the Spanish Armada in 1588, when his fine was remitted.

Of the few reigning queens in the story of British monarchy Queen Victoria is the one we think of as being tough on sexual laxity in high society. But Elizabeth had her share of high-mindedness in this area, too. We have seen her anger at Catherine Grey's pregnancies, both of them. There were several other instances where she considered standards to have been slack, and she was never more censorious – nor more inclined to punish – than when her maids of honour were involved. In 1591 Sir Walter Ralegh, already one of the queen's favourites, with a reputation as a bold sea captain and discoverer, fancied Elizabeth Throckmorton, one of her maids of honour. Elizabeth Throckmorton was the daughter of Sir Nicholas Throckmorton, one of the queen's ablest diplomats. Before long, Elizabeth Throckmorton allowed herself to become pregnant but only because she and Ralegh had already agreed to get married. 'They did marry secretly, but the queen found out and took the highest umbrage at what she regarded as a personal affront. They refused to seek her pardon, whereupon she had both sent to the Tower, Ralegh being put in the Brick Tower, his wife in another place, and they were ordered to be kept apart.' During his spell in the Tower, the first but not to be the only time he was kept there, he wrote a stream of effusive letters begging forgiveness and asking for his release. He was eventually pardoned and set free, but was ordered to leave the court and remained in disgrace for some years. His wife was also released and the two enjoyed years of happiness, until he was arrested and imprisoned in the Tower in 1603 (see pp. 119–124).

Another of the Catholic prisoners in the Tower was Father John Gerard. This interesting figure wrote one of the most fascinating autobiographies to emerge from the first half of the seventeenth century. Born in 1564 and brought up a Catholic, Gerard was sent to Douai in 1577 (the college was moved to Rheims a few months later and he went with it). From 1582 to 1588 he travelled to and from Europe as an underground missionary in England, until in 1588 he became a Jesuit. From then until 1594 he remained in England, generally disguised as a country gentleman, travelling about preaching to and leading discussion with faithful Catholics in secret hiding places. It was a hazardous life, often living from hand to mouth, continually but one step ahead of the authorities who were on to him and trying to entrap him, while he hid in priest-holes, forests, and other uncomfortable places. But in 1594 he was betrayed and arrested, and was taken to the Counter Gaol in Poultry, in the City of London, then moved soon afterwards to The Clink, another London prison (on the south bank of the Thames just below what is now Blackfriars' Bridge). Then in April 1587 he was moved into the Tower and put in a cell in the Salt Tower.

Gerard's autobiography contains a very detailed description of his time in the Tower, which was actually only for a few months, for in October 1597 he succeeded in escaping[1]. When he was taken to the Tower, the Lieutenant, Sir Richard Berkeley, appointed as his personal warder one Bennett, or Bonner, who took him to his cell on the first floor of the Salt Tower. In this cell Gerard found inscriptions carved in the wall. Some were of Henry Walpole, another English Jesuit priest, who had spent a year in the same cell (1594–5) before being taken to York to be executed.

During his short stay in the Tower, Gerard contrived to make extensive contact with friends outside and in other prisons by means of letters in which the visible written lines were harmless comments, requests and pleasantries, but in between which he wrote important messages in invisible ink. This he made by squeezing the juice of oranges which he had sent in to him. It was fortunate for him that Bonner, his warder, loved oranges, so Gerard gave him a number each time a supply was delivered. Gerard stored up the juice until he had enough 'ink' to start his correspondence. For a writing implement he dared not ask for a pen, but instead asked for a number of quills which he could use as toothpicks. To strengthen the deception, Gerard made crucifixes and other ornaments out of the orange peel, and wrapped these in the papers on which the letters were written. Bonner duly delivered the packets, unsuspectingly, and soon the recipients began to reply in the same fashion. To get the invisible ink writing revealed it was only necessary to hold the paper near a naked flame or fire. Gerard kept up this correspondence for nearly six months.

Soon after his transfer to the Tower, Gerard was examined by a high-powered board of commissioners who were investigating the clandestine activities of Catholics in England. The Board consisted of the Lieutenant of the Tower, the Attorney-General Sir Edward Coke, Francis Bacon (the future Lord Chancellor), Thomas Fleming (Solicitor-General) and William Waad, Privy Council Secretary (who later became Lieutenant of the Tower). The examination was rigorous. The Board wanted to find out how far Gerard was implicated in Catholic activities against the government and with whom he had been corresponding in Catholic agencies abroad. They also wanted names of other Catholics involved in conspiracies in England. Gerard always answered that he was not involved in any political activity or plotting and did not believe he should have to give the names of anyone else who might or might not be. So the Board decided to resort to torture. The

1 *The Autobiography of a Hunted Priest*, Johnm Gerard, trans. from the Latin by P. Caraman, Doubleday & Co., New York, 1955.

warrant stated, '. . . cause him to be put to the manacles and such other torture as is used in that place' (the Tower).

The Board's hearings were held in the Lieutenant's Lodgings and after Gerard had been shown the warrant, he was escorted to the White Tower vaults, as he put it, 'in a kind of solemn procession, the attendants walking ahead with lighted candles . . .'. This has been taken by some to suggest that he was escorted along an underground passage from the Lieutenant's Lodgings to the White Tower, but no tunnel has yet been discovered.

Arriving at the torture chamber, he wrote later, he noted that 'every device and instrument of human torture was there. They pointed out some of them . . . and said that I would try them all'. Gerard was told to go up some mobile steps, so that with his arms extended above him he could be hitched to a pair of iron gauntlets round his wrist, suspended from a nail in a pillar which supported the ceiling. Then they removed the steps so that he dangled from his manacled wrists, an excruciating process that after a while led him to faint. To revive him they put the mobile steps under his feet again, then removed them so that he dangled again. He records that this was repeated eight times on the first day. Yet he revealed nothing to his inquisitors.

The next day, the torture was repeated, only this time it was extremely difficult to get the manacles round his badly swollen wrists. He was suspended only twice, because the Lieutenant took compassion and had him taken down. Gerard relates that a few weeks after this event, the Lieutenant resigned from his post because he no longer wanted to be involved in such torturing of innocent men. Other tortures, however, were threatened, including the notorious rack, but the authorities stayed their hand since they had become convinced that he was absolutely determined not to say anything. It was some weeks before he could use his hands again for anything, but after a month he started to do special finger exercises to strengthen them. One thing he wanted to be able to do as soon as possible was to write the letters to his friends, which have been mentioned above.

On the last day of July 1587, after nearly four months in the Tower, Gerard had an inspiration which eventually led to a daring and successful attempt to escape. He knew that there was a fellow Catholic prisoner, John Arden, in the Cradle Tower, which was separated from the Salt Tower only by a garden. They had been able to communicate with each other by signs and notes over the past weeks, but now Gerard asked Bonner to let the two of them meet so that they could celebrate Mass and talk together. Bonner was weak enough, or good-natured enough, to agree – perhaps helped by small bribes – and it was Gerard who was allowed to leave his cell to visit Arden in the Cradle Tower. After a few visits it struck Gerard that as the Cradle Tower overhung the moat between the outer fortifications and the Tower Wharf, a man let down by rope from the Tower could be swung across the moat to the Wharf and spirited away by a waiting boat with its crew. The idea quickly turned into a plan which necessarily involved the help of friends outside, and these were contacted by means of letters with the invisible ink infills. Gerard provides an almost blow-by-blow account of the escape that he and Arden did make by this stratagem, which they attempted on 5 October.

As soon as the two men got away and were safely hidden in a friend's house in Spitalfields, Gerard sent a note by a friend to Bonner in the Tower. In it he acknowledged that Bonner would almost certainly be put to death for letting the two men get away, and Gerard told him that if he also wanted to escape and hide in the country, Gerard could arrange it. The messenger delivered the note to Bonner who could not read, and so had to have it read out to him. He needed little persuading to take up Gerard's offer, and he and the messenger hurriedly left the Tower and ran to a spot outside where another friend had two horses waiting. Bonner was thus spirited away into the country where Gerard arranged for him to have a small pension for the rest of his life.

Mention has been made of the small part of the Tower Wharf played in this dramatic escape. Five years earlier (1592), a programme of works on the wharf was set in motion, which lasted on and off for nine years. These included a new brick wall from the Byward Tower to the water gate, and another to enclose the sluice, and the insertion of two new sluices in the wharf in the area round Traitor's Gate.

The last great event in the Tower's history in Elizabeth's reign was the execution of the queen's favourite, Robert Devereux, Earl of Essex, in 1601. He was the last person to be executed on Tower Green, a 'privilege' usually reserved for noble-women – among whom were Anne Boleyn, Margaret, Countess of Salisbury (see page 84), Catherine Howard, and Lady Jane Grey.

Essex was a courtier of the queen, who distinguished himself at the battle of Zutphen (in the Netherlands) in 1586, where Sir Philip Sidney was mortally wounded. After Robert Dudley, Earl of Leicester, probably the only man whom the queen really loved, died in 1588, Essex became her chief favourite, although he was thirty-three years younger than she. Over the next few years he fought in France, raided Cadiz by sea, attacked the Spanish treasure fleet as it lay to in the Azores but failed to seize any of the bullion, and in 1598 was appointed Lord Lieutenant of Ireland. He was sent out to quell the rebellion led by the Earl of Tyrone, but was defeated several times by the Irish, and then made an humiliating treaty with Tyrone which the queen and her councillors at once repudiated. He rushed home to London to vindicate himself before the queen, complaining that there was a conspiracy to remove him from the court. This may have been true, for he had made many enemies, but he over-reacted and himself formed a plot to rid the queen of some of her councillors, and this involved raising the people of London in revolt. His scheme was thwarted, however, and he was arrested and taken to the Tower where he was imprisoned in the Devereux Tower[2]. In the middle of February 1601 he was tried for high treason and on the 19th sentenced to death. That he was executed on

2 The tower was in fact named after Essex.

117

Tower Green within the Tower precincts was not because he was the particular favourite of the queen but because the authorities feared a major disturbance – perhaps even a rescue attempt – if he were to have been put to death on Tower Hill outside. For his execution on Tower Green a special scaffold was built, and the Tower's garrison was strengthened in case of demonstrations. The entry for the scaffold construction appears in the Exchequer Pipe Office Declared Accounts, as follows:

> . . . makeinge a skaffolde for the beheadinge of the Erle of Essex and a Courte of guarde for the soldiers with seates and restes at the yron gate and boordinge upp the sides makeinge another courte of guarde for the soldiors watchinge and wardinge on the Mounte . . .

Before closing the story of the Tower in the long reign of Elizabeth I, we should relate that during the last years of the reign the first efforts were made to organize the public records that had been accumulating in the Tower. During the reign, records were stored in the Wakefield Tower. One of the keepers, William Bowyer, who held office for several years prior to 1581, spent eight years compiling a digest of the records. This was continued after his retirement by another keeper, William Lambarde, who drafted a Calendar of Records and presented it to the Queen.

We may also mention that in 1597 Hayward and Gascoigne produced a map of the Tower, seen as it were from the air, and which is reproduced as a colour plate. The principal features are marked out in the caption to the plan.

An early 17th century engraving of Robert Devereux, Earl of Essex, the last of Elizabeth I's favourites, who took too many liberties with her indulgence of him and paid the supreme penalty. He was executed on Tower Green, probably to avoid demonstrations from the mob if the execution had taken place outside, on Tower Hill.

VI

Use and misuse in Stuart times

Elizabeth I died in March 1603. She had never married and her successor was a distant cousin, James VI of Scotland, son of the Mary Queen of Scots she had had executed in 1587. James was heir to England by virtue of his being the nearest Protestant in line from Margaret Tudor, sister of Henry VIII and wife of James IV of Scotland. James became James I of England, Scotland and Ireland. He had hardly been on the throne for more than a few months when he clapped into the Tower one of the most famous men of England's history, Sir Walter Ralegh. It was Ralegh's second 'visit' and this time he was to stay for thirteen years. It represented a great fall from his position of high influence and power enjoyed in the last years of the great queen: he had been made governor of Jersey in 1600, and had already been Captain of the Royal Guard for some years.

Sir Walter Ralegh

The circumstances of Ralegh's arrest and trial for high treason have never been fully explained in terms of proven guilt or otherwise. He was accused of being implicated in the conspiracy led by Lord Cobham and known as the Main Plot, whose aim was to depose James and replace him with his cousin Arabella Stewart, a great-great-granddaughter of Henry VII and niece of James's own father, Lord Darnley. The plot was supposed to have involved aid from the Spanish. It seems almost certain that Ralegh was 'framed' by Robert Cecil, later Earl of Salisbury, the new king's chief secretary (and son of the great William Cecil, Lord Burghley), who saw Ralegh as a rival. James, by nature and experience a suspicious man, and easily persuaded that people were often plotting against him, bent to Cecil's influences and allowed Ralegh to be arrested, in July 1603.

Ralegh was taken to the Tower and put in the Bloody Tower to await trial (this was not held until November, and then at Winchester because of an outbreak of plague in London at the time) Almost as soon as he got to the Tower, Ralegh seems to have been plunged into the deepest gloom. Though the full nature of the charges against him were probably not clear to him, they were sufficiently menacing to indicate that he was in very deep trouble. Time and again, day after day, as he alternated between hope and despair – and more often the latter – he would send for the Lieutenant, Sir John Peyton, to seek comfort and re–assurance. Probably Ralegh

A miniature of Sir Walter Ralegh, by the celebrated Elizabethan miniaturist, Nicholas Hilliard (1537–1619).

had never done more than talk openly and indiscreetly about the fact that there was a rival claimant (Arabella), but that of course would have been more than enough to arouse the spitefulness of the king. On one occasion, while dining in his quarters in the Bloody Tower, Ralegh tried to kill himself, by stabbing himself with a table knife, though the attempt may only have been a gesture to get sympathy. No one who has not actually spent time in disgrace in a prison can fully understand what 'attacks of acute melancholy and despair' affect those who have been confined, whether they were guilty or not. For Ralegh, the attempt seems somehow to have helped him, for he began soon to settle down to making the best of a bad job.

At his trial in November the evidence against him was flimsy, though it was pressed in the most aggressively bullying manner by the Attorney General, Sir Edward Coke. Ralegh responded with defiance and bravado – he had always been prone to self-advertisement – but he was inevitably found guilty. Though it was clear that a sentence of death would follow (and it did), Ralegh seems not to have believed the King would permit him to die, and fully expected a pardon. On the day before he was due to be executed, he was reprieved, and taken back to the Tower a week later. Still he was convinced that he would be released, but it became clear that he was going to be confined indefinitely, but with some measure of freedom, within the walls of the great fortress.

Ralegh's time in the Tower is documented in a number of ways, such as details of building works done to make his quarters more spacious, money allowances for servants attending him, facilities for his wife, family and friends to visit, even stay with him, facilities for him to write, carry out chemical experiments, and so forth. Robert Cecil, writing to the English ambassador in Paris, described Ralegh as '. . . lodged and attended in the Tower as well as in his own house. . . . ' Soon after his return from Winchester he was allowed to have his wife, Elizabeth, and his son Wat living in the Tower with him, and in 1605 his wife gave birth to a second son, who was baptized Carew in the Chapel of St Peter ad Vincula (the event is noted in the Chapel Register). He had servants in the house, one of whom acted as secretary. He was also allowed regular visits from other staff from his home in Sherborne in Dorset, until later in the reign of James I the latter appropriated his estates to give them to his favourite, Robert Ker, later Earl of Somerset. This last act reduced Ralegh's income drastically and led to some suffering for his wife and children after they had been forced to leave the Tower (see below).

Ralegh filled his time with writing, chemical and pharmaceutical experiments (he was a specialist in herbal remedies and produced a number of strange concoctions that became well known outside the Tower), and with teaching visiting pupils, the most famous of whom was Prince Henry Frederick, the king's eldest son and heir, who had been born in 1594. Prince Henry, with the active connivance of his mother, Anne of Denmark, visited Ralegh often, sometimes taking friendly notes from his mother to Ralegh. Over the years, the prince learned a great deal in political history and practice, philosophy, ship construction, and science. He is said once to have remarked out loud to some Tower officers, 'No one but my father would keep such a bird in such a cage.'

Among Ralegh's literary works of this period were some fine verses, some political treatises including *A Discourse of War*, and *The Prerogative of Parliaments*, and most famous of all, his majestic *History of the World*. This was begun in 1608 and was written for the Prince. He completed the first volume, which carried the story down to the 1st century BC. For his work he studied quantities of books and documents, many of them brought in for him by academic and other friends. But when Prince Henry died in 1612, ostensibly of typhoid but quite possibly through poison administered to him on behalf of his own father, Ralegh gave up the great work. But the first volume was printed and published while he was still in the Tower, and copies of it have survived to this day.

During the thirteen years of his imprisonment, Ralegh's health, which had not been good when he first entered the Bloody Tower, steadily deteriorated. He wrote much about his complaints. For a time he was partly paralysed as the result of a stroke and for much of the early years he had congestion of the lungs, due largely to the damp and cold in his quarters. Among the factors that contributed to this deterioration, which took its physical toll but left his mental energies unimpaired, were his unending worries about money (the king had reduced him to poverty level), his rough treatment at the hands of Sir William Waad, the new Lieutenant appointed in 1605, whom we have met earlier among the inquisitors of Father

THE
HISTORIE OF
THE WORLD.

IN FIVE BOOKES.

1 IN treating of the Beginning and first Ages of the same, from the Creation unto Abraham.
2 Of the Times from the Birth of Abraham, to the destruction of the Temple of Salomon.
3 From the destruction of Jerusalem, to the time of Philip of Macedon.
4 From the Reigne of Philip of Macedon, to the establishing of that Kingdome, in the Race of Antigonus.
5 From the settled rule of Alexanders Successors in the East, untill the Romans (prevailing over all) made Conquest of Asia and Macedon.

By Sir WALTER RALEGH, Knight.

The true and lively portraiture
of the honourable and learned Knight
Sr. Walter Ralegh.

The title-page of the first volume of Sir Walter Ralegh's History of the World, *which he wrote and which was printed while he was a prisoner in the Tower. There were four further volumes.*

Gerard and whom Ralegh described as a 'beast', and the sharp and sudden reduction of privileges after a visit by members of the Council in 1611 who reported that, among other things, eight years' imprisonment had done little to suppress his pride and passion. He was treated very severely for a time, then this was relaxed, but he does not appear to have been restored to the comfort of the earlier years. His family and servants were sent out and other restrictions were imposed. The timing of this decline in the quality of his treatment, following as it did the early death of Prince Henry, seems more than coincidental. Waad was still the Lieutenant and remained so till 1613–14.

In 1615, Ralegh managed to persuade the king to release him so that he could lead an expedition up the Orinoco River in Guiana, in South America, in search of gold. The king agreed, having found himself very short of money and seeing this as a way out of difficulties. The condition was that Ralegh must not in any way molest the territories of the King of Spain in that region. In January 1616 Ralegh was let out of the Tower. By then he was lame, walked with a stick and was prematurely old. The expedition proved a failure, no gold was found, and over a week-end, while Ralegh was lying in bed ill, some of his men attacked and burned the Spanish town of San Thome. Ralegh returned home to Plymouth, headed for London and was arrested and taken to the Tower (August 1618). This time he was put in the Beauchamp Tower.

The king, meanwhile, had had strong protests from Gondomar, the Spanish ambassador to England, about the assault on San Thome, and by using the suspended sentence of 1603, James had Ralegh executed in Old Palace Yard, Westminster, in October. Ralegh faced his end with great courage. Examining the axe, he exclaimed, 'This is sharp medicine but a sure cure for all diseases.' Then he called out to the executioner, 'What are you afraid of? Strike, man, strike!'

We have some details of the building works carried out on the Bloody Tower to improve and enlarge the accommodation for Ralegh, his family and servants. The Bloody Tower was a gatehouse tower, and the new work consisted of dividing the upper part horizontally into two. The official description has survived: 'Working out of holes in the stone walls in Bloodie Tower for endes of the Beame and joysts to bee laid in for a new floure made there to devide the roome into two Stories for Sr Walter Rawleigh. Working of stone for two newe great stone windowes in the same Tower of two high lightes both full of iron barres and locketts gouted fast wth leade with a Stone table over either windowe. . . .'

The new floor, put in during 1605–6, disappeared much later but was replaced recently, and the Bloody Tower is now furnished in the sort of style that it would have been in Ralegh's time. One of the two stone windows – 'great' seems an exaggerated description today – is almost certainly the window you can see in the west wall. It was put into an earlier period opening. The iron bars and lockets (saddle bars) are still there, too.

For exercise, Ralegh used the garden attached to the Lieutenant's lodgings. For

A contemporary miniature of Arabella Stewart (1575–1615), cousin of James I. She was the daughter of the Earl of Lennox, younger brother of James's father the Earl of Darnley.

the first years he was also able to walk along the wall-walk between the Bloody Tower and the Lieutenant's lodgings, but when Waad took over as Lieutenant in 1605 and began to persecute Ralegh with numerous petty restrictions, a new wall was built high round the garden so that Ralegh could no longer be seen from the Wharf and could no longer exchange the time of day with other Tower visitors. Waad also ordered prisoners to be back in their rooms by 5.00 pm.

Ralegh was the first distinguished prisoner sent to the Tower by the new king, but he was by no means the only one. The conspiracy in which he was accused of being implicated was headed by Lord Cobham who also ended up in the Tower in 1603, and was put in the Beauchamp Tower. This tower was given a 'tourett' (turret-cell) with a lime-and-hair ceiling, in 1606, which he used as a study. Cobham likewise thought that he would be put to death, but was reprieved at the last minute, and he remained in the Tower until he died in 1619. During his confinement he received an allowance of £416 a year, but this was balanced by the government confiscating some of his estates.

Arabella Stewart

In 1610, Arabella Stewart, the woman whom the two men above were alleged to have supported as a rival to the king, herself arrived at the Tower as a prisoner. She had unwisely married William Seymour, fifteen years younger than her, and a descendant of Edward Seymour, Duke of Somerset, Protector of England in the reign of Edward VI, without the permission or even the knowledge of her cousin, the king. As soon as James heard about it he had both of them arrested and imprisoned. Arabella was released before her husband, but he contrived to escape from his room in St Thomas's Tower. By previous arrangement the couple were to meet at Blackwall and take ship to France, but Seymour was delayed for so long that for her own safety Arabella Stewart had to sail off alone. When her ship got her to Calais, she found that the news of her escape had preceded her, and she was arrested and taken back to England. Seymour, however, got away and put in at Ostend, and he remained abroad until the heat was off. Arabella was confined in the Bell Tower, and her regimen was far more rigorous than in the previous confinement, largely through the assiduous attention to duty of Waad. She was allowed few attendants, her food supplies were rationed, and her requests for warm clothing were constantly obstructed. In 1615 she died, grossly undernourished and having lost her sanity. It was one more reflection upon the king and his mean, cruel and unsympathetic nature.

The Gunpowder Plot

Another celebrated prisoner of the king was Henry Percy, Earl of Northumberland, who was held in the Martin Tower from 1606 to 1621 for having allegedly had foreknowledge of the Gunpowder Plot. The charge was one of misprision of treason.

A 17th century Dutch print showing the principal conspirators in the Gunpowder Plot, 1605. Guy Fawkes is third right, Catesby the ringleader is next to him on the right. In describing the plot as the 'unmatcheable powder treason' the artist made a pun without realizing it.

125

This is a page from the House of Commons Journal for November 5th in 1605. The notes in the margin relate to the official search ordered in the vaults of the Houses of Parliament for gunpowder barrels, following the 'tip-off' by Lord Mounteagle.

Northumberland devoted much of his time to forming a literary and scientific circle of friends, both inmates (like Ralegh) and visitors such as Thomas Heriot, the Scottish mathematician who was a pioneer of the algebraic method of calculation. Northumberland had been fined £30,000 as well as put in prison, but he was immensely wealthy, and despite the huge penalty was able to enjoy a life of considerable luxury in the suite he had in the Martin Tower, a life eased along by generous and consistent bribery of Tower officials including, one must suppose, Waad , something Ralegh was unable to do. The Gunpowder Plot – one of the most famous events of English history – whose date, 5 November 1605, is still celebrated all over the country every year, was a conspiracy planned by a number of prominent Roman Catholics in England, with the daring and somewhat unreal aim of destroying the King and Parliament and restoring the Roman Catholic faith in the country. The leaders included Sir Everard Digby, Ambrose Rookewood, Guy Fawkes, Father Garnet (a friend of Father Gerard, see page 126), Thomas Winter,

Robert Keyes and its principal organizer, Robert Catesby. The plan was to blow up the king and members of the House of Lords and the House of Commons as they assembled for the opening session of Parliament on the 5 November in the chamber of the Lords, and to capture James's son and proclaim him king. The conspirators are said to have tried first to dig a tunnel from a nearby house into the House of Lords, but this was not successful. Then they managed to rent a cellar in the basement of the Lords and contrived to convey two tons of gunpowder in barrels into it. But just before the appointed day, one of the conspirators panicked and wrote a letter to a cousin, Lord Monteagle, warning him not to be at the session. Lord Monteagle passed the letter to Robert Cecil, the principal secretary of state, who took it at once to James.

The result was an immediate search of the cellars under the Lords on the eve of the session, and there the guards discovered Guy Fawkes apparently on the point of setting the fuse alight. Fawkes and some others were taken to the Tower, while the main conspirators who got word of Fawkes's arrest fled London for the Midlands where a few days later they, too, were rounded up. Meanwhile, in the Tower, Fawkes had been taken to the vaults of the White Tower and tortured. The actual warrant permitting torture to be applied was written by the king himself and it has survived. Part of it reads, '. . . if he will not otherwayes confesse, the gentler tortures are to be first used unto him, et sic per gradus ad ima tenditur*, and so god spede youre worke. . . . ' We do not know which of the instruments were used, but two signatures of Fawkes have survived from Tower records, one written after some torture and one after much more torture, and the latter very clearly shows that he must have been badly mutilated. Fawkes was then tried, along with the others in the Tower, and he was taken to Old Palace Yard, Westminster, and hanged, drawn and quartered, on 31 January 1606. Among the others were Ambrose Rookewood, who had been held in a cell in the Martin Tower and who carved his name in the wall, and Everard Digby, who carved his name in a cell in the Broad Arrow Tower.

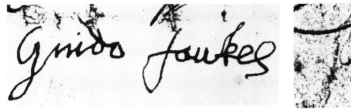 

Two signatures of Guy Fawkes, one of the Gunpowder Plot conspirators and the one whose job it was to be to set the powder alight. Both signatures were written after torture. The first may be presumed to have been written after only a limited amount of pressure, but the second shows only too clearly the extent of Fawkes's injuries and distress.

* 'and so on step by step to the limit.'

Part of the warrant authorizing Tower officials to apply torture to Guy Fawkes. It is written in the king's own hand and personally signed by him.

The Murder of Sir Thomas Overbury

On 14 September 1613, Sir Thomas Overbury, the English poet and courtier, a friend of Robert Ker, Earl of Somerset, the king's current favourite, was found dead in his cell in the Bloody Tower. He had been poisoned, slowly, over a matter of weeks. Ker was anxious to marry Frances Howard, Countess of Essex, the estranged

Portrait of Frances Howard, Countess of Somerset, wife of Robert Ker, Earl of Somerset, the favourite of James I. These two were responsible for the murder of Sir Thomas Overbury in 1613, and they spent six years in the Tower.

A contemporary print of the Earl and Countess of Somerset. The countess was a niece of the Duke of Norfolk, and had married, first, the Earl of Essex, son of Elizabeth I's favourite.

wife of Robert, third Earl of Essex, son of the Essex whom Elizabeth had executed in 1601. Frances Howard was noted for her lax morality but seems to have been infatuated with Ker. She planned to divorce her husband on the grounds of his alleged impotence (an accusation many knew to be absolutely false, Overbury among them). Overbury, who may have had some homosexual association with Ker (who was almost certainly bi-sexual) was determined to stop the intended divorce and the subsequent marriage, and he threatened Ker that he would expose the whole business. He had however not reckoned with the king whose relationship with Ker at the time was very close. Ker persuaded the king to post Overbury as ambassador to faraway Russia, but Overbury refused to go. This was construed as contempt of the king, and he was sent to the Tower, on 21 April. It was not intended that he should emerge alive, but it was not possible to bring any kind of charge against him in court for fear of what he would reveal. He had therefore to be murdered, and it was done by poison.

When the news broke that Overbury had died in the Tower, rumour soon followed that he had been poisoned, but there was no official enquiry for two years. That the mystery was ever cleared up at all was due to a surprise confession by one of the people involved.

Soldiers parading outside the Tower, in the 17th century. A row of cannons is laid out at left. Just inside the walling is a group of houses, probably for Tower officials.

Once Overbury was in the Tower and poisoning was decided as the means for disposing of him, a number of people outside had to be recruited and some suborning had to be done within the Tower. To begin with, the Lieutenant, Waad, was removed (some accounts say he was offered a considerable sum to retire quietly) and replaced by Sir Gervase Elwes who could be relied upon to facilitate whatever was needed in the attendance of Overbury. A chemist's assistant, Richard Weston, was appointed as Overbury's warder. He belonged to a gang of poisoners and aphrodisiac-pedlars in London which was headed by a Mrs Turner who was a friend of the Countess of Essex. Since Ker still professed friendship with Overbury and pretended to him that he was doing all he could to get the King to release him, it was not difficult for sweetmeats and tarts laced with poisons to be sent in to Overbury by Frances Howard (who appears to have been the prime mover in the poisoning conspiracy), and not long after his arrest, Overbury began to receive a regular supply of such 'gifts'. He appears to have had the strongest constitution, for he endured weeks of sustained attempts to poison him to death, '. . . the gang. . . tried every form of poison known to them. They poisoned the victim's food, they poisoned his wine, they mixed arsenic with his salt and added cantharides to his pepper.'

Then, when finally Overbury began to give way under the onslaught, the king's own physician, Mayerne, was sent in to see what was wrong and prescribe for him. More poisons followed, until, on 14 September, an enema containing corrosive sublimate of mercury was prescribed, and the preparation was taken into the cell by an apothecary's boy. This enema proved fatal and Overbury died in the night in great agony.

In the summer of 1615, the apothecary's boy was taken ill and before dying, he confessed that he had taken into Overbury's cell the fatal preparation. This information was conveyed to one of the king's secretaries who decided that before telling his master he would carry out further enquiries of his own. The eventual result was a series of trials of the people involved in the murder, including Ker and Frances (they had managed to get married a few weeks after Overbury's death). They were tried at Westminster Hall in May 1616, and were sentenced, both of them, to death. The king reprieved them and instead sent Ker and his wife to the Tower where they were separated, Ker actually being put in the same cell in which Overbury had been murdered. Both were released six years later. The Lieutenant of the Tower, Elwes, was less fortunate. He was tried for his part in the conspiracy and sentenced to death, and was hanged on Tower Hill.

In 1621, Francis Bacon, Viscount St Albans, Lord High Chancellor, was sent to the Tower and put in the Lieutenant's Lodgings for 'many acts of bribery and corruption', charges to which he pleaded guilty. He was fined £40,000, held in the Tower for a few days, then ordered to retire to his home at Gorhambury, near St Albans, in disgrace. He was later pardoned but never allowed to come back to court or to Parliament. It was a dismal end to one of the most distinguished careers in all

A view of the Tower of London as seen by Hollar, earlier in the 17th century.

English history. When he was in the Tower, he was so overcome with melancholy and remorse that he feared he would die there at once. So he wrote desperately to the king's favourite, George, Duke of Buckingham, begging him to get the king to let him out. In 1623 another great legal figure, Sir Edward Coke, Lord Chief Justice, was sent to the Tower for passionate speeches made in Parliament and outside against the royal prerogative and against interference with the liberties of Parliament. He spent nine months there. In 1624, Lionel Cranfield, Earl of Middlesex, Lord Treasurer, was impeached before the House of Lords for bribery and extortion, charges which had a grain of substance behind them but which were enormously exaggerated as a result of a personal quarrel between him and the King's favourite, the Duke of Buckingham. Cranfield was fined £50,000, stripped of his offices and sent to the Tower where he was held for a few months.

In 1620, the Privy Council received reports that the fabric of the Tower of London was in a poor state, and it appointed a panel of six councillors to make a personal inspection. They were shocked at the condition of the fabric and more alarmed still at the clutter that had accumulated all over the site. The Council thereupon called for a detailed survey and in 1623 the Lieutenant, Sir Allen Apsley, and the Surveyor of the Ordnance, Sir John Kay, produced a report. The site was covered with numerous additional houses and sheds – there were timber yards, coal yards, wheelwrights' works and so on. The moats were almost filled with earth and so had lost their defensive capabilities. The stone and brick work of the main fortress buildings had not deteriorated too far, and the report noted that both the White Tower and the Tower Wharf were in reasonable repair. Repairs and tidying up would cost £7,864. Yet the work was not put in hand before the king's death.

James I died in 1625, and was succeeded by his second son, Charles I, who had the same views about the divine right of kings as his father, and who was even more stubborn in his determination to override the liberties of Parliament. He had long been a close friend of the Duke of Buckingham, by 1625 probably the most hated man in the country, and in a sense inherited him as the royal favourite which he seemed pleased to do. Buckingham had almost carte blanche to manage affairs as he wished, and he did so calamitously, offending people in every direction. Some more spirited members of Parliament impeached Buckingham in the Commons, where-upon the king had them sent to the Tower. One of the MPs was Sir John Eliot. The Commons refused to continue with its work and the king dissolved Parliament, ruling for the next two years without it.

In 1628, Buckingham, who by now had active enemies everywhere, was assassinated at Portsmouth by a Suffolk-born ex-soldier John Felton, who had served with distinction in Flanders. In a way he fulfilled the deep-seated wishes of the nation, and when he was arrested and brought to London, as he came through the streets to the Tower he was cheered and hailed by the crowds. Once inside the Tower he was taken to the White Tower vaults for torture to get him to reveal his accomplices. He insisted there were none (though one man, Sir Robert Savage, had said publicly that if Felton hadn't done it, he gladly would have). Among the officials present at the vault at the time was the Earl of Dorset who threatened Felton with the rack. Felton replied that torture was not permitted by the law of England, and that if he was touched – '. . . if I be put upon the rack, I will accuse you, my lord of Dorset, and none but yourself. . . . ' Hastily, the officials removed him from the vault to his cell. But of course Felton had to pay the penalty for murder, and he was tried and then hanged.

In the same year, the king, more than once refused money supplies by an angry Parliament in the previous two years, once again found himself hard pressed, and he had perforce to accept a Petition of Right before the Commons would agree more money. This document is still widely regarded as second only to Magna Carta in importance.* But, once assured of the subsidies, the king broke his word, dismissed the Parliament and sent eight leading members to the Tower. Among them was Eliot, and this time he was to remain in the Tower for the rest of his life. Eliot was held in the Bloody Tower, probably in the same room occupied in 1628 by Felton. At first, Eliot was well treated, was allowed much freedom of movement and provided with facilities to write, and in his turn there he produced three important political treatises. Then in 1630, the Lieutenant, Sir Allen Apsley, was succeeded by a Lieutenant of the stamp of 'that beast Waad' (Ralegh's words). He was Sir William Balfour. He had Eliot moved from the relative comfort of the Bloody Tower to a much smaller and more austere cell elsewhere, which was cold and damp. This soon began to affect Eliot's health, he contracted consumption and in November 1632 he died.

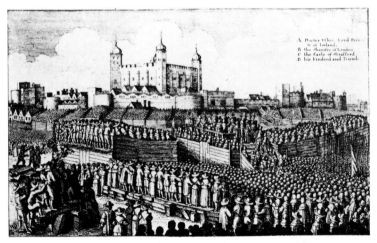

The execution of Thomas Wentworth, Earl of Strafford (Black Tom Tyrant) on Tower Hill in May 1641. The execution 'party' is in the centre of the picture.

* Among its terms: no-one to be forced to pay any loan, tax or benevolence without the consent of Parliament; no-one to be imprisoned without reason shown; no billeting of troops or sailors in private houses; no-one to be tried by martial law.

Agents of Charles I's despotism

From 1629 to 1640, Charles I ruled his kingdoms, England, Scotland and Ireland, without once calling Parliament to session. The history of that eleven years of tyrannical misrule is beyond the scope of this book, but we should mention that the two principal people the king employed as advisers and agents for his arbitrary government were Thomas Wentworth, later Earl of Strafford (who, ironically, had been one of the leading MPs to promote the Petition of Right – and had afterwards changed sides) and William Laud, Archbishop of Canterbury, a high church prelate who spearheaded the government's efforts to stop the growing Puritan movement. Both men ultimately fell foul of Parliament, were tried, imprisoned in the Tower and ended up on the scaffold. Strafford was impeached in 1640 and when the actual form of impeachment fell down, he was brought to the Tower by means of a bill of attainder, which enabled Parliament to both try him and sentence him to death. His case was heard in Westminster Hall over nearly three weeks, and each day he was taken from Traitor's Gate by barge to Westminster, accompanied by a large armed guard which filled five more barges. He was executed in May 1641. Strafford, who did not lack courage at any critical point in his life, was in considerable danger of being lynched by the mob while on the walk from the Tower towards the block on Tower Hill. The Lieutenant, anticipating this, offered him a carriage but Strafford insisted on walking. Apparently, during the execution proceedings, one of the timber stands for spectators, specially constructed on this as on most major execution occasions, collapsed through the sheer weight of the people, and many were injured. Strafford himself affirmed, as he took off his doublet, 'I am not afraid of death'.

Laud, meanwhile, had been taken to the Tower during the Christmas period of

William Laud, Archbishop of Canterbury, and one of the two principal ministers of Charles I during the king's rule without Parliament, 1629–40. Laud was sent to the Tower after impeachment by the Long Parliament, in 1641 and executed in 1645.

Two views of state processions from the Tower of London, in the 17th century. In the top picture, the Tower is at top right, and in the lower, it is at top left.

1640, after a successful impeachment, and he had been lodged in the Bloody Tower. It seems that Laud and Strafford had wanted to meet, but the authorities would not allow it. Laud had to wait nearly four years before he was formally tried at Westminster and sentenced to death, and he, too, walked from the Tower to the block on Tower Hill for execution on 10th January 1645.

Despite the downfall of his two most trusted and reliable advisers who had taken the blame for his arbitrary rule, the king still had learned nothing, still remained blindly wedded to his ideas of dictatorial government. Furious about the death of Strafford and the imprisonment of Laud, resentful of Parliament's cancelling taxation he imposed without its approval, and its abolition of various organs of tyranny such as the Court of Star Chamber and the Court of High Commission, Charles launched on a further series of unconstitutional acts. He tried to bring an army to London to overawe Parliament, and he even tried to get the Scots and the Irish to send forces. Then one day in January 1642 he took a troop of soldiers to the Commons to arrest five leading Members who were among the foremost opponents of his rule. They were John Hampden, Arthur Hazelrig, Denzil Holles, John Pym and William Strode. When the king arrived and stormed into the chamber of the Commons, the five members had already slipped out by another door and fled to the City to take refuge. 'I see the birds have flown' said the king in disgust and turned on his heel as the remaining members shouted and stamped their feet in fury at his invasion of their deliberating chamber. Soon afterwards the king left London, never to return until a few weeks before his execution at Whitehall seven years later. He headed for Oxford where he gathered some forces, and moved northwards to Nottingham where he raised his standard. The departure was the signal for the outbreak of the Civil War. It was now a contest to decide whether King or Parliament should rule the country, which should be the sovereign power in the land. Parliament enlisted a force of 10,000 men from London and the Home Counties, and were offered the support of the resources of the City, the richest part of the kingdom. Even as early as late 1642 it was clear to some that the parliamentarians would triumph.

The Tower in the Civil War

What of the Tower in the eleven years of tyranny and the resulting civil war? The report and recommendations of Apsley and Kay (page 132) were not proceeded with until the 1630s and then only parts were actioned. The proposals about the Tower Wharf were modified in a second report prepared in 1631, this one by the Surveyor General of the King's Works, who at the time was the celebrated architect Inigo Jones, designer of the superb Banqueting Hall in Whitehall, the Queen's House in Greenwich and several other important buildings. He and two colleagues had examined the Wharf and they now recommended major improvements, and these involved among other works the sinking of hundreds of timber piles. In 1636, major repairs were begun on the fabric of some of the Tower's buildings, the principal one being the White Tower. In the year that followed, the master mason, William Mills, replaced stonework damaged through decay and other causes, particularly on the angles of the tower, with new quoins of Portland stone. He attended likewise to the four turrets and the battlements, and to arches, jambs and lintels, making it look something like what can be seen today. He also gave the Tower a new coat of whitewash. Then, in 1638–9, Mills attended to the Bloody Tower and the Beauchamp Tower. By the end of 1640, more than £4,000 had been spent.

Throughout the Civil War and the period of frustrating negotiations afterwards between the defeated king and the parliamentarians, which ended in the king's trial and execution, the Tower was in the hands of Parliament, and there were no attempts to take it. Parliament used it for political and military prisoners, as all preceding monarchs had done. In the first months after the war began, its principal rôle seems to have been to provide arms, ordnance and gunpowder for the parliamentary armies. But towards the end of 1643 parliamentary armies began to gain the initiative through a number of victories over the royalists, won mainly by the Huntingdonshire-born Oliver Cromwell, a cavalry specialist and founder of the New Model Army. Prisoners from the royalist side began to arrive at the Tower and continued to do so until the end of the war. Among the most important was George Monck, a Devonshire-born soldier who had spent several years campaigning in the Low Countries during the Thirty Years War (1618–48). He joined the king's army in 1642 and was made colonel, but at the battle of Nantwich in Cheshire in 1644 he

George Monck, first Duke of Albemarle, K.G., one of Oliver Cromwell's generals who, after the death of the great Lord Protector in September 1658 and the resignation of his son, Richard 'Tumbledown Dick' Cromwell in the summer of 1659, led the movement to offer the throne back to Charles II, then in exile.

was captured by Lord Fairfax, the parliamentary commander who defeated the royalists there. Monck was brought to the Tower and remained there for three years, apparently in straitened circumstances because he was not a man of wealth, but in 1647 he agreed to serve as a commander with the parliamentary army, and thereby secured his release and was then sent to Ireland. We shall come across Monck again later.

By 1647 the parliamentarians were decisively in control of the military situation and had the king as a prisoner at Carisbrooke Castle in the Isle of Wight, with whom they were negotiating a return to the throne on strict conditions. The Tower passed formally into the hands of the Lord Mayor of the City of London and a new Constable was appointed. He was Thomas, later Lord, Fairfax, the commander-in-chief of the parliamentary armies. Fairfax had been a keen parliamentary supporter and a brilliant commander in the field of battle. But his views as to the future of the king were different from the more vigorous and radical parliamentarians who sought to curb the king's constitutional powers drastically, and he found himself becoming disenchanted with the accelerating revolutionary processes affecting the business of government. When it was decided to put the king on trial (and the terms of the indictment were such that only a verdict of guilty of high treason against the State seemed likely), Fairfax decided to pull out of the limelight and he resigned his Constableship. He fell out with Cromwell, by now in fact if not yet in name the leading man in the country, and the latter took over as Constable, holding the office until his death nine years later. In his time, Cromwell established a permanent military garrison in the Tower, but much of the administration involved was

137

delegated to his choice as Lieutenant, Sir John Barkstead, one-time member of Parliament.

In 1653, Cromwell was made Lord Protector, and for the next five years ruled England, Scotland and Ireland with a wise and firm if autocratic hand, and in those years he accomplished much, both at home and abroad. His measures in Britain, though necessary were often unpopular, especially where enforced by the use of the army (which Cromwell often regretted). Abroad, British troops trained and hardened in his New Model Army and the successes they had gained won widespread renown for their fighting qualities. The navy, meanwhile, beat both Dutch and Spanish fleets at sea. New colonies were added to the growing roll-call of British possessions overseas. And Cromwell himself earned the respect and often the admiration of the governments of Europe, some of which turned to him for arbitration in their respective disputes. Yet it has to be said that the country was not happy even if it was ordered and becoming prosperous through expanding trade, and this is reflected in the succession of conspiracies hatched against him from beginning to end of his time. All of them failed for one reason or another, the ringleaders ended up in the Tower, and many of them went from there to their death.

Oliver Cromwell died on 3 September 1658. Although his son Richard was chosen to succeed him in what was not clearly established as an hereditary office, the

A wider panorama of London, in the mid-17th century, drawn as seen from the south bank of the River Thames. The White Tower is the tallest building, in the background. The picture was engraved by Cornelis Visscher.

government was plunged into a political vacuum. Richard Cromwell – to be nicknamed 'Tumbledown Dick' because he showed none of the aptitudes of power that his father had – resigned soon afterwards. There followed a struggle between different elements of the army for control of Parliament and the country, and Monck, whom Oliver Cromwell had made commander-in-chief in Scotland, marched to London and restored order. He organized a general election and the majority of the new members declared that they wanted the restoration of the monarchy, in the person of the executed king's elder son, Charles, then living in exile in Europe. Charles agreed to return and take up the throne, issuing his assent to the terms requested by Monck and Parliament in what came to be called the Declaration of Breda, and at the end of May 1660, he re-entered London to receive a tremendous welcome, 'the ways strewed with flowers, the bells ringing, the streets hung with tapestry, and the fountains running with wine.' It seems that almost the only people who dreaded his return were the surviving signatories of the death warrant that brought Charles I to the block in 1649. They had some cause to be afraid: the god of Vengeance was already abroad in the land.

VII

English Restoration to French Revolution

A gruesome contemporary picture of the revenge and punishment meted out to some of those who signed the death warrant of Charles I. Some of the regicides, as they were called, were hanged, drawn and quartered.

Revenge upon the regicides

Richard Cromwell resigned the Lord Protectorship in May 1659 and retired into private life, withdrawing to the Continent soon after the return of Charles to England. When Richard Cromwell did eventually come back to his native land, in about 1680, he was allowed to live in peace at a house in Cheshunt, where he died in 1712. He had not after all been one of the regicides and he had played no part in his

140

father's revolution or assumption of the sovereign power as Lord Protector. But for the regicides still living in 1660, different fates awaited. Arthur Hazelrig, one of the original five Members of Parliament whom Charles I had tried to arrest in 1642 at the House of Commons, was arrested in March 1660, not for that but for opposing General Monck's scheme for restoring the monarchy. Hazelrig died in the Tower a year later. Also arrested at the same time was Colonel John Lambert, for the same offence. Lambert had served under Lord Fairfax, had led the van at Cromwell's great victory at Dunbar in Scotland in 1650, and after Oliver's death in 1658 he had headed the opposition to Richard Cromwell. For a short while he had chaired a Committee of Safety which ruled the country for a few months while Monck, in opposition to the Committee, plotted the restoration of Charles II. Lambert succeeded in escaping from the Tower. He bribed his bedmaker, an elderly woman, to put on his night clothes and take his place in his bed while he escaped by rope from the window of his cell and got away. He reached the Midlands but was caught and returned to the Tower until the restored king banished him to Guernsey where he languished a prisoner till his death in 1684.

Even while the king was packing up his things in France to come home in triumph to his throne, in May 1660, a fresh set of arrests of prominent regicides was made. Victims had only to have signed the death warrant of Charles I to be branded as regicide. Among the first of this next batch of victims was Colonel Thomas Harrison, who was brought to the Tower on 19 May 1660. Harrison, who had served in the parliamentary army, also captained the troop of guards that conveyed Charles I from Hurst Castle in Hampshire to London for trial in December 1648, and then he signed the death warrant. He also acted as one of the king's judges. Harrison was tried and sentenced to be hanged and quartered, and on 18 October he was dragged on a hurdle to Charing Cross for execution, a few yards from the spot where the king himself had met his execution. Harrison's death was witnessed by Samuel Pepys who wrote that, 'it was my chance to see the King beheaded at Whitehall and to see the first blood shed in revenge for the King'. Another regicide to die was Colonel Francis Hacker, on 19 October. He had commanded the troop of guards at the king's trial in Westminster Hall and who actually brought him out to the scaffold on 30 January 1649.

More than twenty regicides paid the supreme penalty for their part in the trial and execution of Charles I. Each of them was put to death in the most brutal fashion, and the trials and executions were spread over a period of two years, an indication of the virulence of the revenging spirit in the heart of the new king and his government. Sir Harry Vane, for example, a supporter of Parliament, who had been a principal agent in the impeachment of Strafford and his eventual execution in 1641, worked with Cromwell during the Civil War in a political capacity, and yet had no connection with the king's trial and sentence, was arrested after Cromwell's death and put in the Tower in July 1660. Vane had been forgiven by a general amnesty of Charles, Prince of Wales (later, Charles II) who had once promised a 'merciful indemnity to

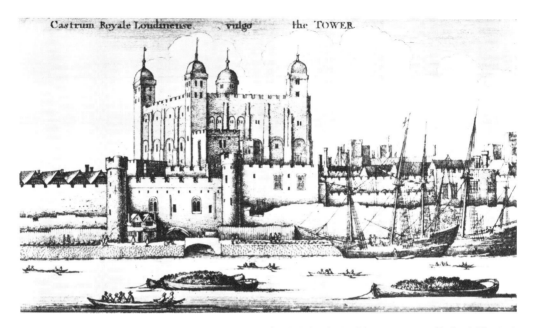

Castrum Royale Londinense vulgo the TOWER

An etching by the Bohemian engraver, Wenceslaus Hollar (1607–77), who lived for some years in England. This is the Tower in the reign of Charles II (1660–85).

all those not immediately concerned in his father's death'. After a few months in the Tower Vane was moved to the Scilly Isles, brought back in March 1662 and executed on Tower Hill in June. The king had said, 'he is too dangerous to let live; if we can honestly put him out of the way.' It was judicial murder.

Meanwhile, in April 1661, the restored king began to make preparations for his forthcoming coronation. Determined at the start of his reign, if not thereafter, to rule as constitutionally as he could, Charles set out to provide Londoners with all the panoply and festivity they could expect at a royal coronation. This entailed coming to the Tower before the great ceremony, and processing from the Tower to Westminster for it. Charles took the barge down the Thames from Whitehall on 22 April. Where he stayed for the night is not clear, but it was not at the Tower.

The coronation proceedings were watched by two of the greatest diarists of seventeenth-century England, Samuel Pepys (1633–1703) and John Evelyn (1620–1706), who were friends, although we do not know if either knew the other was keeping a diary. Pepys and Evelyn were at different points along the route from the Tower to Westminster, Evelyn somewhere in the Strand, Pepys at Cornhill in the City. Pepys recorded a long procession of notable people: 'My lord Monk [Monck had been created Duke of Albemarle] rode bare after the King, and led in his hand a spare horse, as being Master of the Horse. The King, in a most rich embroidered suit and cloak, looked most noble. . . Both the King and the Duke of York took notice of us, as they saw us at the window. . . .' The following day, St George's Day, 23 April, was coronation day and Pepys had a seat in the Abbey, probably by virtue of the fact that his father had been first cousin of Edward Montagu, Earl of Sandwich, who carried the sceptre in front of the king at the actual ceremony.

Evelyn had, after the death of Cromwell, been among the first to urge the restoration of the monarchy. This earned the favour of the king who is said to have wanted to include Evelyn's name among the sixty-odd new Knights of the Bath he wished to create in his coronation honours list. Evelyn, however, declined and remained plain John Evelyn up to his death at the age of eighty-six.

Although Charles II does not seem ever to have stayed in the Tower, a good deal of new building work was put in hand, and a number of repairs and alterations were carried out in his quarter century as king. There were demolitions, too: the entrance to the royal palace area south of the White Tower, Coldharbour Gate, was partly dismantled in 1669, '... taking down the stone walls of the Tower going into Coldharbour where it was ready to fall...' In the 1680s there were further demolitions of royal lodgings and new buildings for the Ordnance were put up on the

The crypt of St John's Chapel in the White Tower was for a time used as an extension to the Armouries. Some of the armour and weapons were set up on display for public viewing, during the middle decades of the 19th century.

site. But if the various royal lodging structures were allowed to run down or were actually pulled down, the Lieutenant's lodgings received a lot of attention during the reign. The old timber-framed structure in the south-west corner of the inner bailey adjoining the Bell Tower was enlarged in 1663 by the addition of two new rooms, one for the Lieutenant and the other for his assistant/secretary. Seventeen years later there were more improvements.

Among other alterations of Charles II's time were changing the use of the Chapel of St John in the White Tower and the setting up of a formal display of armour, which marked the beginning of the Armouries as a museum, making it the oldest museum in Britain – although, of course, some armour had been displayed for nearly a century before that.

The Chapel of St John, which occupies the second and gallery floors of the White Tower, was given a new rôle. It had long been out of use as a chapel; now it was turned into a store for those state papers and records that were kept available for the public to see, antiquaries to study, and so forth. At the same time the bulk of the state papers remained in the Wakefield Tower. The chapel continued to store papers for years, and the archive was steadily augmented as fresh consignments of papers were transferred to it. Not until the mid-nineteenth century were the accumulated heaps of papers removed and the chapel restored to its original use.

The displays of armour which Charles II enlarged had developed from the armours of Henry VIII (there are to this day four personal armours of that king on show, in addition to other armour items). In 1598, Paul Hentzner, a German traveller who came to England for a few months, published an account of his visit, and this included a tour of the Tower.[1] He remarked that visitors to the Tower were required to leave their swords at the gate. He visited the Armoury and described seeing spears 'out of which you may shoot'. He noted that eight or nine men employed all year round were not enough to keep all the displayed arms and armour brightly polished.

In order to emphasize the hereditary character of the monarchy the king sponsored a new display for the public at the Tower. This was the Line of Kings, a development of an idea of Henry VIII's time at Greenwich Palace. The display consisted of a series of figures mounted on horseback, the figures representing the Kings of England in order of succession, 'fully accoutred in armour, purporting to be theirs'. The armour was provided from the Tower Armouries. The dummy kings were mounted on wooden horses, and it was a splendid display. 'Only the most learned antiquary was likely to carp at the fact that all the kings were dressed in complete plate armour, no earlier than the 16th century, and that William the Conqueror was also shown carrying his musket.' The Line of Kings was never complete in historical terms, for it did not include kings whose reputations were unpleasant or embarrassing, such as Edward II and Richard III.

1 *A Journey into England;* Paul Hentzner (trans and ed. Horace Walpole, 1757).

The Tower in the Great Fire of London

On Sunday 2 September, 1666, Samuel Pepys wrote one of the longest entries in the whole of his diary. The first part deserves verbatim quotation:

Some of our maids sitting up late last night to get things ready against our feast to-day, Jane called us up about three in the morning, to tell us of a great fire they saw in the City. So I rose, and slipped on my night-gown, and went to her window, and thought it to be on the back-side of Marke-lane at the farthest, but being unused to such fires as followed, I thought it far enough off; and so went to bed again, and to sleep. About seven rose again to dress myself and there looked out at the window, and saw the fire not so much as it was, and further off. So to my closet to set things to rights, after yesterday's cleaning. By and by Jane comes and tells me that she hears above 300 houses have been burned down to-night by the fire we saw, and that it is now burning down all Fish-street, by London Bridge. So I made myself ready presently, and walked to the Tower, and there got up upon one of the high places, Sir J. Robinson's little son going up with me:[2] and there I did see the houses at that end of the bridge all on fire, and an infinite great fire on this and the other side the end of the bridge. . . So down with my heart full of trouble to the Lieutenant of the Tower who tells me that it begun this morning in the King's baker's house in Pudding Lane. . . and there see a lamentable fire. . . .

A fine painting of London burning during the Great Fire of 1666. The Tower is at right. The flames almost reached the Tower, a hazard very well captured by the artist.

2 Sir John Robinson was the Lieutenant of the Tower at the time. A nephew of Archbishop Laud, he had been a royalist all through the Commonwealth period. In 1660 he was an alderman of the City of London, and brought the City militia over to the king's cause and in support of General Monck. Robinson was made Lieutenant in 1660/1 and held the post until 1678. In 1661 he was also Lord Mayor of London.

Wenceslaus Hollar produced two important etchings of London in 1666, one shortly before the Great Fire of September, and the other soon afterwards. In this, the pre-Fire picture, the Tower is at extreme right. Note also London Bridge, in the centre foreground. Hollar drew the picture from a church steeple in Southwark, on the south bank.

The Great Fire of London had broken out and was already consuming huge areas of densely packed houses in narrow streets. It lasted for three days and three nights and when it finally died out, about four fifths of the City of London had been reduced to ash and rubble. John Evelyn, who also described the Fire in his diary, relates how on the last day (the 5th) it was in danger of reaching the Tower itself. He says that the king went to the Tower by water, and ordered some of the houses near the Wharf but outside the Tower precincts to be pulled down, or blown up with gunpowder to clear a safe space around the Tower. Bayley says that a change in the direction of the wind saved the Tower from being engulfed. Had the fire spread into the fortress, the resulting damage could have been extensive, particularly if the stores of gunpowder in the White Tower and elsewhere had been ignited.

The attempt to steal the Crown Jewels

No account of the Tower's history in the reign of Charles II is complete without mentioning the story of the attempt by Colonel Thomas Blood to steal the Crown Jewels. The Crown Jewels today consist chiefly of a number of crowns, orbs, sceptres, regalia like bracelets, spurs, an anointing spoon, an ampulla for the anointing oil, quantities of gold and silver plate, as well as swords, maces and other processional objects. Most of the objects date from the 1660s or later because older relics – some of them going back to the earliest days of the Tower and possibly even to Anglo-Saxon times – had been destroyed or sold during the Commonwealth period, after the execution of Charles I in 1649. From Norman times at least, the kings and ruling queens of England kept their royal jewels, regalia and ceremonial treasures in the Tower. These were personal assets and could be, and often were, used as pledges for loans for military expenses or for building projects. At first, the jewels stored at the Tower were probably kept safely locked up in a chamber in the basement of the White Tower, under the crypt of the Chapel of St John. Later, a jewel house was built

146

The second of Wenceslaus Hollar's engravings of London at the time of the Fire, this one showing London soon after the conflagration had died out. The extent of the damage to London can readily be gauged by the devastation Hollar depicts in the district between the north end of London Bridge and the Tower (at extreme right).

against the south face of the White Tower. Some regalia were also kept in Westminster Abbey. Early in the 16th century a new Jewel House was built outside the White Tower, on the south side, somewhere near the earlier jewel house. This new building was that built by James Nedeham (see Ch. IV. p. 87), and some though not all of the royal jewels were moved there.

During the earlier centuries it had not been usual for the Crown Jewels to be

A portrait of Colonel Thomas Blood, the Irish adventurer who tried to steal the Crown Jewels in 1671, and who was caught and then pardoned by Charles II.

displayed for visitors, no doubt because of their crucial pledge value and any consequent embarrassment that would arise if any of the items were removed from display, however temporarily. But in the seventeenth century the practice of displaying the jewels to visitors in return for a fee was introduced.

Since most of the Crown Jewels had been destroyed or disposed of during the Commonwealth period, a fresh collection had to be assembled, made up largely from gifts, commissions for new jewels, and a few ancient relics that had survived. Among the surviving old relics were the anointing spoon probably made for King John's coronation in 1199, the ampulla made in the 14th century and a salt that was made in 1572.

The revival of interest in the Crown Jewels after the Restoration of 1660 led to a re-think about where to keep them. At first the jewels were displayed in the old jewel house of Nedeham's time, until this was pulled down. There was at first no official policy to have the jewels on public show, and it was a matter of the keeper finding a source of income. The choice eventually fell on the Martin Tower. The jewels were to be kept in the ground floor chamber in a special cupboard, while the storey above was to be converted into a mezzanine floor with a first floor above, the two floors to be accommodation for a keeper of the jewels. The post was originally called Master of the Jewel House, and the first holder was Sir Gilbert Talbot who declined to take up the accommodation. Instead he put in one of his retired servants, Talbot Edwards, who was to receive no pay but who was allowed to keep fees charged to visitors who wanted to see the jewels. The procedure appears to have been that visitors were asked to pay as they entered the chamber with the jewels, and the door was then closed and locked behind them. Edwards would then open the cupboard to show them the items. The procedure worked satisfactorily for about ten years, but in 1671 a daring burglary was attempted by Colonel Blood.

Thomas Blood was a reprobate Irish adventurer. He had fought on the parliamentary side in the Civil War. He had survived to return to Ireland where in 1663 he made a raid on Dublin Castle with some colleagues and attempted to seize the Lord Lieutenant, the Duke of Ormonde. This failed, but seven years later, Blood tried again to capture the Duke, this time when the latter was in London, and Blood actually captured him but then had to release him.

At seven o'clock on the morning of 9 May, Colonel Blood, disguised as a parson and accompanied by three well-dressed young men, one of whom Blood claimed was his nephew, visited the Martin Tower to see the regalia. Blood had already been there a few days earlier, accompanied by a woman whom he claimed was his wife, and the latter had pretended to be taken ill. Edwards had kindly led the woman upstairs to his wife to look after her, leaving the 'parson' unattended in the jewel chamber. On the second visit Blood brought a present for Edwards' wife as a thank you for her attentions to the 'wife'. As soon as the party entered the jewel chamber, Blood pulled out a mallet from under his cloak and struck Edwards on the head. His accomplices bound and gagged him. Blood then seized the king's crown and tried to

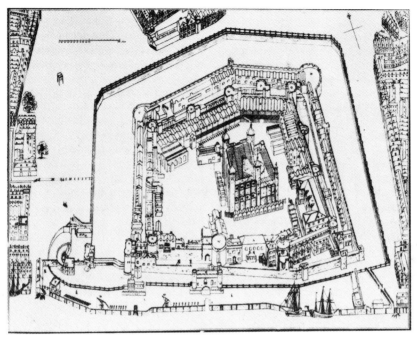

A bird's-eye view of the Tower in 1682. In the centre is the White Tower, with its annexe on the east side. It will be noticed that the annexe takes in the rounded apsidal east extension of the White Tower without affecting its integrity. It also appears that the annexe consists of an inner open courtyard enclosed by three narrow sides of building.

flatten it with the mallet so as to get it into his cassock pocket. His 'nephew' meanwhile pushed the orb into the slack of his breeches. The other two men filed away at the sceptre to cut it in half.

At that moment, however, Edward's son Wythe arrived quite unexpectedly on leave from military service abroad. Immediately his suspicions were aroused, and he rushed into the room to find his father lying unconscious on the floor, bleeding from a head wound. Blood and his gang fled, but three of the four were caught as they tried to get out of the Tower, and the jewels were recovered much damaged.

A report was immediately sent to the king at Whitehall, and Charles sent for Blood for private interrogation. The attempt had the most unexpected sequel. Far from being punished, Blood was pardoned, awarded a pension of £500 a year, and made welcome at court. A day or two later, the diarist Evelyn met Blood at Whitehall, and later wrote down his opinion: 'How he ever came to be pardoned and ever received into favour, not only after this but several other exploits almost as daring, both in Ireland and here, I never could come to understand. This man had not only a daring, but a villainous unmerciful look, a false countenance, but very well spoken, and dangerously insinuating.'

Old Talbot Edwards was not so well treated. He was awarded a grant of £200 but it proved so hard for him to get the actual money that he sold his right to it for half the

The new Armouries block of 1664. This was erected against the inner wall of the Tower on the east side, between Broad Arrow Tower and Salt Tower. It houses armour and weapon displays, over and above those at present on show in the White Tower. The weapon displays include a comprehensive collection of firearms from all over the world, over several hundred years.

amount in cash, and died in some misery in 1674. The affair led to tightening up the procedure for displaying the Crown Jewels and for admitting visitors, and this included the posting of an armed guard by the door of the chamber in the Martin Tower. The jewels remained in the Martin Tower until 1841 when following the great fire at the Tower (see pages 173–176) a new Jewel House was built to house them.

To this day we do not know what really lay behind the Blood episode: naturally enough, tradition has it that the king was party to the attempt because he was desperately short of funds and wanted to sell the jewels but could not do so openly. Recent studies on the matter suggest that Blood was a government spy and had close links with the king's friend and minister, the Duke of Buckingham (son of the Buckingham who had been, first, James I's favourite and then Charles I's, and was murdered in 1628). Blood knew too much to the discredit of both the king and the duke, and so it would not have been safe to bring him to trial.

We might well have known more still if Pepys had not given up his diary in 1669. Pepy's wife died in that year, and he was himself afflicted by an eye disorder that led him to a great deal of anxiety that he was losing his sight permanently, and so he stopped writing the entries. Yet he lived on for thirty-four more years, to become secretary to the Admiralty in 1672, to be put in the Tower in 1679 (accused of involvement in the notorious Popish Plot), to be restored to the Admiralty job in

1684 and also to become President of the Royal Society. His stay in the Tower was short, and during the time he was visited by, among others, his fellow diarist Evelyn, who recorded that on 4 June he dined with Pepys. Evelyn's entry says that Pepys was 'imprisoned by the House of Commons for misdemeanours in the Admiralty . . . but I believe unjustly'. A month later, Evelyn sent his friend a present of some venison, and also dined with him again.

There was one other part of the Tower that received building attention in Charles II's reign, the Chapel of St Peter ad Vincula. Damaged masonry was restored, a small western tower was rebuilt, and inside, a new pedimented reredos in Renaissance style was installed behind the high altar, as well as a new pulpit and lectern. The work was begun in 1670 and continued with intervals until 1676. Possibly it was supervised, or at all events approved, by the new Surveyor-General of the King's Works appointed in 1669. He was Christopher Wren, and he held the office until 1718, almost half a century. In that time he was responsible for the maintenance of the Tower.

Charles II died in 1685. He was succeeded by his brother James, Duke of York, a zealous Roman Catholic who had been a very good Lord High Admiral for some years during his brother's reign. James came to the throne with a considerable measure of popularity, despite attempts in the late 1670s by Parliament to have him excluded from the succession because of his avowed Catholicism. Three years later, when he was compelled to abdicate and even to fly for his life from his own kingdom, there was hardly anyone with a good word to say for him. He had so disgusted the nation by a series of arbitrary and manifestly unjust acts that he provoked a revolution which was completely successful. During his short reign, some of his victims suffered in the Tower of London.

Jacobean Persecution

Almost as soon as he succeeded in February 1685 James revealed himself to be as vain, pedantic and heartless as his wretched grandfather James I and as obstinate as his father Charles I. Despite declaring that he would maintain the government both in state and church as established by law, he embarked immediately upon a policy of restoring the Roman Catholic faith. Before many months passed, he was faced with a revolt. The Duke of Monmouth, the illegitimate son of Charles II, who was in exile in Flanders, returned to England to claim the throne, declaring himself the rightful heir of his father and more particularly a Protestant heir. Calling himself James II, he landed at Lyme Regis in Dorset in June 1685, raised a ramshackle army and got as far as Somerset, but James responded swiftly and sent an army down to deal with the revolt. At Sedgemoor near Bridgwater, Monmouth was utterly defeated, but escaped from the field and went into hiding. A few days later he was caught near Ringwood in Hampshire and brought to the Tower. He begged for an interview with his uncle, the king, who granted it but resolutely refused to spare him. So Monmouth was returned to the Tower to await execution. He was lodged in the

James Scott, Duke of Monmouth, illegitimate son of Charles II and nephew of James II, whom he tried to unseat from his throne in 1685. Monmouth, who was executed on Tower Hill, was the son of Charles by his mistress Lucy Walter. It has been argued that Charles and Lucy were properly married when the king was in hiding during the last months of his father's reign. If this were true, Monmouth was the rightful heir to Charles when the latter died in 1685. Pepys makes several references to the possibility that the king is about to declare Monmouth the legitimate heir, or to say he will 'legitimate' Monmouth. One quote: '. . . he speaks as if it were not impossible but the King would own him for his son and that there was a marriage between his mother and him . . .' The possibility that Monmouth was legitimate – and that James II knew it – may have been why James resolutely refused to spare him after the battle of Sedgmoor, or so it has been suggested.

Lieutenant's house, and on 15 July he was led out to Tower Hill where the executioner made appallingly clumsy efforts to cut off his head. No less than five blows of the axe fell upon him but not one of them accurate enough to decapitate him. By now the crowd, already sympathetic to Monmouth – for he was always much loved by the people – began to advance towards the scaffold and would doubtless have tried to rescue him. On the sixth attempt the axe was brought down properly and the Duke put to death. John Evelyn, who recorded the event, wrote that Monmouth was a lovely person.

Three years later, the king, having alienated most of his supporters as well as the majority of the nation, issued a Declaration of Indulgence which suspended all laws against Roman Catholics, and he ordered the clergy throughout the country to read it out in all the churches. Seven bishops, headed by William Sancroft, Archbishop of Canterbury, formally petitioned the king that they might be excused from the order. The king responded by treating the petition as an act of sedition, and he had them all arrested and taken by barge, all seven in one vessel, to the Tower. Apart from

Sancroft, the six other bishops were those of Bath and Wells, Bristol, Chichester, Ely, Peterborough and St Asaph. They arrived at the Tower in mid-June 1688.

The arrest of the seven bishops had aroused tremendous interest among the people of London. Many could hardly believe their ears when they heard that the king had actually arrested his archbishop of Canterbury. They flocked to the area around the Tower and along the river to get a glimpse of the seven. Hundreds of people took to boats on the Thames and rowed alongside the bishops' barge, cheering them and shouting encouragement and support as the barge neared Traitor's Gate. At the gate, Tower officials fell to their knees to beg forgiveness for having to carry out their duty. Once in the Tower, however, the bishops were treated with some hardness. All seven were crammed into one room in the Martin Tower. When they were ordered to pay fees and replied that these were not due, the Lieutenant, Sir Edward Hales, a Catholic, threatened them that when they returned to the Tower after their impending trial at Westminster Hall, he would put them in irons.

The bishops were tried in Westminster Hall at the end of June, and to the relief and joy of practically the whole nation they were acquitted. Bonfires were lit, bells rung, cannon fired, all over London. It was the signal for the beginning of the end for the king. A number of the leading men from both Houses of Parliament got together immediately and sent an urgent message to the Chief Stadtholter of the Netherlands, William of Orange, husband of James's elder daughter, Mary. They invited him to come to England, 'to defend the rights and liberties of the people'. A few months later, William came, landing at Brixham near Torquay in Devonshire,

Scene of the execution of James, Duke of Monmouth, illegitimate son of Charles II and nephew of James II. Monmouth's attempt to claim the throne in 1685 was unsuccessful. The scaffold was erected on Tower Hill. Such was the popularity of the duke that a large force of armed and helmeted soldiers was assembled to prevent trouble from the huge mob which had gathered to witness the death of their hero.

marched to Exeter and then on towards London, gathering support all the way. By the time he was near Salisbury, it was all over bar the shouting.

The king, only just beginning to realize the enormity of some of the things he had done, hastily tried to undo them, but to no avail. One by one, ministers and friends, generals and admirals, deserted him. Even his erstwhile friend and former protégé, John Churchill (later Duke of Marlborough) abandoned him, and on 11 December James abdicated and fled from London by boat to France. There, he was welcomed by the Catholic Louis XIV, and shortly afterwards given a home at St Germain, outside Paris.

When Monmouth's attempt of 1685 to win the throne of his uncle James had collapsed and he was being hunted for round Wiltshire and Hampshire, the king, thoroughly frightened and very vindictive, decided to deal sternly with the captured officers and men from his nephew's army at Sedgemoor. He sent George Jeffreys, Lord Jeffreys of Wem, his Chief Justice of the King's Bench, down to Somerset to hold a special assize for the trial of as many of the captives as possible. In what came to be known as the Bloody Assize, Jeffreys and four assisting judges heard hundreds of cases, and with little regard for justice and none for mercy passed sentence of hanging on over 300 people and transportation as slaves to the West Indies for another 840. Others still were sentenced to severe floggings, imprisonment in England and other penalties. Jeffreys was rewarded by James with the Lord Chancellorship, and for the rest of the reign he supported the king in every one of his repressive measures. Yet, though presiding over the trial of the Seven Bishops, he does not appear to have attempted to overrule the decision of the other judges to acquit them. When the king decided to flee from England in December 1688, Jeffreys, knowing that the triumphant forces of William of Orange were after him and that he could expect no mercy once he was taken, also tried to escape. Disguised as an ordinary seaman, he was nonetheless detected in a London public house near the river where he was about to embark in a boat for France. He was taken to the Tower to save him from the London mob, and there he was put – appropriately enough – in the Bloody Tower. He was provided with quantities of brandy, to which he was thought to be addicted, and a few weeks later he died.

During the reign of James II, an interesting new building project was begun in the Tower. This was a palatial structure for the Ordnance, whose requirements were increasing gradually over the years and which already occupied several other parts of the Tower. It was soon to be known as the Grand Storehouse (pic. p. 155). It was sited north of the White Tower, where the present Waterloo Barracks block now stands and which replaced it in the 1840s. When the Grand Storehouse was finished, the Ordnance department invited the new king and queen, William III and Mary II, to an opening banquet where they were served by the masons and other workers wearing white aprons and gloves. The building had a fine pediment of carved stone over the central front entrance, and this carved pediment has survived and may be seen today in the present New Armouries.

A late 17th century print of the Seven Bishops who in 1688 were imprisoned in the Tower by James II for refusing to have his Declaration of Indulgence read out in churches in their dioceses. The central figure is William Sancroft, Archbishop of Canterbury, and round him are (clockwise, from centre left) Bishops Thomas Ken of Bath & Wells, Francis Turner of Ely, William Lloyd of St Asaph (in Wales), John Lake of Chichester, Thomas White of Peterborough and Jonathan Trelawney of Bristol.

The liberties of the people were in part restored in William and Mary's reign, but this did not mean a Tower of London empty of prisoners of state. In May 1692 John Churchill, by now Earl of Marlborough, who had risen to prominence in the reign of

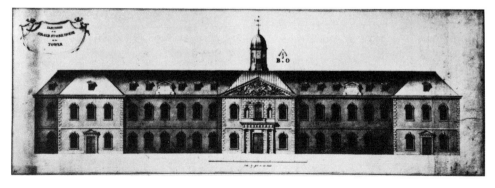

How the Grand Storehouse looked in the mid-18th century. Over the central entrance is the fine stone pediment carved by Grinling Gibbons. When the Grand Storehouse was gutted in the Fire of 1841, the pediment was rescued and is now in the New Armouries.

The Seven Bishops are brought to the Tower by barge, in June 1688. At centre in the background is Traitor's Gate, with troops lined up on either side of the approach. At left in the foreground is a boat containing several well-wishers cheering for the bishops, whose arrest had astonished an already angry and dismayed population in London. Several others boats accompanied the prelates, and they were filled with people shouting encouragement.

James II (he was second in command at the battle of Sedgemoor), who three years later deserted his patron and joined William of Orange, found himself accused of treason (abetting and adhering to Their Majesties' enemies) and was taken to the Tower. He had in fact become the victim of a Jacobite plot: letters had been forged which implied that he had been in treasonable correspondence with the exiled James II at St Germain. It took nearly six weeks for the plot to be exposed, and even then Marlborough was only released on a surety of £6,000. For a long time William III did not feel he could really trust him politically, and almost certainly he never trusted him personally again.

In 1695, Sir Christopher Wren was requested by the Committee of the Council for the Affairs of Ireland to go to the Tower and assess what work was needed and what it would cost to repair the Beauchamp Tower and the Bloody Tower, and to put them 'in a condition to hold Prisoners of State'. He was also requested to survey the ground behind the Chapel of St Peter ad Vincula where it had been proposed to erect a building for keeping prisoners, and to assess what it would cost and how many prisoners it could hold. This was on 15 April, and Wren acted extremely quickly, for only two days later he wrote back to the Committee that he had inspected the Beauchamp Tower and the Bloody Tower, which he said had already been repaired the previous summer, 'being whited, mended and made strong, but to make them fitt for prisoners of State, if by that Expression it be intended that they should be wainscotted and made fitt for hangings and furniture, it may cost £200 or much more but with such walls, windows and winding stairs they never can be made proper with any cost without rebuilding.' He also reported that he had surveyed the ground for the new prison building and reckoned the proposal would cost £600. As to the numbers of prisoners the Beauchamp Tower and the Bloody Tower could hold, and the new building as well, he said he could only say the Beauchamp Tower had a large kitchen, two large rooms and two small servant's rooms, the Bloody Tower a kitchen, one room and one closet, and the new building could have nine single rooms, besides cellars and garrets and a kitchen.

Was the Council expecting a sudden and large intake of important prisoners? This has been suggested by some authorities, but when one considers the total number of rooms mentioned by Wren (excluding kitchens, cellars and garrets), namely, fifteen, it does not seem likely. If a lot of prison space were required in a hurry, there would surely have been plenty throughout the Tower as it was.

In 1695 Isaac Newton, already famed throughout Europe for his scientific and mathematical discoveries and invention, was made Warden of the Mint in the

A very fine cartoon picture of the late 17th century depicting the discovery and arrest of Judge Jeffreys disguised as a sailor trying to get away from England after the fall of his master, James II, in 1688. The inscribed ribbons remind Jeffreys of the worst deeds of James's reign, with which Jeffreys was associated, such as the Trial of the Seven Bishops, the Bloody Assize after the battle of Sedgmoor, and the imposition of a catholic President on Magdalen College, Oxford, against the wishes of the Fellows.

The Tower of London, in a print of the time of James II.

Tower, and given a residence on the west of the Bell Tower, though we do not know if he actually stayed there. Four years later he was advanced to Master of the Mint, a position he held until his death in 1727. This was in addition to the many other duties, official and otherwise that he fitted into a life already filled with scientific research, philosophical enquiry and mathematical invention. During the earlier years of his tenure Newton was instrumental in reforming the minting of the kingdom's coinage, following the passing of the Coinage Act of 1696 by which all the old hammered money was called in, melted down and the metal sent to the Mint in ingots to be re-processed and issued with milled edges. He arranged for more rolling mills to be installed to cope with the work, and by his efforts is said to have created the climate for a period of considerable commercial prosperity. The equipment in the Tower, however, was not enough to cope with the demands of the complete recoinage which the Act required, and additional mints were set up in Bristol, Chester, Exeter, Norwich and York, on a short-term basis until the work was finished. The Tower Mint was thereafter capable of handling the national minting for almost the whole of the eighteenth century, until early in the nineteenth century a new Mint was set up outside the Tower.

William III died in 1702 as the result of a fall from his horse, and was succeeded by his late wife's sister, the Princess Anne, who reigned from 1702 and 1714. Her short reign was filled with the dramatic military exploits of John Churchill, created Duke of Marlborough in 1702, splendidly manifested in the War of the Spanish Succession (1701–13), and of the Earl of Peterborough in the same war, and also by a number of interesting developments nearer home, including the Act of Union between England and Scotland (1707). Yet the involvement of the Tower in the story of England in these years was minimal: perhaps the most famous prisoner was Robert Walpole, later to be Britain's first Prime Minister (1721–42), who when Secretary of State for War was put in the Tower, 'for high breach of trust and notorious corruption', in 1712. His room in the Tower was regularly full of visitors from many walks of life during his months in prison.

In 1704, a House of Lords committee set up to look into the condition of the state records in the Tower was shocked to find those kept in the Chapel of St John in the White Tower (see page 17) were lying about in a confused heap on the floor. The Committee recommended the provision by the Office of Works of proper shelving, and three years later when the Committee paid a return visit, it was pleased to say that 'this Chapel is now made a great and noble Repository, fit to receive many of the Records which now lie crowded in the Chapel at the Rolls.' In about 1712 Wren, in his capacity as Surveyor General of the King's Works, reporting that there was hardly enough room to take any more records transferred from Lincoln's Inn, suggested that a large room on the third floor of the White Tower, next to the Chapel of St John, should be allotted to take records. This was resisted by the Board of Ordnance which had responsibility for the room.

The Tower of London seen from the Thames by the artist Kip at the end of the 17th century. A fine impression of the Tower Wharf is obtained. Note also the Grand Storehouse behind the White Tower, just completed when this picture was produced. On the right hand side of the White Tower can be seen the top storey of the Edward III addition, whose function we have yet to discover in detail.

Queen Anne died in 1714 and was succeeded by a cousin, George Lewis, Elector of Hanover and the nearest Protestant relative available to occupy the British throne. His succession was not achieved without a good deal of opposition from supporters of the Jacobite cause, that is, the party which preferred the continued succession of members of the Stuart family even though they were for the most part Roman Catholic. The Whigs who backed George Lewis, not because they liked him so much as because they disliked Roman Catholics in any shape or form, took various steps to ensure that there was no move to prevent George's accession.

The first Jacobite Rising and the escape of Lord Nithsdale

Early in 1715, a Scottish noble, the Earl of Mar, who had once been a Whig but later came to support the cause of the exiled King James II and (after James's death in 1701 that of James's son James Edward, known as the Old Pretender), raised a revolt in the Highlands of Scotland. At the same time, Edward Radcliffe, Earl of Derwentwater, an English peer who also espoused the Jacobite cause, organized an army and took it to Scotland to help. But the Duke of Argyll defeated Mar at the battle of Sheriffmuir, near Stirling, and Derwentwater's force, which now consisted of several more Scottish lords, moved south into England but was defeated at

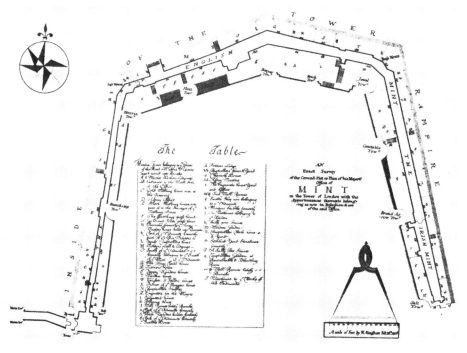

An 'exact survey of the Ground Plot or Plan of their Maiesties Office of Mint in the Tower of London with the Appurtenances thereunto belonging.' This was drawn by William Allingham in 1701. It shows the extent of the activities of the Mint and the amount of accommodation needed at the time, during Sir Isaac Newton's tenure as Master of the Mint.

A drawing of St John's Chapel, in the White Tower, when it had been abandoned for religious use and made over to storing public records. This conversion was done in the later 17th century and for the next two centuries it remained a record store. Visitors who had bona fide *reasons for inspecting public records were admitted to see them in this chapel.*

Preston. Mar got away from Sheriffmuir, but the Derwentwater party was captured and most of them taken to the Tower, with their hands tied behind their backs. In February 1716, they were taken to Westminster Hall for trial, were found guilty and condemned to be hanged, drawn and quartered, the manner of death for some of the lords including Derwentwater being changed to execution on the block. One of these lords was William Maxwell, Earl of Nithsdale, and only days before the date set for his execution he planned and pulled off a daring escape, with the help of his brave young wife.

Nithsdale was, like Derwentwater and others, confined in the Lieutenant's Lodgings. On the eve of his intended execution, the door of his room opened and two women came in. One was a servant, a Miss Hilton; the other was his wife, Lady Nithsdale. To his surprise, the servant began to undress. Then he noticed that she was wearing two sets of clothing. When she had discarded the top garments, she left. A short while later, Mrs Mills, another servant, appeared at the door. From her cloak she took a hood, a scarf and a pair of shoes. Lady Nithsdale told her husband quickly to don the garments and then he left the room with Mrs Mills.

161

An engraving of James Radclyffe, third Earl of Derwenter (1689–1716), whose mother was an illegitimate daughter of Charles II. Derwentwater was brought up with the Old Pretender (James Edward Stuart, son of James II) in France, and naturally became one of the leaders of the 1st Jacobite Rising, of 1715. He was captured at the battle of Preston, lodged in the Tower, tried for treason and beheaded in 1716. His colleague, the Earl of Nithsdale, similarly condemned, managed, however, to escape from the Tower the night before he was due to go to the block.

Wending their way out of the building they reached the Bulwark Gate without attracting any notice and were allowed to go out. Meanwhile, Lady Nithsdale, still in her husband's room, was waiting to give the other two enough time to get away. Then she left the room and followed the same route as the others until at the Bulwark Gate she was challenged. She lifted a handkerchief to her eyes, and a sympathetic guard let her out to a waiting carriage. Nithsdale, meanwhile, has reached some lodgings in Soho which his wife had taken, and there he changed his clothes and put on the dress of a servant to the Venetian ambassador who was about to leave for the continent. By this means Nithsdale got out of England altogether and arrived weeks later in Rome.

Lady Nithsdale, meanwhile, went northwards to Scotland to her husband's country seat in Dumfriesshire, gathered up some possessions and clothes and set out for Italy, to join her husband. They remained there for thirty-three years until Nithsdale died. It was one of the most audacious escapes ever undertaken from the Tower. Sadly, Derwentwater was not so lucky: he was executed the day after Nithsdale's escape.

A variety of works were carried out in the Tower in George I's time. In 1717 the upper storeys of the Middle Tower were rebuilt and while this was being done the builders refaced the tower at all its levels with Portland stone. In 1724, improvements were put in hand on the Jewel Chamber and accompanying quarters in the

Martin Tower, and a new kitchen was installed. By this time the jewel display appears to have been kept permanently behind a very strong screen of stout iron bars (and something of what it may have looked like at the time may be judged from the 1841 drawing by Cruickshank (see page 175). The screen does not seem always to have prevented attempts at theft, for in 1815 a demented woman got her hand through and damaged one of the crowns. Many of the windows in the White Tower were enlarged.

George I died in 1727 and was succeeded by his eldest son George II (1727–60), with whom he had been on the worst possible terms for several years. George, too, was threatened by conspiracies on behalf of the Jacobite cause, as we shall see. In 1743 the Tower witnessed an extraordinary event. More than 100 men of the Scottish regiment, the 43rd Highland Regiment (later known as the Black Watch), mutinied while on duty in England. The mutiny collapsed and 107 men were rounded up and brought to the Tower for trial. They were marched through the streets of London in June, and from the 8th onwards they were tried, in batches of fifteen to twenty per day. All were sentenced to death. The trials of all except a few were held in the Lieutenant's lodgings. Three more men were tried in the Horse Guards building in Whitehall.

The authorities then realized they were faced with having to execute over 100 people, even for the eighteenth century a horrendous idea to contemplate. They were got out of their predicament, however, by a letter from the king's secretary in

The Tower in the time of George I (1714–27). The tower at extreme right is Lanthorn. The king's standard – disproportionately large – flies from a pole on top of the White Tower which at the time was also known as the Magazine, that is, arsenal.

An engraving of the scene where the 100 or so Scottish Highland regiment mutineers were escorted to the Tower as prisoners, in 1743. Note that the men are wearing regimental kilts. Three years later, after the Second Jacobite Rising was crushed at the battle of Culloden in 1746, Scottish Highlanders were forbidden to wear national dress, which included kilts.

The three Scottish regiment mutineers selected to die before a firing squad in the Tower, 19 July 1743, (right to left) Samuel McPherson, Malcolm McPherson, Farquhar Shaw. The ring of men round the three victims are the 100 or so other mutineers who were spared, and they are flanked outside by royal troops.

Hanover (where the king was at the time), in which he said that while an example would have to be made – and three ringleaders should be picked to be shot by firing squad – the remainder could be spared the death penalty but should be posted overseas. The three 'sacrificial' victims were Samuel MacPherson, his cousin Malcolm MacPherson, and Farquhar Shaw, and they were shot by firing squad in front of the Chapel of St Peter ad Vincula. There are two sad ironies about this story. One was that the men ordered to form the firing party that day were fellow Scotsmen, of the Scotch Regiment of Guards. The other was that one of the main causes of the mutiny in the first place had been that the men did not want to serve overseas!

The following year, Captain George Anson, a bold sailor and navigator in the tradition of Drake, returned to Spithead, near Portsmouth, after a voyage round the world. He had set out in 1740 with six ships, with orders to attack Spanish shipping in Pacific waters, as a contribution to the British effort in the war with Spain. During the voyage, Anson lost five ships and several hundred men, but he succeeded in capturing a prize Spanish ship, the *Nuestra Senora de Covadonga*, which was carrying £500,000 of treasure. From Spithead, he brought his own ship and the prize ship up the Thames and disembarked just in front of the Tower, to unload the treasure at Tower Wharf on to a queue of waiting wagons, which were to take it to the Tower Mint. News of the immense treasure had already reached London from Portsmouth, and when Anson arrived he was greeted by a huge crowd, cheering as it accompanied the wagons on their journey towards Traitor's Gate. Anson was promoted to rear-admiral.

The wagons carrying the treasure from Captain Anson's ship into the Tower from Tower Wharf, 1744.

The execution of Lords Kilmarnock and Balmerino, on 18th August 1746 at Tower Hill, They were two of the leaders of the Second Jacobite Rising. The scaffold is at right, surrounded by a company of guards. The steep bank in the foreground is the outer bank of the Tower's moat.

The Second Jacobite Rising

A year later, the Second Jacobite Rising broke out when Prince Charles Edward (Bonnie Prince Charlie), the Young Pretender and son of James Edward, the Old Pretender, landed off Moidart in West Scotland with only seven followers, and in very quick time succeeded in scrambling together a large army of Scots greatly angered at the disadvantages that had resulted from the Act of Union with England in 1707. Charles Edward entered Edinburgh without a fight and proclaimed his father (still living in Rome) James III. He marched out of the city at the head of a larger army and defeated a government force at Prestonpans. From there he headed for the border with England, crossed it and got down as far as Derby, with practically no resistance. His progress was so fast that it is said that George II in London was actually packing his bags in readiness to flee to Hanover, his other kingdom. But at Derby, Charles Edward waited for the English to rise in his favour but in vain. Englishmen had done so much better out of the Act of Union that they had no intention of putting their gains at risk. His commanders pressed him to return to Scotland to fight it out there.

The next year, the final and inevitable confrontation took place, and at Culloden in north-east Scotland the Duke of Cumberland outgeneralled his opponents and won a crushing victory, which he marred appallingly by ordering 'no quarter' for the Scottish wounded men and prisoners on the field of battle. Bonnie Prince Charlie got away but many of his principal supporters, chiefly peers and Highland chiefs, were caught and taken to London, to await trial. They were lodged in the Lieutenant's Lodgings in the Tower. Among those taken were the Earl of Kilmarnock, Lord Balmerino, the Marquis of Tullibardine, and Simon, Lord Lovat, who was over eighty years old. Some of the leaders were tried in Westminster Hall in July, and

Kilmarnock, Balmerino and Tullibardine were found guilty and were executed on 18 August. Later, Lord Lovat was tried, also at Westminster, and he was found guilty and sentenced to death. Lovat had a long and tarnished reputation as a man of no morality, capable of rape, treason and other crimes. He was executed on 9 April 1747, and was the last person to be beheaded on Tower Hill, indeed anywhere in England.

George II was succeeded in 1760 by his grandson, who became George III and who was to reign for sixty years. In that time he became one of the most popular kings of British history.[3] In this long reign few people were imprisoned in the Tower. The Menagerie continued to house the royal collection of animals but this began to decline year by year at the end of the century. The Mint's rôle increased, but by the 1780s it was clear that it was taking up too much space, to the detriment of the defences of the fortress, and this problem came more strongly into focus from the dangers of invasion from France during the later part of the French Revolution and the earlier part of Napoleon's dominance of France (about 1795–1806), and plans to move it out of the Tower were considered in detail and eventually carried out. The Record Office grew in importance and its space requirements expanded, but that problem was not solved until the middle of the next century. But the department whose rôle developed more than any other was the Ordnance Office, which seemed

This is an engraving of Simon Fraser, Lord Lovat (1667–1747), who at 79 was one of the leaders of the Second Jacobite Rising, 1745–6. He was captured and held in the Tower during his trial at Westminster, and he was executed in May 1747. The etching was done by William Hogarth at St Albans, when the troop conveying Lovat to the Tower stopped there for some hours.

3 That is, among ordinary people, a popularity testified in a number of ways, such as the widespread erection of obelisks and other monuments throughout the country in celebration of the king's recovery from illnesses.

to need more and more space and take up more and more employment as its responsibilities extended far beyond the fortification and ordnancing of the Tower – as it began to be responsible for defensive fortifications all round the country. The headquarters of the Ordnance Board had moved out of the Tower to Westminster as early as 1714, but still Ordnance demands dominated the Tower. To take one example, the needs of the Record Office for more space were often frustrated by the Ordnance, in one way or another.

Censorship

In the early 1790s the government of William Pitt became increasingly frightened that the spirit of the French Revolution would find its way into Britain. It was a fear exacerbated by the growth of political clubs in the country, whose aims included agitating for extending the vote, at the time exclusively the right of landed individuals. The government, in a panic, passed a number of repressive acts. Some had quite ludicrous results, such as making it illegal to speak in public about parliamentary reform, or to drink to the health of the French Republic. These political clubs, while not banned at first, were carefully watched by government spies, and in many cases the government even arranged for *agents provocateurs* to join clubs to try to get them to break the law, so that the ringleaders of opposition could be arrested and tried for sedition or treason. In 1794, a number of social reformers of high reputation, respectable men who themselves had the vote and believed that the franchise should be extended, and who had been organizing societies for reform,

The execution of Lord Lovat on Tower Hill, in 1747. A leader of the Highland Scots in the Second Jacobite Rising, he was the last person to be publicly executed on Tower Hill. The executioner raises the axe (D), and the old rebel's head fell into the cloth (C).

A view of the Tower from the north-west, engraved in 1753.

were suddenly arrested and taken, first to City prisons, and then on to the Tower. They included John Horne Tooke, one-time friend and supporter of John Wilkes, and John Thelwall, founder of the Corresponding Society, a reforming political club.

While in the Tower, the prisoners were not allowed to have any writing materials, were not permitted to communicate with anyone without an order from the Privy Council, and they were forbidden to have or to read newspapers. Even a copy of Shakespeare was taken away from Thelwall. The prisoners were eventually tried for high treason but were acquitted. Public interest in their fate was intense, and it is hard to say what might have followed a guilty verdict for any of them.

Before the arrests of the club leaders, several precautions had to been taken to ensure the safety of the Tower in case of any armed rising of the mob, presumably following the episode of the storming of the Bastille in Paris on 14 July 1789. The Tower's garrison was greatly enlarged. Hundreds of men were employed to repair fortifications, battlements, etc. The moat was cleared of debris, and mountings for the Tower cannon were refurbished. It is interesting to study the figures for expenditure on the Tower at the time. From 1783 to 1794 they were never more than £700 in any one year, and as little as £300 in 1793. Then there is a massive increase: 1795 – £3,800; 1796 – £2,100; 1797 – £2,100; 1798 – £2,100. How much of these figures relates to military-type works we cannot fully identify, but the pattern suggests a much closer attention to keeping the Tower in good shape from all points of view than before 1795. The figures from the beginning of the nineteenth century are larger still, as will be seen in the next chapter.

$\mathcal{A}$ vast national historical museum

The radicalism of the political clubs in Britain which had so frightened the government of William Pitt in the 1790s (see page 168) was not dampened by the deepening involvement of Britain in the struggle against Napoleon Bonaparte. Even when Napoleon was finally defeated at the battle of Waterloo in 1815 and subsequently banished to the south Atlantic island of St Helena, and the distressed working population of Britain, rural and urban, might have looked forward to better times, such times did not come. Peace there was, but plenty there was not: stagnating trade refused to pick up, a run of bad harvests led to the iniquitous Corn Law which made farmers and landlords richer but ordinary people poorer and more destitute, and the mechanization of the means of production drastically reduced the need for handmade goods, resulting in much urban deprivation. As the grievances multiplied the government's reaction to them was once again repression. This provoked riots, violence, marches, protest meetings – and in turn more repression, in which the military played its part by the charging and slaughtering of unarmed demonstrators on a wide scale. It also stimulated the proliferation of political clubs and societies devoted above all else to working for parliamentary reform.

An Age of Repression

In 1817, Habeas Corpus Act was suspended. In 1819, the Six 'Gag' Acts (as they became known) were passed, among which were measures that prevented public meetings of more than fifty people at a time without special permission (rarely granted), imposed heavy duties on newspapers and pamphlets to discourage publication of material that aired the grievances, and allowed magistrates to order searches of private houses for weapons. These were another example of panic legislation, but this time there was no French revolutionary spirit abroad to justify it, as the fall of Napoleon had brought about the return of reactionary monarchies and governments everywhere.

In 1820, a dangerous conspiracy was hatched in London. It had the aim, no less, of the murder of the entire Cabinet of Prime Minister Lord Liverpool, when the members were to dine at the London home of Lord Harrowby, in Grosvenor Square, early in March. If successful, the conspirators were to head for the Tower, take it over, and then proclaim a republic. The ringleader was Arthur Thistlewood (1770–

1820), a Lincolnshire-born soldier and trouble-maker who had spent time in Paris during the Terror of 1793–4 and was greatly influenced by French revolutionary ideas. In 1816 he was involved in the Spa Fields riot in London, when the mob broke into several gunsmiths' shops and helped themselves to weapons. For his part he was sent to prison but released soon afterwards. His family were tenants of Lord Harrowby's and so he was familiar with the layout of some of Harrowby's houses, notably the one in Grosvenor Square.

The conspirators met several times, and for the last time a day before the attempt, that time to pick up the arms and ammunition required for the next day. This last meeting took place in a room above a stable in Cato Street (now Homer Street), just off Marylebone Road in central London. Unfortunately for the conspirators, someone had tipped off the authorities, and when the conspirators assembled that night, a posse of police was waiting for them. There was a terrific shoot-out, splendidly depicted in the artist's drawing below and in it Thistlewood killed one of the constables, and got away. But the next day he and his fellows were taken and put in the Tower. Thistlewood himself went to the Bloody Tower, the others were separated and put in various other parts. A few days later, they were tried, and Thistlewood and four others were sentenced to be hanged, outside Newgate Gaol. Two more were transported for life.

Some authorities believe that the Cato Street Conspiracy caused widespread alarm round the country, much the same as the Gunpowder Plot of 1605, and this is to some extent reflected in some of the newspaper accounts and commentary of the time.

An artist's impression of the ambush of the Cato Street conspirators at their meeting on the day before their projected scheme to murder the Cabinet as its members were to dine at Lord Harrowby's house in Grosvenor Square the next day.

171

While the Tower played no significant rôle in the nation's affairs throughout the Napoleonic period, except of course to continue to house much of the Ordnance's offices and stores and workshops, there was a steady flow of expenditure upon its buildings and facilities from 1800 onwards. At £1,700 for 1800, the expenditure never fell below £1,000 before 1815 (in 1812, it was as high as £5,100); it averaged £1,350 a year between 1815 and 1825, dropped to a little over £500 a year to 1832, rose again after that and between 1838 and 1848 it was on average £1,100. These relatively large amounts are reflected in a number of works and repairs.

New lease of life for the Menagerie

By the end of the previous century, the Menagerie was already looking very run-down, and the animals seedy. By 1815 it is recorded that the complement consisted of only one lion, two lionesses, one panther, one hyena, one tigress, one jackal, one mountain cow and a large bear. Seven years later, the complement had sunk to a grizzly bear, an elephant (where was he/she in 1815?) and one or two birds. The animals were housed in a semicircular building, two storeys high, the upper floor being an open area, the lower divided into two areas for sleeping. This building may have been the original barbican of Edward I's time, or a similarly shaped structure raised on the site of the original.

The entrance from outside the Tower into the Royal Menagerie which occupied the remodelled remains of the Lion Tower, or Barbican, of Edward I. This is how the Menagerie was seen towards the end of the reign of George III (1760–1820).

A wire-frame representation of an elephant, clad in elephant armour brought to England in the 1760s by Robert Clive, victor of the battle of Plassey in 1757 (which added a large part of India to the British Empire). The armour may have been a trophy from that campaign. It is at the New Armouries.

In 1822, a new Keeper of the Menagerie was appointed. He was Alfred Cops, and in his time he is said – by Bayley in his *History and Antiquities of the Tower of London* (1830 edition) – to have built it up into one of the finest collections in the universe! This was a last-ditch attempt to revive the Menagerie as a national collection of animals, but late in the 1820s animals began to be assembled in Regent's Park prior to the creation of a new Zoological Gardens there, and among them may have been some Tower Menagerie inhabitants. The move to Regent's Park was the result of the attempt by the then Constable of the Tower, the great Duke of Wellington, victor of Waterloo and holder of a variety of offices of state, to get the Menagerie out of the Tower altogether. And in 1834 the collection was moved to the Zoological Gardens.

The other feature which the Tower had accommodated for so long was the Mint, and this was also moved out. The process was a long drawn-out one, spreading over twenty-five or more years, from the 1780s to 1810–11. A new Royal Mint was set up outside on Tower Hill, in 1806, and by 1811 all the apparatus and offices had been removed from the Tower itself.

The fire of 1841

On the night of Saturday 30 October 1841, a very serious fire broke out in the Bowyer Tower (on the north side of the inner curtain) and in no time spread to neighbouring buildings, engulfing some, threatening others. The Bowyer itself was almost completely destroyed. One of the adjacent buildings which caught light was the Grand Storehouse (or Great Armoury) which stretched from east of the Chapel of St Peter ad Vincula across the inner ward to a point below the Brick Tower. On its north side the Grand Storehouse abutted on to the Bowyer Tower. It had long been used to store small arms (there were stands of over 150,000 weapons), but it also housed a number of trophies captured in battle, such as enemy cannon. One treasure was the wheel from Nelson's flagship at the battle of Trafalgar, HMS Victory, and this was destroyed. Indeed, the whole Storehouse was gutted. Its burning was described in George Cruikshank's *Omnibus*, a periodical at the time edited by Laman Blanchard and illustrated by the great Cruikshank and others. Cruikshank himself visited the scene of the fire the very next morning and talked to many of those who had been through the whole drama.

The raging fire spread to the Brick Tower, next eastwards along the inner curtain and destroyed it. Damage was also done by the intense heat to the north side of the White Tower, many yards away south, and the lead pipes were melted. At one time it seemed as if the whole fortress would be consumed by the fire. Then, suddenly, the cry went up that the Martin Tower was threatened. That was where the Crown Jewels were housed. At all costs they must be saved!

But here the Tower staff and the firefighters from the London Fire Brigade Establishment (forerunners of the famous London Fire Brigade) ran into great trouble. No one had the keys to the Jewel Cage, with its iron bar grilles, nor did anyone know where they were. Security arrangements had been tightened and tightened over the years since Colonel Blood's attempt to steal the Crown Jewels, and now the keys were the sole responsibility of the Lord Chamberlain, who was accountable to no one except the monarch. There wasn't time to find him, for there were no telephones, nor fast motorcycles for messengers to reach him. So the Master of the Jewel House, Lenthal Swifte, and the chief police officer on the scene, Superintendent Pierse of the City of London Police Force, realized there was only one thing for it. The cage must be broken into. Its bars would have to be prised apart, and bent so as to let someone in to hand the jewels out. One of the firefighters took up an axe and another a crowbar, and between them they managed to get some of the bars loose enough to edge them outwards and make a space for Superintendent Pierse to get through to the display area. There, he passed out the regalia, item by item, 'Orbs, diadems, and sceptres – dishes, flagons and chalices – the services of court and of church, of altar and of banquet, were sent forth. . . .' The heat from the burning Martin Tower, meanwhile, had been growing more and more intense, so that firefighters had to play water on the walls to try to cool it down. Even the Superintendent's coat got scorched by the heat, as he gallantly grabbed one item after another and passed it through the opening – a scene vividly drawn by Cruickshank and reproduced on page 175.

The regalia were all saved, and taken to the Governor's house to stay there until

An etching by George Cruikshank, showing Superintendent Pierse, of the Metropolitan Police, breaking into the jewel cage holding the Crown Jewels in the Martin Tower, during the 1841 Fire, to rescue them. Through his devotion to duty, and at extreme danger to himself, the whole regalia was saved. Cruikshank visited the damaged parts of the Tower of London the next morning and made several drawings. These were published soon afterwards.

they could be moved to a firm of crown jewellers who looked after them in their cellars for several months while a new Jewel House was built. This was raised very soon after the fire, outside the inner curtain wall, south of the Martin Tower, but it was not a successful replacement, and in 1852, not long before he died, the Duke of Wellington recommended that it ought to be pulled down. Yet it was nearly twenty years before his advice was followed. It was demolished in 1870, soon after the Crown Jewels had been moved out of it to a specially reinforced upper room in the Wakefield Tower, where a central case with a surrounding grille (the Jewel Cage) was constructed to house the display. At the same time, the residence of the Keeper was transferred to St Thomas's Tower where the quarters were connected with the Wakefield Tower by a bridge reconstructed upon the remains of a much older one put up by Edward I. Before this alteration in the Crown Jewels' accommodation, it had become customary to appoint as Keeper a retired military officer, and the first was Colonel Charles Wyndham. By the 1960s, when the Tower, already one of the most popular tourist attractions in the United Kingdom was receiving well over a million visitors in a year – and most of these wanted above all else to see the Crown Jewels – it was clear that the Jewels would have to be moved again, and in 1967 a new Jewel House was erected at the Waterloo Barracks (the building that replaced the ruined Grand Storehouse.

The 1841 fire was finally overcome about ten hours after it had broken out, and the trail of destruction it left was extensive. Bowyer and Brick Towers were more or less ruined, Martin Tower was damaged, and stretches of walling in between had been affected by the various firefighting and rescue activities. There was the melted lead damage on the White Tower's northern face, and there was damage to the Chapel of St Peter ad Vincula. Worst of all was the ruin of the Grand Storehouse, which emerged as no more than a roofless and floorless shell, with almost all its contents destroyed or damaged, except what was able to be got out by many heroic rescue attempts during the conflagration. After the fire there were several sell-offs of relics to the public. Some of the cannons that survived (and can be seen today elsewhere in the Tower precincts) bear marks of damage from the great heat of the fire.

Victorian rebuilding and tourist promotion

It was fortunate for the Tower that its Constable at the time was the great Duke of Wellington. By the 1840s he had become arguably the most famous and the most widely respected man not only in Britain but also in Europe. He was also one of the most influential men in the kingdom, and it was mainly at his instigation that a considerable programme of rebuilding was commissioned, not only to replace the destroyed and damaged structures but also to repair or replace many other features that had fallen down, or were otherwise decaying as the result of long-term neglect. The programme was ambitious and it occupied the remainder of the nineteenth century. The chief architect was Anthony Salvin (1799–1881), who already had work at Balliol College, Oxford and restoration work at Norwich Castle great tower to his credit. He was to be supervisor of the programme almost up to his death, and after him other distinguished architects were appointed to continue.

The 1841 fire could be seen as providential in some respects. By the 1830s the fabric was clearly very run-down all over the place. This was due partly to the changing rôles of the fortress over recent centuries, and also to the divided nature of the responsibility for the fortress's upkeep. It had long ceased to be a castle in the proper sense of that term (whose definition is given on page 5) and was not even a royal residence in any sense any more.

It had for some time housed the national arsenal, controlled by the Office Board of Ordnance, and as such played an important part in Great Britain's rise to world power, and during some of this time it had been a garrisoned fortress needed for the maintenance of law and order in the capital, particularly during the unsettled years of the campaign for Catholic Emancipation (1823–29), the campaign for Parliamentary Reform (1830–32) and the rise of the Chartist Movement (1837–39). Yet in these years the fabric had deteriorated at the expense of the needs of the departments that used the site. At the end of the eighteenth century the site was largely shared between the Royal Mint and the Ordnance. When the Royal Mint was finally moved out in 1810–11, all that remained as the responsibility of the Office of Works were a few of its buildings such as the quarters occupied by the Record Office, the Menagerie (and we have seen on page 172 how that was in decline) and a variety of residential quarters for Tower officials and warders. The Ordnance occupied the bulk of the remainder of the site. In these years the Ordnance allowed some unfortunate alterations to the White Tower, including on the west side the erection of a small guardroom building which Bayley described as 'contemptible', and, on the south side, parts of the base were cut away to allow the erection of a Horse Armoury.

In the years following the fall of Napoleon and the end of the long war with France (1815), there was a revival in interest in the Tower of London as a national historic monument. The causes of this revival lie in the euphoria accompanying the national relief at the triumphant conclusion of the struggle with France, the neo-Gothic revival in architecture and decorative arts, and in neo-medievalism. In 1825, John Bayley produced his two-volume work on the Tower, *The History and Antiquities of the Tower of London*, which was for a long time to be the standard work on the subject, despite the later publication of a variety of other works. The two volumes were reprinted in a single volume in 1830, the same year in which another work, *Memoirs of*

Striking coins in the Royal Mint in the Tower. This is a print by Rowlandson, possibly executed by him in the Tower only a few months before the Royal Mint was finally moved out altogether, in 1810–11.

The Tower of London

the Tower of London, by John Britton and E. W. Brayley, appeared. These two books started a process that has eventually brought the Tower to the pinnacle of tourist attractions in Britain, and put it among the most popular buildings in Europe.

The growing interest in the Tower was fed by a repetition of a multitude of stories of human and usually tragic interest about the prisoners confined in the Tower during its long history, which served in some respects to obscure other much more positive historical memories, and in particular its fascinating and important architectural history. In 1841, William Harrison Ainsworth (1805–82), a popular Victorian novelist who specialized in works centred on famous historical characters or historical buildings, produced a lengthy novel, *The Tower of London: a historical romance*, which originally appeared in a magazine in serial form, with illustrations by Cruikshank. It was the first of a succession of general books on the Tower emerging over the next century and a half. Harrison Ainsworth's book was a mix of fact and fiction – indeed, he never attempted to say it was anything else – and it was to be read widely. While it did little to enhance the real history of the Tower, it certainly stimulated the development of the Tower's popularity as a tourist attraction, and this cannot have escaped the notice of the Duke of Wellington and the committees associated with him, which were involved with pushing for the overhaul of the Tower after the 1841 fire, an event which also kindled a spate of artistic illustrations of the disaster and its consequences, one or two of which are reproduced in this book.

The largest of the improvements initiated by the Duke of Wellington after the 1841 fire were the barracks that were raised on the ruins of the Grand Storehouse. Wellington laid the foundation stone in 1845 and appropriately they were originally called the Wellington Barracks, and later the Waterloo Barracks and are now known as the Waterloo Block. These barracks were built to accommodate about 1,000 men, but were never fully used. The building was constructed to look like a mediaeval military fortress, with tall towers at each end and in the centre enclosing the entrance (a reproduction great gatehouse), and with battlemented parapet all round the top.

Salvin's principal works at the Tower were the restoration of the Bowyer, Brick, Beauchamp and Salt Towers. He rebuilt part of St Thomas's Tower over Traitor's Gate, supervised the works for rehousing the Crown Jewels, and restored both the Chapel of St John in the White Tower (following the close interest in the project by Queen Victoria and her husband Albert, the Prince Consort) and the Chapel of St Peter ad Vincula. The last work was a major interior alteration and was carried out in 1876–7. In some mediaevalists' eyes, some of the Salvin restorations testify to a nineteenth-century idea of mediaeval building rather than an accurate reproduction of what mediaeval building was really like, and they are much regretted.

When Salvin finally retired from his long involvement with the Tower, in 1877, his place was taken by Sir John Taylor, who carried on the great programme for the next two decades. Under him, the Broad Arrow Tower received an extra floor, at the top, whose room is described as 'thoroughly disagreeable' by purists. The Lanthorn Tower, which had been badly damaged by a fire in 1774 and pulled down three years

This is how the White Tower looked in 1821. It is different in some respects from its present appearance. The principal difference is the huge extension along the eastern side. This was added, it is believed, in the 14th century, though its windows appear to be of much later date. The entire structure was pulled down in the mid-19th century, and no traces of it remain. So far, it has not even been investigated archaeologically. Its removal certainly left us with a much purer view of what the White Tower looked like in its early glory.

later, was rebuilt from scratch, not on the ruins but slightly to the north of the original foundations. The Cradle Tower, which Edward III added in the fourteenth century to provide an extra water access on the river side, had been truncated during the war with Napoleonic France to produce a gun platform. It was heightened again to about what it probably was. The turrets of the White Tower were also restored.

The Tower of London has more than once been the victim of bomb outrages. At 2 o'clock in the afternoon of Saturday 24 January 1885, when the Tower was filled with visitors and tourists, as it was on most Saturdays, suddenly, a violent explosion rent the air. It came from the second storey Great Hall (or Banqueting Hall) of the White Tower. Sheets of flame lit up the rough walls and flashed upon the suits of armour on display. For a moment there was silence as the dust settled, and then panic broke out as the visitors, screaming and shouting, fought to get out of the building.

Tower officials took swift action. The Tower guards, called to arms, closed all the Tower gates. The fire brigade was sent for, and a thorough search was made in the lower floors of the White Tower and elsewhere. Meanwhile, in the Great Hall, officials found a shambles of armour, guns, swords and other relics lying in heaps all over the place. The windows were blown out: part of the wooden floor was torn up and smouldering at the edges. Warders and guards began to stamp out the flames and the charring edges of wooden cases, rifle stands and furniture, as they waited for the firemen to come, and when the brigade arrived, the fires were brought swiftly under control. Other warders, meanwhile, went round looking for casualties to bring them aid. Miraculously no one was killed, and only a few were seriously hurt. But many sustained cuts and bruises, and a lot of visitors were very frightened, suffering from shock.

The cause of the explosion was soon discovered. A bomb made from dynamite (the relatively new high explosive invented by Alfred Nobel, the Swedish manufacturer) had been planted behind some stands in the Great Hall, and the fuse had been lit shortly before 2 o'clock, timed to explode the bomb at 2.00, when a large number of people could be expected to be in the White Tower. Through their prompt action in closing the gates, the guards were able to trap the culprit, who was a Fenian extremist. The Fenian Brotherhood was an Irish revolutionary movement founded among Irish emigrants in the United States, which spread to Ireland itself, and members committed acts of terrorism in Britain to draw attention to the cause of Irish independence. In some respects they were the equivalent of the IRA terrorists of the 1980s, though of course the latter have no cause to fight for independence, as Ireland won it in 1921. This Fenian terrorist had been involved in a similar bomb attempt in central London two years earlier. He was tried and sentenced to fourteen years penal servitude. The White Tower bomb exploded at about the same time as another Fenian bomb set off in the Houses of Parliament on the same day. Nearly ninety years later, another terrorist bomb was exploded in the White Tower, killing one person and injuring over forty others, and that may have been the work of the IRA.

The Tower of London in the present century

In the present century the Tower's principal rôle has been more as a vast national historical museum than anything else. Yet that is not to say its other remaining rôles are unimportant, nor that there have been no dramatic events associated with it. During the First World War, parts of the Tower were open to visitors regularly, such as the White Tower and the Wakefield Tower (where the Crown Jewels were displayed), and these continued to be open after the first German air raids on London. Only one bomb actually fell anywhere near the Tower, and that was in the north-west on Tower Hill, on what was once the moat that was filled in and grassed to make a parade ground in the 1840s. Eleven spies caught acting for Germany were brought to the Tower in the four years 1914–18, to be shot before firing squads on a small rifle range between the Martin and the Constable Tower, on the outer ward. All had been held in custody elsewhere to begin with, and were tried and sentenced, and then spent their last evening in the Tower itself.

There was one celebrated state prisoner who was confined in the Tower for a time, in 1916. He was Sir Roger Casement, the Irish-born patriot who had served the British government with some distinction for many years and had then retired to join the Irish struggle for independence. Casement, who was born in 1864 and who was knighted in 1911, then went to America to whip up support for the Irish campaign, and when the First World War broke out in August 1914 he returned to Europe and headed for Germany where he did the rounds of British prisoner-of-war camps to talk to Irish soldiers, to persuade them to abandon their loyalties to Britain and fight for Ireland in an uprising that was being planned and which would be backed with German money. In April 1916, Casement set out for Ireland in a German submarine and landed in Kerry, with a quantity of arms and cash. But he was very soon detected by local police still loyal to Britain, and eventually was sent to London where he was tried, found guilty of treason and sentenced to death. He was also stripped of his knighthood and suffered other indignities. Before the trial he was kept in St Thomas's Tower. After the trial he was moved to Pentonville Prison where in August he was hanged. Fifty years later, his remains were disinterred and taken back to Dublin amid rejoicing and celebration: the Irish had not of course seen him as a traitor but as a martyr.

By the year of the outbreak of the Second World War, 1939, aerial bombardment had become a much more deadly and more sophisticated form of warfare. Judging from the experiences of Spanish civilians during the Spanish Civil War (1936–9), in which German and Italian air force bombers, supporting the nationalists under General Franco, carried out many intensive air raids on Spanish cities, the British authorities realized that London would in the event of war with Germany become a principal target for air attack, and that no buildings would be likely to be spared simply because they were historic. The Tower would be as vulnerable as any other, and when war was declared on 3 September, the Tower was closed to the public for the duration of the war. The Crown Jewels and some of the more valuable other relics such as mediaeval armour were moved to a safer place outside London.

During the war, particularly in the autumn and winter of 1940 when London endured a number of devastating air raids by German bombers, the Tower was hit several times by high explosive and by incendiary bombs. Mercifully, the damage was relatively slight. One building destroyed was a bastion on the north side of the outer curtain. This had been one of Salvin's creations of the 1840s, and to some it was no tremendous loss! Sadly, however, twenty-three people were killed in these air raids, some of them in the area of Tower Wharf.

In the spring of 1941, the Tower received a distinguished prisoner, no less than the Deputy Führer of Nazi Germany, Rudolph Hess, at the time No. 2 to the Führer, Adolf Hitler. How he came to be in Britain, let alone the Tower of London, at the height of the war with Germany, is an extraordinary story.

On Sunday 11 May, Winston Churchill, Britain's wartime prime minister (and in the opinion of this author, the greatest Englishman of all time), was staying the weekend in the Oxfordshire country house, Ditchley Park. During the day he received a telephone call from the Duke of Hamilton (in Scotland), who passed him some sensational news. Churchill asked him to come south to see him and when the duke came he reported to Churchill that Rudolph Hess, Hitler's Deputy Führer, clothed in the uniform of a junior officer of the Nazi German air force, the Luftwaffe, had flown to Scotland in an aeroplane and had baled out over Scotland. When he landed by parachute, Hess had injured his ankle, and so he was easily captured and taken to a military hospital near Glasgow. Hess had asked to be taken to see the Duke of Hamilton, whom he knew slightly, and the duke went to the hospital to see him. Then Hamilton rang Churchill at Ditchley.

It appears that Hess was extremely worried about the war between Britain and Germany and wanted to do something to bring it to an end, if he could. But he had also to admit that he had come over to Britain entirely on his own authority, and without the knowledge or agreement of his chief, Adolf Hitler. The upshot of

During World War II the moat which had been drained in the middle of the 19th century and thereafter used as a miltary exercise ground, was turned over to allotments for vegetable growing.

Photograph of a bastion built on the north of the outer wall of the Tower, during the Salvin rebuilding work after the 1841 Fire. It is seen largely destroyed as the result of an air raid by German bombers in 1940. The building behind is the Waterloo Block. The bastion was not rebuilt. Purists had never liked it in the first place.

Hamilton's visit to Churchill was that Hess was taken to the Tower of London, where he was confined in the Governor's House for a few days. Then he was moved to another prison, and yet more prisons, and remained in captivity until October 1945, when he was moved to the cells at Nuremberg in Germany to await trial, along with many of his colleagues, for crimes against humanity perpetrated during the war by the Hitler régime. It was but one example of Churchill's magnanimity that he instructed Anthony Eden, then Foreign Secretary, that among other things, Hess's 'health and comfort should be ensured, food, books, writing materials and recreation being provided for him . . . He should be treated with dignity as if he were an important general who had fallen into our hands.'[1]

As Churchill wrote later on in his war memoirs, he was glad not to have been responsible for the way Hess was treated after the war. In his view, Hess had atoned for his moral guilt for German war crimes and crimes against humanity 'by his completely devoted and frantic deed of lunatic benevolence.'

1 Min. of 13.5.41, PM to Foreign Secretary.

When Churchill died at the end of January 1965, he was given a state funeral. Part of the obsequies included a cortège after the service in St Paul's Cathedral down to Tower Pier by Tower Wharf, where a barge took his coffin across the Thames to Waterloo Station, from where it was carried to the little country churchyard of Bladon in Oxfordshire, near Blenheim Palace, where he had been born in November 1874.

After the explosion in the White Tower, in 1885, the *Morning Post*, one of the country's leading national papers, had expressed the country's relief that the Tower had been 'saved to the inestimable benefit of a grateful nation that looked with pride upon the achievements of its past. It is to be hoped that this outrage will not deter visitors from enjoying the pleasures and lessons that the Tower has to offer us all.' It did not deter them, nor indeed did German bombs, nor yet the IRA bomb attempt of 1974. As the present century enters upon its last decade, over 2½ million people are visiting it in a year. This is a greater number of people than that of the entire population of England in the years of the reign of William the Conqueror who started it all, so soon after his decisive victory near Hastings in 1066.

Index

Note: page numbers in italic refer to illustration captions.